DANGEROUS BETRAYAL

DANGEROUS
BETRAYAL

THE VENDETTA THAT SANK TITANIC

BILL BLOWERS

New York

DANGEROUS BETRAYAL
THE VENDETTA THAT SANK TITANIC

© 2016 BILL BLOWERS.

Published in New York, New York, by Morgan James Publishing. Morgan James and The Entrepreneurial Publisher are trademarks of Morgan James, LLC. www.MorganJamesPublishing.com

The Morgan James Speakers Group can bring authors to your live event. For more information or to book an event visit The Morgan James Speakers Group at www.TheMorganJamesSpeakersGroup.com.

A **free** eBook edition is available with the purchase of this print book.

CLEARLY PRINT YOUR NAME ABOVE IN UPPER CASE

Instructions to claim your free eBook edition:
1. Download the BitLit app for Android or iOS
2. Write your name in **UPPER CASE** on the line
3. Use the BitLit app to submit a photo
4. Download your eBook to any device

ISBN 978-1-63047-574-1 paperback
ISBN 978-1-63047-575-8 eBook
Library of Congress Control Number:
2015902152

Front Cover Painting by:
Ken Marschall

Cover Design by:
Rachel Lopez
www.r2cdesign.com

Interior Design by:
Bonnie Bushman
The Whole Caboodle Graphic Design

In an effort to support local communities and raise awareness and funds, Morgan James Publishing donates a percentage of all book sales for the life of each book to Habitat for Humanity Peninsula and Greater Williamsburg.

Get involved today, visit
www.MorganJamesBuilds.com

Habitat
for Humanity®
Peninsula and
Greater Williamsburg
Building Partner

To the memory of 1,517 innocent men, women, and children who lost their lives in the freezing North Atlantic in the early morning hours of April 15, 1912.

FOREWORD
By E.J. Stephens
Historian and Author

The creation of prose, whether based on fact or fiction, is always a challenging endeavor, but when an author can cleverly combine the genres, true magic emerges.

In *Dangerous Betrayal: The Vendetta That Sank Titanic*, Bill Blowers has exhaustively researched seemingly unrelated facts surrounding the *Titanic* disaster and woven them into an intriguing narrative that leads to a frightening possibility.

Titanic was built at a time when mankind was shifting faith toward the twin modern religions of science and machinery. Hard lessons learned by generations past were quickly forgotten, and respect for the hazards of sailing the North Atlantic was replaced by the illusion of safety granted by massive steel hulls and steam power. Nowhere was this more evident than in the errors in judgment made by the builders, owners, and crew of *Titanic*.

Dangerous Betrayal uncovers a vendetta against *Titanic's* financier, J.P. Morgan. The ingenious plan collides with nature, resulting in a tragedy of catastrophic proportions.

A masterful mingling of fact and fiction, *Dangerous Betrayal* presents a story written so seamlessly that the reader is left pondering the question—did this really happen?

Preface

Dangerous Betrayal: The Vendetta That Sank Titanic, based on the *Titanic* disaster, is a work of historical fiction.

The narration of the details of *Titanic's* creation, the events surrounding the sinking of the ship, and the impact with the iceberg are approximations of historical events. As the story unfolds the author interjects events, situations, and characters whose occurrence and/or existence may be fictional in nature.

The scenario described in this book is chillingly possible.

BOOK 1

CHAPTER 1
April 14, 1912—11:50 PM

T*itanic* was motionless on a silky smooth, freezing North Atlantic, her bright lights little more than beacons calling attention to her pathetic crippled state.

Viko had done the impossible. He had disabled the great ship mid-ocean, pulling off the greatest kidnapping in history. *RMS Titanic* was adrift and silent, unable to proceed forward, rendered crippled and mute by the destruction Viko had wrought.

Everything had worked exactly as planned. The ship's steering mechanism had been destroyed and her Marconi wireless was unable to transmit calls for help. Both had been reduced to little more than mangled collections of scrap iron, copper, and cordite residue. Damage that was irreparable at sea had been inflicted by two carefully placed explosive charges, detonated by wireless signals from the nearby *Californian*. Until he arranged for her rescue, *Titanic* would wander aimlessly about a freezing ocean, the money and prestige of her hapless passengers now meaningless as they faced the harsh reality of their hopeless situation.

The cold clear air gave Viko Tesla a perfect view as he stood watching through his binoculars, savoring his victory. His was a perfect vantage point to watch the aftereffects of his handiwork on the so-called "unsinkable" ship. He smiled to himself. *Titanic* might be unsinkable, but she wasn't unstoppable. He had proven that conclusively.

Titanic was five miles to the northeast. From his perch high on the upper decks of the *Californian,* Viko had watched as she came to a most unscheduled stop. Her lights were shining like a crown of jewels, outlining her superstructure against an ink-black, star-studded sky. She was motionless, her officers daring not to proceed westward without an operational rudder.

His tension subsided as the full realization of his conquest seeped through his body. The freezing air around him became clouded with the fog of his breath as he released the pent-up air from his lungs. He thought back over the events of the past few hours and weeks, of how everything had fallen into place. When the ice pack forced Captain Stanley Lord to stop the *Californian* for the night, it was stationed directly in the path of the approaching *Titanic,* the perfect place for Viko to carry out his vendetta. Nature was conspiring with him against his enemies, cooperating to bring justice where mankind had failed.

With little more than the push of a button—the action that triggered his wireless—Viko Tesla had brought J.P. Morgan's most ambitious financial venture to a pathetic stop. *Titanic,* man's latest testament to luxury, speed, and oceangoing safety, had been turned into a floating pile of worthless iron.

Delicious thoughts of retribution ran through Viko's mind. *Let's see how they fare when their money, influence, and prestige can reach no further than the frozen railings of their precious ship. How little their luxuries will mean to them as Titanic runs out of coal, when the heat stops flowing, as they have to eat cold food, maybe even raw meat, bitter food served in freezing dining rooms appointed with meaningless tapestries and stiff frozen furniture to remind them of their useless wealth.*

He had warned Morgan, told him to leave his uncle alone, but the fat little bastard laughed at him—dared to call him a *little pissant.* No one took him seriously. But now they belonged to him. He, Viko Tesla, had stripped away the victory of their finest hour and would hold them hostage until the day they would pay him the ransom of their humility, on their knees before the man they had tried to destroy.

Once again his mind drifted to images of his uncle, the world-famous Nikola Tesla. How Viko loved and despised him in a jumbled mass of confused feelings of protectionism and disenchantment. Nikola was at once the most brilliant technical mind alive, yet at the same time the victim of his own naiveté. He was such a small man in the ways of the world—but he would be ignored and shoved aside no longer. Not after this eventful night. And Nikola would be the most shocked of all because Viko had done this by himself in complete secrecy, knowing that Nikola would never have allowed such a thing to happen.

When *Titanic* was finally located, its position discovered through the amazing technology that Tesla himself had created, then those sniveling barons of power would be at Nikola Tesla's feet in thanksgiving.

One a.m.

Viko peered through his binoculars at the stationary ship. He watched as their panic took over, as they fired flares into the clear night sky.

He went into the wireless room and put on the Marconi headphones. In the stillness of the room he listened intently. There was not a sound; *Titanic* was unable to transmit. The explosive charges had worked just as he had planned. *Titanic* was stationary and silent, stranded in the middle of the North Atlantic.

Two-twenty a.m.

He watched as the lights of the ship seemed to be turned off, first the steerage deck, then second class, and finally first class until she went totally dark and was no longer visible in the distant darkness. They were obviously reducing the ship's electrical demands to preserve their limited supply of electricity.

Viko chuckled to himself as he let his fertile mind imagine the newspaper headlines that would brandish the news of the sudden disappearance of the ship everyone had been talking about. Panic would grip the financial centers in London and New York when it was revealed that J.P. Morgan was among the missing. What would happen to the fortunes of the likes of John Jacob Astor? He was sure that religious leaders would decry the gluttonous appetites of the first-class passengers and point accusatory fingers at such sinfulness as the reason why God had inflicted his wrath upon them.

In his delirium it was all too perfect, and he had brought it about—his own solitary effort!

As he contemplated all he had accomplished and the unexpected events that had helped carry it out, Viko began to think that perhaps God agreed with him. Morgan and his ilk deserved punishment.

He smiled.

He was in charge, in control—the fate of the *Titanic* and her passengers was in the palm of his hand.

CHAPTER 2
April 14, 1912—11:35 PM,
Aboard *Titanic*

Back in his room, Thomas Andrews was exhausted and angry. Would he ever be freed from the interference of Ismay? From the first day he was introduced to J. Bruce Ismay five years earlier, he had been forced to put up with his meddling. At first it was *Titanic*'s design. Then after construction began he was constantly interjecting himself where he had no place being. He interrupted with nitpicking comments, always trying to cut costs in the ship's superstructure so that he could add more luxury to first class. On more than one occasion Andrews had faced a mutiny from his workers if he did not put a stop to Ismay's overbearing idiotic interruptions.

It wasn't Ismay's constant interruptions as much as his overbearing personality. Either by word or deed Ismay never failed to make all around him aware that he was the CEO of White Star Line, that he was the final approval on everything, and that they, no matter their title or position, were simply minor cogs in his operation. He had a unique ability to make all who met him dislike him intensely. The last thing Andrews needed was a daily reminder of Ismay's self-appointed position of second in command to God himself.

Andrews lay down on his bed and closed his eyes. He stroked his temples, attempting to drive away the tension and headache that had settled in. How could Captain Smith have allowed Ismay to get away with this increase in speed? Was he spineless in the face of the chairman of White Star Line?

The speed increase was going to damage *Titanic*. It would be no simple repair. The engines had been lowered into the hull before the superstructure above them was built. To repair them, the stern would have to be dismantled. At a minimum, *Titanic* would have to go back into dry-dock. But if the worst thing happened, if the engines seized up at sea, the ship would need to be towed to the nearest port.

Andrews forced himself to calm down. *It's just a ship—theirs, not mine. Let them run her as they please. I have done my job and I have done it well.* But with his inbred dedication to his work, such effort proved futile, much like trying to convince a mother to stop worrying about a daughter just because she reaches the age of eighteen.

The rhythm of *Titanic's* engines relaxed Andrews as he lay there. The gentle vibration rippled through the steel hull like the gentle breathing of a child asleep in his arms.

What was that? He heard something, or perhaps felt something was more like it. Maybe the engines had skipped a beat, making a popping sound. Or perhaps it was a dull explosion far away, lasting only a fraction of a second, followed by the steady vibration of the engines again. Had he actually heard something? He was tired, but also a trained engineer and a professional. He knew the feel and sound of the ship, and the noise he had just heard didn't belong.

His telephone rang. Andrews sat bolt upright, startled by its loudness. This was the first time he had been rung-up on the voyage, and the unexpectedness of it rattled him. He almost fell in his haste to answer the call. At this late hour, the phone ringing could only mean serious trouble somewhere in the ship.

It was Fourth Officer Boxhall. "Get up here right now! We have lost control of steering."

"What do you mean lost control? That's impossible."

"I am telling you, sir, we can't control the ship."

Surely Boxhall had to be mistaken. The steering mechanism, newly conceived for this class of ship, was based on electrical control from the wheel to the rudder control steam engine. Gone were the endless mechanical links and steam pipes that required constant maintenance. It was an ingenious system and one guaranteed to work through the most dreadful of circumstances.

Andrews ran out of his room leaving the phone receiver hanging by its cord. He took the stairs two at a time, rushed along the portside railing, and burst into the bridge control room to find the helmsman, Robert Hitchens, spinning the wheel from side to side with no effect on the ship. It was loose in his hands, turning freely with no resistance. Unknown to them, the mechanism under the deck had been ripped apart by an explosion, the sound that Andrews had heard.

"What happened?" Andrews barked.

"We were steaming along steady-as-she-goes, and suddenly the wheel jerked in my hands. There was an explosion, a loud popping sound from below decks, and the wheel went limp. I instinctively tried to turn it but it had no effect on the ship."

"Get Smith up here at once and stop this ship!" Andrews shouted to Boxhall.

Joseph Boxhall stood resolute. "We are steaming at full speed under direct orders of Captain Smith, and this ship will not stop without his order."

"You fool! We may be out of control! We can be turned by ocean currents."

"We don't know that we are out of control, and we will not change course without a direct order."

Andrews couldn't believe what he was hearing. This was not a military ship in a battle condition, it was a passenger ship full of innocent sleeping passengers—and it was out of control. The largest inhabited floating vehicle ever set upon the sea was speeding through the ocean with no control over its direction, and Boxhall wouldn't stop it? Who needed a commander to explain this? How could protocol and chain of command stand in the way of common sense?

Andrews could take no more of this claptrap. "Stop the ship, you fool! You'll kill us all!"

"Mr. Andrews, may I remind you that you are simply a passenger on this ship and I, as the officer on duty, am in charge. I will not be spoken to in this way. You will stay in your place, and you will do your damned job. Now find out why we have lost rudder control! I have direct orders that this ship is not to stop but is to remain at full speed, unless directly ordered by the captain. Do I make myself perfectly clear, Mr. Andrews?"

Thomas Andrews did not give a whit about Boxhall's blustering. He had no fears whatsoever. His only concern was the safety of the ship and its passengers. He walked up to Boxhall, stood six inches from his face, and in a voice that reverberated through the bridge shouted, "Get off your constipated British arse, get Captain Smith on the telephone, and stop this ship RIGHT NOW! Do I make myself PERFECTLY clear, Mr. Boxhall?"

Boxhall turned white. As he tried to stammer out a reply, a shout came down the telephone line from Fleet in the crow's nest.

"Berg! Berg, dead ahead!"

Lookouts Fleet and Lee, half frozen from the cold wind screaming through the lookout post, were doing their best to stare ahead into the darkness. With no binoculars to shield their eyes they were looking directly into a twenty-four-knot wind with an air temperature of about 25º F. The cold air stung their eyes, and the exposed skin of their cheeks and foreheads had lost feeling. It was difficult for them to speak.

At first Fleet wasn't sure what he saw; it was actually more what he didn't see. The calm glassy surface of the sea had been alive with the reflection of stars from the sky above. Now there was no reflection. He was looking into nothing, a black hole, a shadow almost—a mass that seemed to be growing in size by the second. As he continued to stare ahead, the shadow on the sea loomed up like a mountain, and as he pointed ahead both he and Lee realized they were staring at a huge iceberg about two miles ahead and directly in the path of *Titanic*.

"Berg! Berg, dead ahead!" came the shouting voice from the lookout as they continued to ring the bell that meant extreme danger. The huge hulk of the iceberg grew out of the sea like a kraken from the deep preparing to strike. They could see its crags and peaks as the distance between them closed at an alarming rate.

Boxhall spun away from Andrews. Looking out through the windows of the bridge, he shielded his eyes from the running lights and saw the beast approaching. Hitchens at the wheel stood frozen in place. His hands gripped the wheel awaiting a command to evade impending disaster.

"HARD A-STARBOARD, HARD A-STARBOARD!" shouted Boxhall. Hitchens spun the wheel as hard and as fast as he could to the left, but the wheel spun freely with no effect. The ship continued straight ahead. They had no control. They were rushing headlong, at the maximum speed as dictated by Ismay, into a floating mountain of impenetrable ice.

Andrews rushed to the engine order telegraph (EOT) and slammed it from full ahead to full reverse in an attempt to stop the ship. The command was registered immediately in the bowels of the ship. Harold Ostermann, in command of the engine room, rushed over to the EOT, looked incredulously at the "full reverse" position, and after a few seconds of disbelief, acknowledged the command and shouted to his crew, "FULL ASTERN! EMERGENCY! FULL ASTERN!"

It was impossible to immediately reverse huge steam engines churning out fifty-nine thousand horsepower. To their credit, the crew were able to bring the engines to a complete stop and then start them up in the reverse direction, but this took nearly forty-five seconds. By then the distance between *Titanic* and the iceberg had been cut in half. It was a heroic move but it did little to save them from the impending collision. There was no steering control, and the massive forward energy created by the speed increase from eighteen to twenty-four knots had nearly doubled the forward momentum of the ship. *Titanic* didn't have a chance.

Boxhall, livid that Andrews would attempt to usurp his authority, tried to shove him away from the EOT but was restrained by other members of the crew.

Hitchens, still trying to control the direction of the ship, shouted, "Andrews is right! If we can't steer, we must stop."

Up in the lookout, Fleet and Lee watched in horror as the iceberg raced toward them. "Turn, turn!" they shouted into the phone as they braced themselves for impact. As she neared the iceberg, *Titanic* seemed to rise slightly from the water, with a noticeable turn to port. It seemed that the ship was finally turning. In reality the ship had struck a sunken part of the iceberg and was riding up and over an underwater shelf of ice. The force of the impact against the hull pushed her to the left.

As *Titanic* ground her way along, the immense lateral pressure on the hull of the ship, magnified as it was by the excessive forward speed, was more than she had been designed to withstand. It caused the ship to be lifted up and shoved to the side, and for three hundred feet, steel plates below the waterline bent inward. Rivets tore loose, and tons of subfreezing seawater poured into the ship.

Far below, on deck F, the rushing seawater engulfed a few steerage passengers in bed. Luxury cars stored in the forward hold were quickly swallowed in brilliant green seawater, and wooden boxes of cargo and passenger trunks floated around them.

A few first-class passengers enjoying nightcaps and cigars in the lounge on the promenade deck became aware of the commotion. Several rushed out to see what had happened. The iceberg had passed by, scraping itself along the starboard side of the ship, and ice littered the deck. Some began to play with it, making snowballs and having fun. A few looked aft and saw the iceberg disappearing into the night behind them.

"We've struck an iceberg!" someone shouted.

On the bridge, Boxhall had come to his senses and was about to order the engines brought to a full stop when Second Officer Charles Lightoller ran onto the bridge, still in his pajamas. Seeing that *Titanic* seemed quite normal, he ordered that the ship proceed forward but at a reduced speed.

Thomas Andrews, his mind racing through the possibilities of damage to the ship, objected. "If the iceberg has breached the hull, moving forward will only cause her to take on water at a faster rate. Furthermore, we have no rudder control."

Lightoller, remaining calm and professional, stood fast to his decision and suggested that Andrews find out what damage, if any, had been done. A command was sent to the engine room ordering half-speed ahead, and Lightoller went off to get Captain Smith. Andrews organized a group of crewmen into groups of two, sending them to various sections of the ship, with instructions to return in ten minutes. Andrews went to his room to gather his blueprints.

— ◈ —

Captain Smith had been jolted awake. He got out of bed and opened the door just as Lightoller rushed up to waken him.

"Sir, we need you on the bridge. We've struck an iceberg."

Captain Smith found everyone standing around the ship's wheel as the pilot, Hitchens, moved it back and forth.

"What the hell has happened?"

"A berg, sir, we've sideswiped a berg. I tried to port around it, but the steering mechanism seems to be broken. We have slowed the ship."

"Close all the watertight doors. Lightoller, wake up all crewmembers and tell them to stand by."

"Shall we alert the passengers, sir?"

"No, not now, not until we assess the damage. After all, this ship is unsinkable."

Fifteen minutes later a stunned group of officers stood around the map table looking at the blueprints before them. Damage reports were in and Andrews had drawn a line along the hull where it appeared the ship had struck the iceberg. Andrews stood in silence, staring at the prints and shaking his head in disbelief. Smith had to ask him three times before he responded.

"How bad is it?"

Andrews was pale white. "It is very bad. We aren't going to make it. It's a fatal blow, sir. She's going to founder."

"But how? What about the watertight doors and the bulkheads?"

"Thanks to Lightoller, the doors have been closed, sir, but the bulkheads are useless in the face of this much damage. The rivets are torn out over three hundred feet of the hull. *Titanic* was designed to remain afloat with any three compartments flooded, but five have been breached. The ship will fill and lower at the bow. As it does the water will reach the top of the first watertight section, spill over to the second, and flood the next and then the next until she goes down. There is no saving her. Of this I am absolutely certain."

CHAPTER 3
April 14, 1912—11:50 PM,
Aboard *Titanic*

Two Hours Thirty Minutes to Sinking

Bruce Ismay rushed onto the bridge; he was in his pajamas and slippers and had just thrown an overcoat on in his haste. "What happened, why did we slow down? What is going on, and why wasn't I informed of this before the ship was stopped?"

How typical of Ismay, Andrews thought, talking as though all decisions on the ship had to pass through him. "We have struck an iceberg, and we are going to sink. Thanks to the excessive speed the damage is very bad. There is a three-hundred-foot opening in the starboard side of the ship, and seawater is pouring in faster than we can pump it out."

"But what about the watertight compartments? This ship is unsinkable!"

Andrews walked up to Ismay, his voice full of contempt. "I assure you, Mr. Ismay, this ship will be on the bottom of the ocean before dawn. Yes, there are watertight compartments. *Titanic* was designed to remain afloat with any three

15

flooded, but these openings are allowing water into five of them. It's just a matter of time."

Turning to Captain Smith, Andrews added, "I suggest that we start alerting the passengers and lowering the lifeboats."

Recalling the argument he had had when Ismay reduced the number of lifeboats from forty-eight to sixteen, Andrews turned back to Ismay. "And you, Bruce, you might want to think about how you are going to explain to half the people on this ship that they are going to be dead in a few hours. We only have lifeboats for eleven hundred souls."

"I will have none of that insubordination on this ship, Mr. Andrews!" Captain Smith said, shocked to hear Andrews speak so critically to the chairman of White Star Line. "I demand that you apologize immediately to Mr. Ismay."

Andrews was in no mood to take orders from anyone.

"That's rich, Captain Smith, especially coming from you. It is because of you and him that we were traveling so fast. Me apologize? Never! Now, I suggest that you start getting passengers out of bed."

Andrews's words had a chilling effect on the entire room. Several seconds of tense silence followed. Smith knew that Andrews's stinging accusations were painfully truthful. He knew that his first duty was to his passengers, and he had erred in allowing Ismay to talk him into the excessive speed, but he could still do his best to save as many passengers as possible. Smith openly apologized to his crew for his transgression and gave orders to alert the passengers and get them up on deck.

Ismay would hear none of this. How could these people be so stupid? This was the *Titanic*, the unsinkable *Titanic*. "No, we will not alert the passengers." Turning to the crew, who were watching this unfolding tragedy, he ordered, "Get this ship up to speed NOW!"

Captain Smith walked up to Ismay. "You arrogant bastard. You think that your money and your bluster can save this ship—that because you say so this ship will not sink? Well, Bruce, let me be the first to tell you that you are not God. Your position as chairman means nothing on this ship. If you are not out of this room and off this bridge in five seconds, I will have you thrown overboard and you will drown with the supreme knowledge that you were the first victim of *Titanic's* sinking—how is that for a first on your beloved *Titanic?*"

Ismay bristled. He would not stand for this. He raised his hand and pointed directly into Smith's face. This was met with a sharp blow to his face as Smith exhibited his supremacy at sea. "Now get him the hell out of here before I throw him into the sea myself," Captain Smith growled.

Sharply focused by Captain Smith's actions, the officers turned back to the table where the blueprints before them spelled their doom. They looked to their skipper for direction. Smith did not hesitate. With forty years at sea under his belt, he knew their best hope lay in an orderly, calm, and organized gathering of everyone on deck as they prepared for the worst. He did not delude himself that the ship would remain afloat; Andrews was much too professional and deliberate to predict such a terrible fate if he did not truly believe it. However, Smith was hopeful that they had enough time for another ship to get to their location and take on the passengers and crew before the ship foundered.

He sent for Jack Phillips, the head wireless operator, and gave him specific orders to begin transmitting a call for help, and he asked him to use both the standard CQD distress call and the new SOS emergency distress call. He gave Phillips the map coordinates of their location, 41.46 N 50.14 W, with the directive that these should be sent over and over again. Given their powerful transmitter, Smith was certain that other ships would race to their aid in plenty of time.

What neither Smith nor Phillips knew was that, just as *Titanic's* rudder controls had been disabled, the wireless also had been rendered practically unusable. The sabotage was more extensive than anyone could imagine. And as if things were not serious enough, they were now several miles north of the coordinates being transmitted. The compass mechanism had been deliberately altered, also sabotaged, making it impossible for them to know their exact location in the North Atlantic.

Orders were given to rouse all the crew and to organize some of them into teams that would go from door to door telling people to get up, get dressed, and come out on deck bringing their lifejackets with them. Others were sent to the boat deck with instructions to uncover the lifeboats and prepare them to be lowered to the loading decks where people could more easily board. He asked Officer Boxhall to locate the distress rockets and to stand by for orders to begin firing. In addition to this, Boxhall was to uncover the Morse lamp so that visual signals could be sent to ships as they neared *Titanic*.

Everyone had left the map room except for Smith and Andrews. Smith asked quietly across the table, "Tell me, Thomas, in your best professional opinion, how long do we have?"

"Sir, I pray to God that I'm wrong, but with the number of openings in her side, perhaps no more than three hours before she goes under."

Smith's external air of confidence disappeared. The responsibility that sat on his shoulders felt like the entire tonnage of *Titanic* was pressing down on him. He buried his face in his hands. "Three hours to get twenty-two hundred people to safety. Three hours to get those people into lifeboats that can only carry eleven hundred. My God, what have we done?"

His worst nightmare had become a reality.

Dazed with the enormity of the tragedy unfolding before him, Smith withdrew into himself. The strength and command-presence he had exhibited just a few minutes before evaporated. He left the bridge and immediately encountered a crowd on the deck.

"What has happened?" they asked. "Why have we stopped?"

People were beginning to panic. Smith looked without seeing. He walked through the crowd as if surrounded by a personal fog. He was overcome by shock, visibly aged from moments before. It was Thomas Andrews, following Smith from the bridge, who addressed the crowd, his natural leadership ability showing through as everyone gathered around him.

"The ship has struck an iceberg. We are taking on water and the ship is sinking. Go to your rooms, get your families, and get to the lifeboats. Dress as warmly as possible, and don't worry about your belongings. Leave them in your rooms and lock the rooms as you leave."

Exhibiting surprising self-control, everyone in the crowd grew quiet; Andrews repeated his plea to them: "For God's sake, go. Be quick about it."

In the wireless room, Phillips was sending distress signals, albeit inconsistently. In 1912 there was no international agreement on what constituted a distress signal. The typical distress call at the turn of the century was CQD, but in 1908 SOS had been adopted as the universal prefix for distress messages. Due to nationality issues, engrained usage, and just plain stubbornness, many operators had continued to use CQD. *Titanic's* operators were exhausted and confused. They had been up for over eighteen hours, sending trivial social messages from passengers.

There was also something wrong with the Marconi wireless set. Jack Phillips was attuned to the various sounds the transmitter made as he keyed in messages, and there was a different sound than there had been just a half hour earlier. Before, when he tapped the key, he could hear a definite "thump" from the large transmit coils within the apparatus. The sound had been explained to him as the surge of current caused by the powerful transmitter as it charged the antenna with each key depression. The machine was an extension of Phillips's arm, like hearing his own heartbeat, an echo of acknowledgment.

As he sent the distress signal the sound from the coils was noticeably quieter, only a whisper of its former self. As Phillips thought about this, he remembered the change had occurred just before they struck the iceberg. Perhaps the collision had disrupted some of the power fed from the ship's electrical generator?

Receiving stations located on the New England coast began to have difficulty receiving the code being sent by *Titanic*. The easternmost station on Nova Scotia replied:

TITANIC – YOU ARE BREAKING UP – HAVING DIFFICULTY READING YOU – PLEASE RESEND

Stations farther south along the Atlantic Coast lost all contact. They had been receiving and passing on *Titanic* messages all evening, and the sudden interruption of communication in the middle of a message was causing messages to become garbled.

No one suspected, or ever would, that it was part of a deliberate plan formulated to make *Titanic* invisible to other ships at sea, to make her disappear, vanish until such time as an unknown perpetrator decided to play his final card in a deadly game of vengeance.

The first step in Viko's elaborate plan had nearly succeeded. In ten more days he would cause earth-shattering news to be published. But he had made the same mistake as the builders of *Titanic*; he didn't consider the power of nature over the feeble power of man. The possibility that a huge chunk of floating ice would turn his plan of salvation for his uncle into a death scenario for 1,517 innocent people had never been considered.

CHAPTER 4

April 15, 1912—12:15 AM,
Aboard *Titanic*

Two Hours Five Minutes to Sinking

C aptain Smith regained enough composure to tell his officers to get people into the lifeboats and to care for the *women and children first*. At this directive, Officers Lightoller and Lowe took over command of the boat deck. They went from lifeboat to lifeboat telling the crew to start preparing them and repeating Smith's order that it was to be women and children first. Amid all the confusion, this order was twisted into *women and children only*, heaping more tragedy onto the already deteriorating situation. Lifeboats, many less than half full, were lowered into the water with spaces that could have been filled with the many men who watched with great anxiety as their loved ones drifted away into the cold dark night. The crew was unwilling to fill the boats to their capacity of sixty-five people because of the unfounded concern that the boats would break in half if they carried that much weight as they were lowered eight stories to the water below.

The lifeboats had been tested at Harland and Wolff Shipyards with seventy full-grown men in each, but once again, the curse of error stacked on error continued, and many unnecessary deaths occurred because of the lack of the crew's training. Many of them had been on the ship for such a short time that they were no more familiar with her than the passengers.

As the first lifeboat was lowered to the boarding location the crowd surged ahead to get on. Lightoller shouted out, "Women and children first!"

This slowed the surge, but one man, dressed in his tux with a heavy overcoat, rushed forward shouting "Let me aboard. Do you know who I am?"

"I don't care if you are Jesus Christ himself, get back and let the women board."

The man kept coming, but a hard left to his chin dropped him to the deck. That seemed to knock some sense into the crowd, and a somewhat more orderly boarding process resumed.

Bruce Ismay was still trying to get the ship underway. This was his ship, or so he thought, and if he said it would survive, then by God it would survive. He returned to the bridge and demanded of Quartermaster Hitchens, "You know who I am, now get this ship's engines restarted and underway immediately!"

Hitchens had no such authority. Only the officer in charge of the bridge could give direction regarding heading or speed. Ismay, between his general ignorance of shipboard procedure and his overall expectation that the sun rose and set at his beck and call, continued to bluster about how the ship was unsinkable. What was wrong with everyone? Why didn't they know this! He screamed to everyone on the bridge, "Get this ship underway; I demand it!"

He went so far as to threaten everyone on the bridge with immediate dismissal if they didn't acquiesce to his demands. He was summarily thrown out for the second time with the added assurance that he would indeed be tossed overboard without hesitation if he returned to the bridge or attempted to interfere with ship operations one more time.

Ismay tried to stop the wireless operators from calling for help. He didn't want the world to know that *Titanic* was in trouble. He told Phillips to stop sending the CQD immediately and to resume the transmitting of the passenger personal messages. Phillips just looked at him, unable to believe what he was hearing.

Ismay's final threat, that this would be Phillips's last job on a White Star Line ship if he did not stop transmitting the CQD, fell on deaf ears as the haggard wireless operator turned back to his transmitter key and continued to send the message:

CQD – TITANIC DOWN AT THE HEAD. WE ARE SINKING COORDINATES 41.46 N, 50.14 W URGENT – CQD.

Ismay managed to find another way to interfere with ship operations. He went to the boat deck and decided to help with the loading of passengers. His attempt at helping was just a cover for his selfish plan to save himself. Not coincidentally, he was one of the few first-class men who survived the sinking. He knew that lifeboat capacity was well below that required to accommodate everyone. It was his directive months earlier—over vehement objections from Thomas Andrews—to reduce the number of lifeboats from forty-eight to sixteen. His reasoning was that forty-eight boats limited the space on the promenade deck for first-class passengers to stroll about.

Fifth Officer Harold Lowe was busy organizing the loading and lowering of lifeboats. But what started out as an orderly process quickly turned into confusion and a near catastrophe after Ismay showed up and attempted to take over. Ismay started shouting "Lower away, lower away!" The crew manning the ropes became confused because as he shouted this, Lowe was telling them to wait until more passengers could board the lifeboat. The aft end of the lifeboat began to lower while the crew on the bow end held fast, nearly dumping its load of passengers into the water sixty feet below. Lowe grabbed Ismay by his collar and gave him a choice. "Get the hell out of here or so help me God I will throw you overboard myself!"

Ismay slinked away, waited till the last moment, and quietly stepped into the last boat as it began its descent.

CHAPTER 5
April 15, 1912—12:45 AM,
Aboard *Titanic*

One Hour Thirty-Five Minutes Remaining

Water was splashing over the bow. The slant of *Titanic's* deck was noticeable. It was obvious there was no saving the ship. The only hope for survival for the nearly twenty-two hundred passengers and crew aboard was escape to the safety of the lifeboats, or for another ship to come to their rescue.

Captain Smith ordered distress rockets to be fired at five-minute intervals. The rockets shot up into the night sky like Fourth of July fireworks and exploded in a shower of brightly glowing magnesium—the unmistakable and universally accepted symbol of extreme distress, one that all ships' crews recognized.

Smith went to the wireless room. "Mr. Phillips, have any ships replied to our distress calls?"

"Several ships have replied, but most are just asking for a repeat of the message. Some are reporting trouble receiving us and requesting that we repeat the CQD. I think the transmitter is damaged or has somehow lost power."

First the ship's steering and now her wireless? What else could possibly go wrong? Was *Titanic* cursed?

Shortly after the collision, the officers had noticed the lights of a ship off the port side of *Titanic*, about five miles away. It was stationary. They assumed it had stopped for the night. Why wasn't it moving toward them? They had been sending wireless distress signals constantly but had received no reply from the nearby ship. Smith was sure that once the rockets were seen, she would come to their aid, and yet the mystery ship remained stationary.

"Sir, we should try the Morse lamp," Officer Boxhall suggested.

Smith concurred.

They repeatedly sent distress signals that any observer on the other ship should have seen and clearly understood. Nothing. No response. They were either being ignored or everyone was asleep. Surely the ship's lookouts could see *Titanic*'s lights burning brightly. No one could miss the rockets' flash and shower of bright sparks.

On board the *Californian*, Viko was watching the scene through binoculars but ignored the rockets and the distress signals of the Morse lamp. From his vantage point, the first step in his plan was working perfectly.

CHAPTER 6
April 15, 1912—1:20 AM,
Aboard *Titanic*

One Hour to Sinking

T he majority of *Titanic*'s passengers could not understand the concern. The request to board the lifeboats seemed unnecessary. The deck was tilting noticeably, but *Titanic* was still afloat. Electric lights illuminated everything as if it were daylight. The band played popular songs, and some of the men joined in a makeshift barbershop quartet. The ship seemed like the place to stay. Why get into those flimsy lifeboats and be lowered to a freezing ocean when staying aboard was much safer and a good deal warmer?

Passenger Archibald Butt, an advisor to President Taft who was returning from an official trip to Great Britain, did not really believe the ship would founder. He remained convinced that *Titanic* was unsinkable. He had heard Captain Smith himself say with firm conviction that the danger of ships going down at sea simply no longer existed.

Others, however, did not share in this sense of comfort that the great ship would not be lost. They looked around and saw everyone in lifebelts. If they were far enough forward they could see that the bow of the ship was underwater. They watched as lifeboats were systematically loaded and lowered into the sea. They saw the brilliant bursts of the distress rockets being fired every five minutes into the sky. They knew better. There was no question whether the ship was going to sink. It was only a matter of when.

The icy cold air was nothing compared to the cold they would feel when they had no choice but to jump into the sea and the subfreezing water came in direct contact with their skin. That feeling, that kind of cold, is unimaginable, like the stabs of a thousand sharp knives.

Men, knowing they would never live through the night, gallantly told their wives and children to enter a lifeboat—they would be getting into a later one, they said.

Isidor Straus of Macy's fame and Ida, his elderly wife of forty-seven years, were returning from a long vacation in the south of France. The officer in charge encouraged Ida to board a lifeboat. She refused to leave her husband's side.

Jack Phillips and his assistant wireless operator, Harold Bride, continued sending distress signals even as water filled the wireless room. Phillips did not attempt to save himself even after being told to abandon his position. Bride did survive, although he suffered from severe frostbite and exposure.

Second Officer Charles Lightoller, in his position as an officer, was personally responsible for saving countless lives, but in particular for his actions after the ship's sinking for his direct assistance in saving twenty-seven men from a freezing death. Initially thrown into the water as the ship went down, and narrowly escaping drowning himself, he was able to swim a short distance to the upside-down collapsible boat D and drag himself up onto its inverted bottom. Several other men were already there.

His natural leadership abilities took hold. In a feat of creative ingenuity, Lightoller directed the men to stand and arranged them in two lines. Although the boat was upside down, he was able to maintain its balance by having the men shift their weight from side to side as the sea gently rolled the boat.

Lightoller kept the men busy and alert, despite the fact that they were ankle deep in water and could feel nothing from the knees down. He was dressed only in thin slacks and a sweater, soaked in freezing water and fully exposed to the cold air. He kept the boat upright with his sense of command and duty and his knowledge of sailing. A few of the men eventually died from exposure, but most survived and forever owed their lives to him.

All told, 1,517 people died that night. Neither the great ship nor any of those unfortunate souls would ever see another dawn. They would never again see another relative, know what warmth felt like, or continue a life on this earth. *Titanic*, said by many to be the most magnificent ship ever built at any time in the history of shipbuilding, would never carry another passenger, nor awe the public with her beauty and magnificence.

The world changed at two-twenty on the morning of April 15, 1912. More than *Titanic* went to the bottom of the Atlantic Ocean. The faith of the modern world in man's ability to perform any task, overcome the forces of nature that rule this planet, or have any real control over his destiny, died that early morning with her.

CHAPTER 7
April 15, 1912—12:15 AM,
Aboard *SS Carpathia*

Rescue

C*arpathia*, fifty-seven nautical miles to the south, was one of the few ships close enough to *Titanic* to rush to her aid. Like most others who heard the wireless call for help, her captain, Arthur Rostron, did not believe his messenger, Samuel Perkins, who woke him from a deep sleep.

"*Titanic*? Impossible! Get back there and confirm it."

The message had to be a mistake. There must have been another ship with a similar name, or a simple error in wireless coding. But the message came back the second time, very weak, but unmistakably from *Titanic*.

"WE ARE DOWN AT THE HEAD – HURRY"

Rostron immediately changed *Carpathia*'s heading from southeast to northerly, which would take them to *Titanic*'s coordinates. He issued orders to prepare the ship for survivors and went to the bridge to personally take over the rescue mission. *Carpathia* had a cruising speed of fourteen knots. It would take about four hours to get to the site of the disaster.

A second message had said "COME AT ONCE – WE ONLY HAVE A FEW HOURS"

Captain Rostron ordered all shifts of stokers to the engine room. He had all heat and hot water turned off throughout *Carpathia*, with one exception: make coffee, lots of it, and strong. He directed that all of the ship's crew be rousted from bed and gather in the main dining room where he explained that they were on the way to the rescue of a sinking ship, none other than *Titanic*. They were ordered to gather all the blankets, linens, towels, and spare beds and set them up in the main dining room. *Carpathia* was already at capacity, and room would have to be made for well over a thousand people.

Rostron directed the crew not to disturb the sleeping passengers. In the morning they would ask passengers to share their quarters. To the credit of the crew, everyone volunteered their berths and for the rest of the voyage slept in small groups huddled on the cold decks of *Carpathia*. He ordered that all unnecessary lighting be turned off and all steam directed to the engines. With all available power directed to the engines, *Carpathia* managed to increase its speed to seventeen knots and raced northward to attempt a rescue. In a matter of thirty minutes Rostron had transformed *Carpathia*, a small luxury liner, into a rescue ship and, by directing all the heat from her boilers to the engines, a fast one at that.

He took the added precaution of having all the searchlights brought forward and directed at the sea ahead of them. Doubling the lookout watch, he warned them to be especially vigilant lest *Carpathia* fall victim to the same fate as *Titanic*.

Two hours into their rush north, the sea became dotted with small icebergs, growlers, many too small to be of consequence, but then they began to see the big ones, some towering one hundred fifty feet above the water. As the lookouts called out iceberg locations, the helmsman skillfully navigated around them, never losing speed.

Carpathia arrived at the coordinates of *Titanic*'s last known location and the ship slowed to a stop. Except for the icebergs, there was nothing there—no lifeboats, no *Titanic*. The coordinates, 41.46 N by 50.14 W, had been in error.

Due to a faulty compass the ship had been five miles farther north than her reported position.

Captain Rostron was puzzled. Just then, one of the lookouts saw a green flare on the horizon to the northwest. *Carpathia* fired off a rocket in reply, which was immediately followed by another flare in the same vicinity as the first. He assumed they had found *Titanic*. As *Carpathia* moved cautiously in the direction of the flare, Rostron directed the wireless operator to signal that they were nearby and ask for confirmation of the coordinates of *Titanic's* location.

Carpathia's wireless operator had been trying to contact *Titanic* throughout their rush north and had not received a single reply after the last weak message that they were well down at the head. A few other ships sent messages back that *Titanic's* wireless signal had been lost at two-eighteen a.m. The only sound in his earphones was static. Another green flare shot up off in the distance. Could it be that *Titanic* could receive but not transmit? Rostron directed the pilot to steam toward the flare's location, and once again he cautioned the lookouts to keep a careful watch for the icebergs surrounding *Carpathia*.

As the first pink glow of dawn lit the sky, they spotted lifeboat number two. It was the source of the flares they had seen. The pilot pulled *Carpathia* alongside, and as the ship's crew tied the lifeboat on, the White Star Line emblem next to the name "TITANIC" could clearly be seen.

The first officer shouted down, "Where is the ship? Where is *Titanic*? We cannot locate her, and she isn't replying to the wireless."

The reply he received chilled him to the bone.

A woman on the lifeboat shouted back, "*Titanic* is gone, at the bottom of the sea. We have just watched our husbands and children die."

Rostron couldn't believe what he was hearing; surely this had to be a mistake, a terrified passenger speaking of her worst fears. He went to the side of the ship, and as he assisted the survivors on board, he spoke with a group of them, repeating his question. "Where is *Titanic*, what happened?" As the survivors told of the tragedy he was able to piece together that she had struck an iceberg at about eleven-forty p.m. and foundered at two-twenty a.m., taking most of the passengers and crew with her.

Carpathia moved through the ice field, located sixteen lifeboats, and brought the survivors on board. A breeze picked up, causing a light chop to develop, making the rescue effort more difficult. Collapsible lifeboat C with twenty-two aboard was practically full of water, and the survivors were in bad shape. One had frozen to death and several were suffering from severe frostbite. With the sea choppy, the chance of capsizing increased alarmingly, and they would have been lost if the helmsman of *Carpathia* had not moved the big ship to shield them from the waves as they were lifted one at a time in a rope sling.

When Bruce Ismay came aboard, he demanded to be taken to private quarters. He required several visits from *Carpathia's* doctor to administer medicine and sedatives. He was reported to be sitting on the edge of his bed looking straight ahead with lifeless eyes, or with his head buried in his hands. He did, however, manage to have several wireless messages sent ahead to White Star's New York office requesting that he be given an immediate berth on the *Cedric*, being prepared for a crossing back to Great Britain. He didn't want to face the anger of New York investigators. These were all signed "Yamsi," fooling absolutely no one as to the originator.

The most incredible story of survival is of one of the cooks aboard *Titanic*. Before jumping or falling into the sea as the ship went down, he drank almost a fifth of whisky, an amount that one would expect to be enough to kill him by itself. He was in the water the entire time. He swam alongside collapsible lifeboat D until it was rescued. He reportedly suffered no long-term ill effects of more than four hours in twenty-eight-degree water. He found his way to *Carpathia's* galley where he stripped off his wet clothing, wrapped himself in blankets, and stretched out in front of the open door of a large warming oven, recovering fully from the ordeal.

Officer Lightoller, after a cup of hot coffee and a change into dry clothes, went to the bridge to help Captain Rostron in any way that he could. They scanned the sea with binoculars and could see no more survivors. Based on his estimate of the lifeboat loading, Lightoller was confident that they had unloaded all of the lifeboats, and both he and Rostron were aware of the grim truth: there could be no more survivors in the water. *Carpathia* carefully threaded her way farther north where the debris field continued to rise from the sunken ship.

Rostron and Lightoller tallied the numbers and approximated that they had brought 700 people on board, corrected later to the exact count of 705. The full impact of the tragedy hit Lightoller. There had been more than 2,200 people aboard *Titanic*. He had been so busy helping others all night that he had not had the time to think about the loss of life, only to save those he could. Overcome with grief and fatigue, and chilled to the bone, he began to sob and shake uncontrollably. Rostron offered him his handkerchief; someone threw a blanket over his shoulders, and the crew in the bridge remained silent out of respect for this gallant man's grief.

Carpathia moved through floating deck chairs, wooden furniture from one of the dining rooms, lifebelts, and the remains of a collapsible lifeboat. As they searched, the red, white, and blue barber pole from the men's hair salon bobbed to the surface. A few pieces of clothing drifted alongside, but strangely there were no bodies in sight. A woman's straw hat floated next to an oil-soaked baby blanket, silent testimony to the terrible tragedy.

The *Californian*, motionless, just a few miles distant, was preparing to get underway and her wireless operator, Peter Evans, was surprised that Viko was nowhere to be found. As soon as he heard over the wireless of the sinking that had occurred during the night, he went to Captain Lord with the news. Lord was horrified that he had not been notified of this and asked for Viko to be sent to him immediately.

Viko had vanished, and with him had gone the mysterious trunk that he kept nearby at all times. A search of the entire ship did not locate him. Lord began to suspect the worst: that perhaps Viko had fallen overboard during the night, and that no one was awake to help him.

Captain Stanley Lord, although completely innocent of the *Californian*'s failure to come to *Titanic*'s aid, spent the rest of his life linked to the loss of life that fateful night.

CHAPTER 8
The Beginning—White Star Line

I n 1868, Thomas Ismay and William Imrie formed Ismay, Imrie & Co. to operate steam-powered ships across the Atlantic. They arranged for Harland and Wolff Shipyards of Belfast, Ireland, to manufacture their ships, resulting in a highly successful partnership for both firms. They settled on the name White Star Line with Ismay, Imrie & Co. as the parent organization.

Thomas Ismay had started as a young man with a dream, a willingness to work hard, and a love of the sea. He was justifiably proud that by 1899 he had created the most successful steamship company in Great Britain. Although a tough businessman who could compete head-to-head with the most ruthless of his day, in his personal life he was a kind and benevolent man who treated his workers fairly, donated willingly for the betterment of those of lesser means, and took his role as an influential resident of Liverpool seriously.

Unfortunately, Thomas's qualities did not extend to his son, Joseph Bruce Ismay.

Thomas was determined that young Joseph would receive the finest of educations and exposure to the upper crust of British society in preparation for the day when he would head White Star Line.

Thomas had achieved great wealth but was looked down upon because he actually worked to obtain his money. He spoke with the wrong accent, enjoyed the wrong foods, and dressed as he pleased. These habits were passed down to Bruce, who, when sent to the finest boarding schools, found himself isolated by the stigma of his parentage. His schoolmates ridiculed the way he spoke, poked fun at his lack of the proper pedigrees, and questioned why his family did not vacation in the correct ski lodges of Switzerland, or the proper villas in the south of France. He was miserable at school and had great difficulty learning anything. His stern father would hear none of this—told him to be a man, to learn from his classmates and get on with it.

At some point, possibly while at boarding school, Joseph decided that his name would be J. Bruce Ismay, and he would no longer reply if addressed as Joseph. From that moment onward, the future J. Bruce Ismay began to form.

He had few if any friends. Bruce avoided social occasions at any cost, became increasingly isolated and self-centered, and was highly critical of everyone. In general, he proved very difficult to get along with.

Bruce used his unusual height as a weapon, delighting in staring down at those he deemed to be lesser people. He was rude to anyone he considered below him, such as his father's valet and household staff. His father gave him a job at White Star Line largely because no one else would hire him, but with the strict admonition to his staff that Bruce should receive no special treatment. He was given a desk in a corner area of a large open office among other clerks who soon found their attempts to befriend him were not reciprocated.

Bruce was habitually late for work. He sat at his desk facing the wall, doing little or nothing, and rarely spoke to anyone except to complain about noise, tobacco smoke, a wastebasket that had not been emptied, or some other triviality. He particularly annoyed his father with his habit of arriving at work and walking through closed doors into Thomas's private office, despite what might be going on in there, and hanging his coat and hat on his father's private coat tree.

Most who knew Bruce considered him to be little more than a spoiled brat. In modern, less polite society, he would be known by cruder names.

— ☉ —

Thomas enjoyed a good pint at the pub, and despite his wealth he enjoyed the company of his workers much more than the stuffy and self-absorbed society types his wife kept introducing him to. It bothered Thomas greatly that his son was more like those societal snobs than like himself.

It troubled Thomas that his lifelong dream of turning the reins of White Star Line over to his oldest son was never going to materialize. Bruce had learned nothing of the shipping business. His only connection to it was his birthright. Thomas knew that in the hands of someone like Bruce, White Star Line would falter and fail, and after spending a lifetime building the company, Thomas was not about to let it be destroyed.

Thomas decided to look elsewhere for a successor. The workers at White Star Line who had to put up with this overgrown brat were about to mutiny. Thomas's head clerk had expressed exasperation to him several times, but despite stern warnings to Bruce to straighten out and learn something, nothing changed.

Thomas made arrangements to speak to his attorney and began the difficult task of changing his will. As originally written, it stipulated that Bruce would obtain controlling interest at the time of Thomas's death. He also drafted a termination letter, the hardest one he had ever written, clearly outlining the reasons for Bruce's dismissal.

That night, Thomas went to bed early, complaining of continued indigestion that had been plaguing him for a few days. The next morning he didn't come down for breakfast. His wife found him in bed staring up at the ceiling with lifeless eyes. He had passed away during the night of a massive heart attack.

At the age of thirty-seven, a totally unprepared, incapable, and inept J. Bruce Ismay became the head of White Star Line.

Within the short span of a year, White Star Line was in trouble. Bruce struggled each day to make the simplest of decisions. He could not overcome his years of isolation from others or bring himself to trust anyone, demanding to make even the smallest of decisions himself. The result was a stranglehold on the business. Docks were backed up with cargo and luggage piled to such depths that items either spoiled or were lost. Competition from other shipping lines, mostly German, began to bleed away White Star Line's lucrative business.

Money stopped coming in, and the financial position of White Star Line became precarious.

American industrialist J.P. Morgan stepped into this mess and quickly took over. He became the largest stockholder of White Star Line, allowing J. Bruce Ismay to retain his position as chief executive officer and managing director of the International Mercantile Marine. Morgan, quite aware of Ismay's ineptitude as a manager, made certain that his position of CEO was in name only and installed capable people in critical positions to ensure that White Star Line would recover and thrive.

Morgan was a leading American industrialist and financial genius who controlled much of United States manufacturing, and did so with legendary ruthlessness. His most powerful weapons were his trusts, or perhaps better described as monopolies. He had immense wealth and would simply destroy all competition with predatory pricing or physical intimidation, ultimately controlling entire manufacturing sectors. A physically unattractive person, he was nevertheless respected (or at least feared) by his competitors.

Morgan decided that newer ships were needed to compete with the German upstarts. After ruminating for weeks, the ideas for three new luxurious ships began to take form and shape.

Over a three-week period in January and February of 1907, evening meetings were held at Ismay's home in London. In attendance were the executives of Harland and Wolff, J.P. Morgan's London bank manager, and Thomas Andrews, chief designer of Harland and Wolff Shipyards.

They discussed first-class suites of three and four rooms, located such that their wealthy occupants would have complete privacy, including private decks where they could enjoy the sea air without interference from second and third class passengers. These suites would have adjoining accommodations for servants who would naturally be traveling with their employers. Ismay wanted luxurious carpeting throughout all of the first-class dining and gathering areas. The ships would be the first to have indoor swimming pools and gymnasiums where passengers could work with professionals toning their bodies. There would be onboard hospital facilities to provide medical attention when needed and to assist the infirm who wished to travel abroad.

The main first-class dining room would rival the finest restaurants in Paris with its appointments and furniture. The best chefs would prepare delicacies from around the world to meet the demanding palates of distinguished guests. Refrigerated storage for all manner of perishable food from the finest caviars to the best cuts of aged beef was a necessity. The ships would be equipped with the latest electrical appliances, including a telephone system.

Ismay, in one of his rare benevolent moments, did not forget the third-class passengers, the steerage hordes who would represent the largest percentage aboard. They would have accommodations, although many notches below first and second class, that would be better than they had seen in their entire lives. They would receive good food and their own promenade deck, but with precautions taken in the construction to ensure they would never mingle with the upper-class passengers.

Andrews listened to Ismay ramble on. It was obvious that Ismay understood luxury but had little concept of what it took to build a ship. Andrews found this to be both amazing and amusing. After listening for about a week to the sometimes outlandish requests for luxury, size, and appointments, Andrews offered an observation.

"Mr. Ismay, with all due respect to your desires and obvious knowledge of the tastes of the royalty that will sail on these ships, do you realize that to include all that you are asking, these ships will have to be over nine hundred feet long, perhaps ten to twelve stories high above the water line, with the largest steam engines ever conceived? These will be the largest single standalone structures ever built! They will be complete floating villages."

In complete seriousness, Ismay replied, "Mr. Andrews, I like to think that they will be complete floating cities."

And with that sobering reply, Andrews was tasked with laying out the initial plans for a new class of ships dubbed the Olympic Class. Andrews's considerable talents as an engineer and designer would be tested as never before. He was determined that this new class of ships would not only be the most luxurious ships afloat, but also the safest. He would put behind once and for all the fears of ocean travel.

Three ships were planned, *RMS (Royal Mail Steamer) Titanic* and her sister ships, *RMS Olympic* and *HMHS (Her Majesty's Hospital Ship) Britannic*. Of the three, *Titanic* was to be the showcase luxury liner. She would be a floating palace that would race passengers across the Atlantic in record time and afford them such luxury and comfort that when they arrived at their destination they would not want to disembark.

CHAPTER 9

April 1907,
White Star Line Conference Room

E ight months had passed since that culminating Friday evening at Ismay's London home. For that entire time Andrews had been consumed with the task Ismay had placed before him. He transformed what was often a jumble of conflicting thoughts and wishes into a giant workable steamship. Unlike Ismay and the other executives who sketched, talked, dreamed, and demanded the biggest, fastest, most luxurious vessel ever contemplated, he had to be concerned with the reality of steel, rivets, steam power, and tens of thousands of construction details.

The blueprints he unrolled on the huge mahogany conference table excited him more than he had ever been in his highly successful career. All of his designers and drafters at Harland and Wolff had worked long days and weekends to complete the preliminary plans. Andrews knew he had carried out the directive (more like a command) from Ismay to the best of his ability, but even now, as he awaited the arrival of the executive committee, the plans before him staggered even his considerable imagination.

The only negative about such an assignment had been Ismay himself. Thomas Andrews understood that Ismay was the customer and certainly had the right and the responsibility to ensure he was getting his money's worth (actually Morgan's money's worth). As the design progressed, Ismay's constant interruptions of the work became unbearable. Ismay knew nothing of the design process, yet he continually asked inane questions, insisted on influencing basic design steps, questioned the materials being proposed, and made a general pain-in-the-ass of himself.

The executives arrived for the unveiling of the plans. Before them lay the blueprints for *RMS Titanic*, the most luxurious ship yet conceived. Andrews explained the plans, at first haltingly, and then with growing confidence.

The marvels of *Titanic* would go well beyond her size and appointments. The technology to be employed opened a new era in ship design. These would be the first ships to use electrical remote control of what had been previously mechanical functions.

The name *Titanic* was fitting. She was going to be enormous: 882 feet long, 92 feet wide, 60 feet from the water to the boat deck, with a displacement of 66,000 tons. She would be 11 stories high (175 feet) from keel to the top of the masts. This monster would be propelled through the sea by two reciprocating engines and one turbine type engine that could produce a combined total of 59,000 horsepower. Her top speed was predicted to be 25 knots. When filled to capacity, she would be capable of carrying 3,547 passengers and crew.

Unbelievable as it sounded, *Titanic* was predicted to be unsinkable. Cleverly designed bulkheads placed throughout the length of the ship divided her into sixteen watertight compartments, any three of which could flood with seawater while protecting the rest of the ship.

Luxurious details that would rival a European mansion were to be included in abundance. Refrigeration would provide fresh meat, vegetables, and ice cream as well as fresh flowers for the first-class tables. Electrically powered lighting throughout the ship would illuminate every hallway and room. Fans would force fresh air through ducts, keeping the ship free of unpleasant odors and smoke. And one of the most intriguing additions would be telephones. First-class passengers could call ahead for dinner reservations, to plan a massage, even to order flowers! They could contact friends in other rooms to arrange a card game or meet for tea.

RMS Titanic and her sister ships would be man's largest and most complex mechanical creations.

In anticipation of the total completion of the design process, orders were issued at Harland and Wolff that Yard 401 was to be prepared for the most ambitious shipbuilding project yet attempted. On March 31, 1909, construction began. The crew at Harland and Wolff raced headlong into the construction of three massive iron machines, one of which would become the sarcophagus of 1,517 souls on her maiden voyage, loudly proclaiming the end of man's belief that he could accomplish anything without first considering the dangers involved.

There was a downside to each marvelous untried addition being built into *Titanic*. Serious men took great care to ensure that ships were built to withstand the forces that an angry sea could bring forth. Historically, changes came about slowly and after much deliberation. It was the use of technology, especially electricity, that made *Titanic* vulnerable to accidents. The inherent redundancies and resilience of the many proven mechanical systems that had been well known and in use for years were gone. The ship would depend upon a steady and never-ending supply of electricity for her operation and safety. This would be exploited at a future date by a brilliant but misdirected mind, intent on extracting measured revenge against J.P. Morgan.

BOOK 2

CHAPTER 10
Nikola Tesla

A s Ana Tesla went about her daily chores she prayed that the stifling heat would break. It had been unbearable for weeks, and as she approached the end of her ninth month of pregnancy, the humidity made her feel like she was moving in slow motion. The hot summer day was typical for Smiljan, a small town in the Lika region of Croatia. Ana had told her husband, Milutin, earlier that morning that this may be the day, and asked him to remain near home in the event she might need him. Having already given birth to two children, daughter Christina and three-year-old son Dane, she recognized the signs that nine months of pregnancy were about to come to an end. Her back was sore, and every once in a while she felt pressure in her abdomen.

Ana was at the stove when a large amount of water ran down her legs and spread across the floor. Christina, fixing vegetables, was standing right next to her. This was the sign the midwife had told Christina to expect, and although only a girl of twelve, she knew her mother's labor had begun in earnest. She ran to the barn to get her father.

Milutin sent Christina to fetch the midwife. He carried Ana to her bed and helped her out of her soiled garments. He took her hand and prayed that she would not suffer needlessly. Milutin's soft voice and his easy way with prayers helped Ana relax as she was assured that God would watch over her in her struggle to deliver her third child.

As if nature had been called to add drama to the entrance of a new life into the family, thunder and lightning crashed as a powerful summer storm unleashed its full fury. Christina did her best to comfort young Dane, her toddler brother, who was terrified of the crashing sounds coming from the sky.

At exactly midnight, on July 9 1856, Ana delivered a healthy baby boy; Nikola Tesla arrived into the world. At that precise moment the thunder and lightning abated, followed by a heavy summer rain.

Christina and the midwife bathed tiny Nikola in warm bathwater and wrapped him in a soft blanket. Christina and Milutin took turns holding the tiny infant and smiling at his bright dark eyes that seemed to follow them around as he took in his first views of the world.

The experience of her mother's labor and delivery deepened the bond between Christina and Ana. The miracle of new life touched Christina deeply, and from that moment on she shared in the love for Nikola that normally only comes from a mother to a son.

For the most part, Nikola's early years were idyllic, if a bit frustrating for his parents. He exhibited an insatiable curiosity, and regardless of the constant reprimands from his father, he never stopped exploring the world around him in the fields and town of Smiljan, or the world he discovered in the books of his father's library.

Milutin got up early one Sunday morning to prepare for his Sunday sermon. He went into the kitchen and found five-year-old Nikola asleep at the kitchen table with his head resting on the open pages of a book of Greek mythology written entirely in the original Greek. A Latin Bible and a Latin book of canon law lay half-opened in front of him.

"Nikola Tesla," he shouted in anger. "How many times have I told you to leave these books alone?"

Nikola jolted awake. His initial look of confusion was replaced with fear as he realized that he had been caught once again disobeying his father's very clear and direct admonition that these valuable books were not to be touched.

Milutin Tesla was a loving but stern father. He and Ana had many discussions about how to deal with this curious and incorrigible boy they had brought into the world. Their older son, Dane, now eight, rarely disobeyed. He was quiet and reserved, the one destined to follow his father's footsteps into the Orthodox priesthood.

Milutin was about to grab Nikola by the shirt and take him out for a solid whipping, but the look of fear in the boy's eyes touched something in his heart. Using every ounce of willpower, he forced himself to hold back, taking a deep breath. Nikola sat as still as a statue, not knowing what was about to happen. Was he about to get another spanking?

Nikola struggled to explain why he had once again disobeyed. He lowered his eyes and they filled with tears. His shoulders started to shake.

The commotion in the kitchen awakened his mother. She got out of bed and stood in the doorway, watching the tears stream down her son's face. She walked to the table, sat next to Nikola, and pulled him to her breast as she stroked his hair and whispered his name. "Nik, our poor dear Nik, whatever are we to do with you?" She rocked gently back and forth, looking pleadingly into the eyes of her husband, silently asking *what are we to do?*

Nikola said, "I'm sorry, Papa, but these books have told me so much. Their stories make me wonder about the world and about God in heaven."

"What do you mean, they tell you things? These books are in Latin and Greek."

At that, Nikola flipped a few pages back in the book that had been his pillow and began to read aloud a tale of the Greek god Poseidon and his struggles to control his domain of the seas.

Milutin grabbed the book from Nikola and began to read, first silently and then aloud as he haltingly translated what Nikola had just read with ease. He was struggling to translate the Greek, at which point Nikola recited from memory the story on the pages before Milutin's eyes.

Milutin closed the book of Greek mythology and reached for the Latin Bible. He opened to a random page in the New Testament, one of St. Paul's letters to the Corinthians. He turned the book to Nikola and said, "Read this."

Nikola immediately began to read the text before him, translating into his native Croatian tongue. The translation was flawless.

Milutin closed the Bible. "What else does it say?"

Nikola continued from memory, flawlessly and without hesitation, giving a word-for-word translation of St. Paul's letter. It was perfect. Even the inflection was correct.

Milutin asked him, "How many times have you read this?"

Nikola thought for a moment. "I think just once a month ago. Since then I have been reading about the Greek gods."

Tears rolled down Milutin's face. He shook his head as he realized that this incorrigible boy of five had taught himself both Greek and Latin, just by reading these books.

Finally Milutin spoke. "Nikola, come here, come over here to me."

Ana looked at her husband, and her eyes pleaded with him to be lenient. She had just witnessed something she did not understand, but knew in her heart that it was a sign of genius.

Nikola walked slowly around the table to his father. Milutin gently placed his hands on Nikola's small shoulders. "My dear boy, how we have misunderstood you. Can you forgive me for trying to take away these treasures from you? Go ahead, you may read any of my books, whenever you want. But there is no need to stay up all night and strain your eyes by candlelight."

Nikola wrapped his small arms around his father's neck, squeezed as hard as he could, and then turned to his mother asking if he could have something to eat. Ana's face broadened into a huge smile as she laughingly said, "How typical of a little boy, thinking about his stomach at a time like this."

CHAPTER 11
Depression and Despair

Five years later, Nikola was out in the barn playing in the hay with a few of his friends when he heard a loud cry from his mother. Running into the house he found Ana kneeling on the floor holding the lifeless bloody head of his older brother Dane to her breast, sobbing and screaming "No, no, dear God, no, this cannot be!"

Standing before her was the farmer who lived next door, his own clothing stained with blood. He was rocking from foot to foot in a nervous frenzy, tears streaming from his eyes, and in his hands he held his hat which he kept wringing and squeezing like a rag. He was trying to speak, but all he could do was stammer. "I, I don't know how it happened, oh God, I am so sorry, I found him next to the wall, he was not moving. Oh my God, no. Oh my God, no! What am I going to do?"

Dane loved animals, especially the horses next door. Their neighbor, Mr. Gavran, had a large vegetable farm and a pasture with horses. Dane had learned to ride early and loved to be carried bareback on a large black horse that ran like the wind. The huge animal would wait for Dane, almost like a dog might, swishing its tail and snorting with anticipation whenever Dane came into view. They would run through the woods, jumping the low stone walls that marked property lines until both Dane and the horse were exhausted.

Dane had gone out as usual that afternoon, but this time the horse came home alone, overheated and clearly agitated. The horse, normally quite docile, was snorting, tossing its head around, and pawing at the ground.

The farmer got on his own horse and after a search of the meadows and hills found Dane's lifeless body slumped next to a stone wall. There was blood on the wall, and Dane lay in a spreading pool of blood from a deep gash in the side of his head.

Nikola just stood there in shock. He was frightened. Blood was everywhere. At first he thought it was his mother who had been hurt, but as she continued to rock back and forth on her knees, holding Dane against her, it was obvious that it was Dane's blood on the floor before him.

Ana's cries continued. "Dane, oh my Dane, oh no, this cannot be!"

Young Nikola knew right then that Dane was dead, that his big brother was gone. He ran from the house and raced to his father's office. By the time he got there his face was streaked with tears and dirt. His father looked up and was about to scold Nikola for disturbing him, but when he saw the tears and heard the sobbing, he said, "Nik, what is it, what's wrong?"

Nikola could only say one word over and over as he pointed to the door. "Dane, Dane, Dane."

Together they ran home to the scene of a tragedy that would be burned into Nikola Tesla's memory forever. Dane was dead. His mother, Ana, was lying on the floor beside him, her dress soaked in blood. She wailed and screamed, cursing a God who would take away her son. Dane, a young boy full of promise and goodness, only thirteen years of age, had been taken from her, and with him went a part of Ana's heart and mind.

After the terrible loss, Ana withdrew into herself. Dane was her favorite, and his loss proved to be a blow from which she couldn't recover. Bouts of depression that had occasionally gripped her in the past deepened and became a constant part of her life. She grew distant and isolated from her husband

and children. She had little to do with Nikola or his sisters, abandoning the care of her family to Christina. She began to resent Nikola for the loss of Dane, causing him extreme pain and a sense of guilt because he was alive and Dane was not. In the depths of her depression, she would lash out at him. At other times she spoke to him as if in a dreamlike state, calling him Dane, apparently unable to accept that Nikola was alive and her favorite son was gone.

From that time onward the life of Nikola Tesla became an increasingly solitary existence.

A few months after Dane's death, Milutin came home one afternoon quite excited. He had a letter from his bishop and was anxious to share its contents with Ana. He had news that might lift her spirits.

They were going to move to the town of Gospic. Milutin had been offered a large parish, quite an honor for a priest his age. He felt that this move would be good for Ana, getting her away from the memories of Dane's loss that imprisoned her as certainly as the bars of a cell. Milutin was also pleased for the educational opportunity this move offered Nikola.

Milutin gathered the family together in the parlor of their small home and read the letter aloud to everyone. Ana didn't react. She listened to what he was saying but remained quiet and withdrawn. Nikola listened intently. He understood immediately, and his fertile mind began to analyze what this might mean.

By this time, it was well known that Nikola was a genius. He had been placed in the local school when he was six and in less than a year mastered every course, and read every book, learning German, French, and a smattering of English. His mathematical skills were beyond anything the schoolmasters had ever seen. He only had to read a math problem, close his eyes and think for a few seconds, and he could give an answer.

Despite his superior intelligence, Nikola was insecure. He had a few close friends, and the thought of moving away and losing them caused him much anxiety. Had it not been for his closeness to Christina, he might have done nearly anything to keep from going away to another town and the unknowns that waited there.

Shortly after they moved to Gospic, Nikola experienced the first of what was to become a lifelong series of out-of-body experiences.

His first day at his new school had not gone well. Nikola had been placed in a class filled with students six years his senior. The teacher was not prepared to deal with the effect of this diminutive genius being dropped into a class with much older students, who upon seeing young Nikola in their midst, did their best to make fun of his small stature.

His new teacher was skeptical of the decision to put such a young person into the class and was quite open about it, adding further to Nikola's embarrassment and insecurity. He managed to get through his first day, quickly filling in the answers to a test he was given to measure his abilities. When Nikola raised his hand after just twenty minutes, the teacher got up to see what the question might be and was completely shocked to see every question answered, every problem solved completely and correctly. The teacher was overwhelmed. No student had ever completed the test in less than two hours.

Nikola had not wanted to move away from his familiar surroundings. This first day at school seemed to be a confirmation of his worst fears. He was taunted and made to feel like he didn't belong. He hurried home and rushed to his sister Christina, wrapping his arms around her and sobbing. "Tell Papa I want to go back home. I don't like it here!"

Christina could do little more than comfort him, as she knew very well that the family would never go back to Smiljan. Their mother seemed to be smiling a little more each day, their father had a new larger parish, and it had come with a house that was larger than the cottage that a family of seven had managed to squeeze into back in Smiljan. No, they would not go back. She simply said, "This is our new home, and you must learn to like it here."

Nikola looked up at her, took his arms from her, and sat on the floor in the farthest corner of the kitchen. He pulled his knees up to his chest, wrapped his arms around his legs, pressed his head back into the corner, and sat motionless.

At first Christina thought he was thinking about what she had just said. She was used to his brilliant mind pondering problems as he sat motionless. She let him sit there for a few minutes while she puttered about the kitchen. "Well, Nik, what do you think, can you get used to this place?"

Nikola didn't answer. He didn't move or react in any way. His eyes were focused straight ahead as if looking at something on the other side of the room. She went over to him and gently put her hand on his shoulder and then pulled it back, alarmed. He was cold.

She waved her hand in front of his eyes; there was no reaction. "Nik!" Still no response. She raised her voice and shouted at him, "Nikola, Nikola Tesla, answer me!"

Ana was in the next room. Hearing the alarm in Christina's voice, she came into the room. "Chris, what's wrong, what has he done?"

Christina was bent down, her hand on Nikola's forehead, and at that moment she understood what was happening. When her mother was grieving for Dane she would become lifeless, and her body seemed to become like ice—she was cold to the touch. It was the same thing, but now it was Nikola. Christina grabbed her mother's arm. "Momma, he is in a trance or having a seizure. What should I do?"

As they looked at him, his eyes would occasionally blink and remain closed for a few seconds, accompanied by a shudder or jerking of his body. It was as if he was seeing something that no one else could see.

Christina ran to get her father. She interrupted a meeting of a committee that Milutin had formed from a group of the oldest members of his parish. In the room with him were the mayor, several members of the town's governing body, a doctor, and one of the prominent landowners in the area. Milutin was not happy to have his oldest daughter burst into the room.

"What is the meaning of this? These are important men of the city. How dare you—"

But before he could get out another word, Christina grabbed his arm and pulled him around to face her. "Papa, you must come immediately, it's Nik. There's something wrong with him. He is not moving and he is cold, like Dane was in his casket. He's sitting in the corner not moving, maybe not even breathing. Momma is in one of her moods and doesn't seem to care. Please, you must hurry!"

"I'll be right there. Go back and wrap him in a blanket and try to warm him up. Let me excuse myself from these men."

Milutin explained that his son had suddenly taken ill. The doctor offered to accompany him and the others told him to hurry off to tend to the boy.

When they arrived they found Nikola sitting at the table furiously writing on a large piece of paper, a blanket draped over his shoulders.

"I thought you said he was sick, not moving."

"Papa, I came back like you said and I found him like this sitting here at the table. I threw a blanket over him as you asked. Feel his forehead. What is happening to him?"

The doctor put his hand on Nikola's forehead and pulled it back in surprise. It was very cool. His clothes seemed to be drenched, as if he had fallen into the nearby river. Nikola was in some sort of trance, completely oblivious to their presence. He continued to write and make strange drawings on the paper.

The doctor looked down at the paper. "He is writing in Greek! The boy is writing about water and water pressure being used to spin a wheel or a disk. Very strange indeed."

Before them, Nikola, ten years of age, had just outlined a water turbine design that was revolutionary in concept. It would be more than a hundred years before this concept was adopted as the motive force for seagoing recreational vehicles.

Nikola suddenly came out of his trance, put down the pen, and looked around. "Papa, has the storm passed? The lightning was very strong. The bright light hurt my eyes." He looked at his father, the doctor, and his sister standing there with concern and questions in their eyes.

The doctor spoke first. "Hello Nik, I am Dr. Vendar, and your father has asked me to take a look at you. How are you feeling?"

Looking at Milutin and Christina and then back at the doctor, Nikola answered, "A doctor? Why? I'm not sick. I feel fine."

"Nik, look at yourself, you are very wet and very cold, but there has been no rain at all. So unless you fell in the river today, you have been perspiring profusely."

"But where did the lightning come from? My eyes are still sore and wherever I look I see little green dots where the bright flashes stung me."

Neither the doctor nor Milutin could explain Nikola's questions about the lightning. They knew that something unusual had happened to him. The drawing before them could not be explained away. It was the work of a genius. The doctor spent the next half hour examining him but found nothing out of the ordinary. He could do little else but suggest that Nikola get into some dry clothes, lie down, and take a nap. Nikola's temperature had returned to normal and any lingering effects of the episode were gone. But the drawing on the table was the key to the puzzle of what had just occurred, one that neither the doctor nor Milutin could answer. It was a map that led to a buried treasure, one that would remain locked in Nikola's head for years to come.

Nikola's "lightning bolts" were bright, unexplained flashes of light that would appear in his head during periods of extreme stress or creativity. Interestingly, Ana complained of similar flashes in the depths of her depressive grief. These flashes of light would be a part of Nikola's life forever.

Christina never forgot this moment. There was a pattern to these strange episodes. Nikola would first experience deep, debilitating depression then he would become completely nonresponsive and statuelike. These periods of catatonic behavior were always accompanied with the complaint that he saw very bright lights, his temperature would drop, and his body would perspire profusely. The creative outpouring following these incidents resulted in gigantic leaps of creative thought, and later in his life, massive writings of his philosophies of social fairness and equality.

CHAPTER 12
Nikola Tesla—Genius

N ikola continued at the school in Gospic. During his last two years, he became an assistant, often better at teaching concepts of chemistry and physics than the teachers themselves. His natural curiosity and his bent for mischievousness constantly got him into trouble, but the schoolmaster had given up trying to discipline him. It simply didn't work.

Milutin allowed his son to graduate just before his sixteenth birthday. The awards and accolades Nikola received took nearly half the time allotted for the entire graduating class. It was with a mixture of extreme pride and great relief that the schoolmaster announced, "And we wish the very best for Nikola Tesla as he moves on to Austrian Polytechnic Institute for his continued education."

Nikola's family, minus Ana, sat in the front row. What should have been a joyous moment was dulled by Ana's absence. She was home in bed, slowly dying of a broken heart. She was never able to break free of the pain caused by Dane's death. Nikola, flushed with pride at his accomplishments, and resplendent in his graduation gown with medals hanging from his neck, was missing the only thing he really craved: the love and acceptance of his mother.

That fall, Nikola bid farewell to his family and the town of Gospic. Milutin, although still concerned about Nikola's well-being, had consented to his son's leaving home as soon as he reached the age of seventeen. The institute was anxious to receive this young genius and had reassured Milutin that Nikola would be well supervised and given special guidance and counseling when needed. They were well aware of the potential problems that awaited a young man of seventeen entering a world of boys two to three years his senior.

Austrian Polytechnic Institute

In class, Nikola was always alert, the first with answers to the most complex of questions. His analytical abilities were beyond the grasp of everyone.

He brought on the ire of one of the school's most respected professors, Dr. Hochstein, openly challenging the professor's theory that DC (direct current) was the natural state of electricity. Nikola, working on his own, had theorized that AC (alternating current) held the real benefits for mankind. AC was the natural state of all energy, and he was not at all bashful about correcting others who did not agree with him, even the most highly regarded, experienced, and respected professors.

Nikola held firm to his theory and openly stated that AC power would overshadow DC and become the world's preferred source of electrical energy, and he was right. Not because of strong opinions, not because of overbearing ego, but because he could prove it.

Unfortunately, he was just a student, a young brash student at that, and he was given the option of accepting what he was being taught or leaving the class. Despite his massive intellect and proof, at least to himself, he backed down, accepting that his time had not yet come.

As his first year at the institute approached its end, Nikola was clearly suffering physically from his lack of adequate nutrition and sleep. The chancellor wrote to Milutin, expressing his concern for Nikola's well-being. Milutin asked newly married Christina and her husband Branko to travel to Austria and bring Nikola home.

Christina was shocked at Nikola's appearance. He looked like a walking cadaver. He had never been particularly heavy or muscular, but now he was little more than skin and bone. Over his vociferous objections, Christina made him get into bed, and while she prepared hot soup for him, Branko went for a doctor.

The doctor's reaction to Nikola's condition was predictable. "This boy needs to get home, get some food and sleep, and receive a doctor's care until he regains his strength. What has happened to him? Why hasn't he been eating?"

The doctor was familiar with malnutrition and expressed that perhaps Nikola could not afford to eat properly. When Christina explained her brother's study habits, his incredible intellect, along with his inhuman ability to drive himself, the doctor suggested they get him home and nurse him back to health before he killed himself and that incredible intellect ceased to exist. They remained at the institute for another three weeks at Nikola's insistence so he could complete important laboratory work. Between the two of them, Christina and Branko made sure that Nikola got at least six hours sleep and two meals each day.

Christina and Branko spoke to the institute's chancellor explaining that Nikola needed to go home until he regained his strength. They were reassured that his place in class would be waiting. But the chancellor did advise them, "When young Nikola has sufficiently regained his strength, his father needs to explain the value of showing respect to his elders, especially his professors. His theories of electricity are not in concert with modern progress. He is here to learn, not to teach."

Christina knew that the chancellor and the institute professors did not understand her brother as she did. Nikola had never been wrong, a simple fact these men had yet to learn.

When they arrived back in Gospic there was black everywhere. As they rounded the last corner Christina broke into tears and sobbed uncontrollably. The family home had a wreath on the door. No one needed to tell Christina that her mother had passed away.

The house was filled with mourners. Milutin was on his knees before a beautiful coffin surrounded by white flowers. He was praying for his beloved Ana, lying motionless before him, a smile on her lips for the first time in years. Christina wrapped her arms about her father's neck, and the two of them held each other as she sobbed uncontrollably. Nikola stood back. His eyes, filled with tears, were fixated on his mother.

Nikola stepped forward and softly placed his hand on his father's shoulder. He didn't know what to say. Milutin turned toward him. His eyes widened at his son's emaciated appearance.

"My God, boy, what have you been doing? Is this what happens when I let my only living son go away by himself? I should never have let you go!"

It was the wrong rebuke at the wrong time.

Nikola's mood darkened with each goodbye and condolence. An ache that could not be salved filled his heart. His mother was gone to the grave, her soul gone to a place his father called heaven. He had been taken from the institute by force. How little his father understood of the workings of his mind, the depth of his intellect, or the gift of knowledge that had been taken from him. He was only seventeen, still considered to be a child, and therefore subject to his father's will.

Is this what happens when I let my only living son go away by himself? I should never have let you go! rang in Nikola's ears.

Nikola felt as though his educational future had been cut off forever. Until he was twenty-one, he would be under his father's thumb, forced to be whatever helping hand was needed. No, this he would not do. He would not have his vision limited by that of a smaller intellect, even if that intellect was his father's, well meant, but miniscule in comparison to his own.

Nikola decided to leave. He knew how to live in the world. For the past year he had done perfectly well by himself. Why remain? No one needed him, and most likely, no one would care where he went, or why. He knew more than nearly everyone about the primitive machinery being installed to generate and use electricity, and such knowledge would land him a solid, well-paying job wherever he went.

He remained at home, sleeping and eating well, rebuilding his strength and health, avoiding his father as much as possible. As part of his preparation to leave, he would regularly borrow a horse from a local friend and ride through the countryside. This was part of his plan to get away unseen, but it also reinforced his belief that he was destined to live a life of solitary existence, depending on no one but himself for his security, shelter, and well-being.

Two weeks after his mother was laid to rest, at three in the morning, Nikola quietly gathered his few belongings, went to the barn, and rode off into the night. He went across the countryside to a nearby town where he could catch a train that would take him out of the country to the mountains of northern Italy. His last act had been to stop at his sister Christina's house and leave a letter on her doorstep. He expressed his sincere thanks for her kindness to him, promised that he would stay in touch from time to time, and included instructions that would lead them to the horse so it could be returned to its owner.

CHAPTER 13
Tesla the Recluse

Nikola settled in the Italian Alps town of Lecco, at the southeastern end of Lake Como. He found employment working with draftsmen and engineers, laying out plans for a DC electrical generating plant. He quickly became frustrated with the overall plans, which to him seemed primitive at best. Nikola learned that the "Italian method" of decision making was a series of expletive-laced screaming matches where logic and reason were buried under emotional outbursts. He felt betrayed by fate. He was the lowest ranking person in a group of men who did not possess half his understanding of electricity.

One man, Mario, could not help but notice Nikola's unhappiness. As they were leaving work one Friday afternoon, Mario asked him, "Nik, how about we stop and have a beer on the way home?"

Surprised by the friendly offer, Nikola readily agreed.

"Nik, here's to our friendship." Mario raised his glass and Nikola did the same. Nikola had his first taste of beer. He found it deliciously bitter and sweet at the same time.

"So tell me, Nik, why the long face?"

Nikola drained his glass. He told Mario of the death of his mother and the death of his brother Dane. He spoke of being forced to leave the institute by his overbearing father. He was tired of being a freak of nature, a biological oddity, taller than everyone, and cursed with a superior intellect. He was living in his own isolated prison, at arm's length from everyone around him—and on he went.

Hours later and emotionally drained, Nikola finally stopped talking. To his surprise, he had finished five glasses of beer. He felt strange, kind of woozy, and yet relaxed at the same time.

"Nik, I think we'd better get you home" were the last words he remembered as Mario helped him stagger to his apartment.

A loud pounding on his door awakened Nikola the next afternoon. His head hurt and his mouth felt like someone had stuffed it full of cotton. Mario was standing there trying hard to suppress laughter as he looked at his poor hungover friend. "I thought I had better come by and make sure you were all right."

After a cup of black coffee, Nikola started to feel a bit more human. He was hungry, in fact famished. He invited Mario to lunch at a nearby *ristorante*, and the two of them strolled down the street on a beautiful sunny day.

Taking their time with the meal, they sat and talked while enjoying delicious Italian food. As Nikola settled the bill Mario asked, "Do you have plans for tonight? I am getting together with my cousins for our Saturday night game of cards. My sister will be making pasta for everyone. Her sauce is the best in the city. My brother will be there and he will bring wine."

Mario's family was warm and inviting, if perhaps a little too loud. They welcomed Nikola with hugs and kisses, and glass after glass of wine. As the evening wore on, they invited him to join in the card games. Nikola's mind was as sharp as ever and he quickly mastered the games. He found he could determine his odds of winning by watching the cards as they were discarded. When the evening finally ended at three in the morning, Nikola held most of the money.

Mario asked, "Are you sure you've never played cards before?"

Nikola became a regular at the local tavernas. He was good at cards, but due to his late hours and drinking, he was showing up later and later for work, disheveled and smelling like a brewery. He was ultimately dismissed for showing up in such a sorry state.

He found that in a few hours of playing cards several nights a week he could comfortably support himself. He would sit down at a table of strangers, act like a rookie and an easy mark, but at the last minute produce a winning hand, leaving the others cursing in Italian as he left with a pocket full of lira.

Nikola's gambling nearly cost him his life when he unknowingly sat down at a table with the brother of a man he had beaten a few nights before. As Nikola walked home after his usual "beginner's luck," he was nearly stabbed in the back. He managed to escape the attacker, but six hours later he was on a southbound train quite fortunate to be alive. He had purchased a ticket on *the next train out* without regard for its destination.

Most of the train's passengers were headed for the seaport town of Civitavecchia, a shipping port on the Tyrrhenian Sea, which had been in use since the days of the Roman Empire.

Nikola hadn't bathed in days. His body odor, mingling with the sickening stench of alcohol, caused others to move away from him. He made a quiet vow that he would get off at the next stop, regardless of where it was.

He found his way to the shipping docks of Civitavecchia where he would spend the next two years. He located a pensione, took a long bath, and went to bed, sleeping well into the following afternoon. He wandered out, found a busy taverna, and enjoyed a hearty meal and a bottle of Chianti. In this seaside city he could be completely anonymous. No one would find him here, and he could easily make enough money as a gambler.

He preferred the company of the sailors, drunks, and prostitutes. They had no aspirations beyond the next drink, the next meal, or the next job on whatever ship would hire them. But, most importantly, they had no desire to hurt him, to take anything from him, or to treat him like he was some kind of freak. He was nothing more than a momentary friend, the source of the next drink, or a pigeon to be fleeced in a card game.

Whenever his memory took him back to his family or his life of learning, he turned to the bottle to bury the pain.

Days turned into weeks and weeks into months, and before he realized it Nikola had been living as a recluse for nearly two years.

One Thursday afternoon as he was eating a bowl of *pasta e fagioli*, his eye caught the headline of the previous day's newspaper lying on the corner of the bar. The title of an article, *First AC Electrical Power Plant Construction*, leapt off the page. A flood of memories rose to the surface. He grabbed the paper and read about an experimental electrical AC generating plant.

The article went on for several pages and provided a rather comprehensive explanation of the process of generating electricity. It included a comparison of DC power versus AC power. Nikola devoured each word like a hungry person eating his first food after weeks of starvation He agreed with everything that was written. Yes, this was exactly as he had predicted two years ago.

As he continued to read, he found that he could predict, word for word, the contents of each paragraph. And then, almost like an explosion in his mind, it hit him—these were his exact words! His photographic memory, capable of recalling the tiniest events of his life, suddenly focused with precision. He was reading the contents of the thesis paper he had written two years earlier while at the Austrian Polytechnic Institute, presenting his arguments defending AC electricity's superiority over DC electricity. A professor, Dr. Franz Hochstein, was credited for the technical content of the article.

Nikola was livid. This was the professor who had demanded of the chancellor of the institute that Nikola Tesla be condemned for his behavior, especially for his lack of respect for his elders.

Nikola went directly to his pensione. He gathered up his belongings and walked several blocks inland to the better part of the city. He rented a hotel room for one night, purchased an entire new set of clothing, and arranged for it to be delivered to the hotel. He threw his tattered clothes into the fireplace and soaked in a hot tub for hours, washing off months of grime and filth. He dressed in his new clothes and paused for a few minutes to enjoy the experience of new cloth against clean skin.

He walked to a barbershop, got his hair cut, and had his beard shaved completely off down to smooth skin. As he got up to leave and as he was giving the barber an extra-large tip, the barber commented with a smile and a bow, "Grazie! But don't wait so long to get your hair cut next time."

As Nikola turned toward the door, he saw someone in the mirror that he had not seen in years. Standing there was his old self, a young good-looking tall man, with dark hair, a ready smile, and eyes that sparkled with purpose and intent.

CHAPTER 14
Retribution

Professor Hochstein didn't notice the tall young man enter the lecture hall and take a seat in the last row. Nikola Tesla listened and watched as Hochstein expounded on details of AC's superiority, especially for long-distance power distribution, simply repeating word for word the arguments Nikola had confronted him with over two years earlier. Hochstein had never expanded upon (or clearly understood for that matter) the theoretical arguments Tesla presented. If he had, he would have realized that Tesla's early work overlooked important limitations of AC that had to be considered if it was to reach its full potential.

As Hochstein wrapped up his comments, Nikola stood up and, using the full power of his deep voice, asked the question, "Excuse me, Professor, but aren't you overlooking the fundamental principles that will limit the distance AC can travel? What you propose will not work."

"Young man, I don't know who you are. Do you realize who I am?"

"I know exactly who you are; you are a fraud! Nothing more than a thief who takes the work of others and claims it for himself. Now, as I said, you are making a basic mistake. If you had done anything except claim my work as your own, you might have known this."

The crowd in the lecture hall turned around to see this outspoken stranger. They snapped back around as Hochstein, red with fury, shouted, "Get this imposter out of here! The work I am presenting here is sound, and I will not be questioned by some upstart."

Nikola shouted back, "I am no imposter. My name is Nikola Tesla. The original work you claim as your own is my work, submitted to you over two years ago when I was a young student of yours. How is your memory, Professor? Better than your honesty, I presume?"

Hochstein was speechless. Beads of sweat formed on his forehead as his muscles tightened, causing visible shaking of his rigid arms. He shouted, "I said get this imposter—" but was cut off by the audience.

"Let's hear him out. Let him speak!"

Nikola strode to the front of the room. He turned to the crowd. "I am the originator of everything that Professor Hochstein claims as his own work. For those of you who wish proof of this, I ask you to go to the office of the chancellor and locate the records of my attendance at this institute. You will find that I was reprimanded because I disagreed with the professor's arguments of the superiority of DC over AC, and you will find my paper in which I put forth every argument presented to you as the original work of Dr. Hochstein! This man is a fraud and a liar."

A collective gasp came from the crowd at such an accusation. Sweating profusely, obviously in extreme discomfort, Professor Hochstein again attempted to have Tesla removed, but the crowd was not about to listen to his objections.

Tesla spent the next thirty minutes explaining the oversights and half-truths in Hochstein's claims, convincing everyone that only the original creator could have such insight. As he completed his explanation, several hands shot up, and for another half hour he answered questions and expanded on his dissertation. One by one they began to see the veracity of Tesla's technical argument and the increasing belief among them that he had indeed been the original creator of the arguments promoting AC power as the superior form of electricity.

— ◇ —

Hochstein did not show up at his office the next morning and for two weeks missed all of his lectures.

Tesla had a basic belief in the goodness and honesty of others. He was shocked and disappointed that a man of Professor Hochstein's stature would stoop to such depths. It was difficult for him to understand why Hochstein, being a scientist himself, couldn't have simply stated that it was indeed Tesla's work he was promoting. This was an important lesson but unfortunately one that Tesla would never understand, and as time would tell, it would ultimately be the cause of his downfall.

The morning after his confrontation with Professor Hochstein, Nikola went to the chancellor's office, obtained copies of his grade reports, and boarded the next train to Prague.

The turn of events had a profound impact on Nikola Tesla. His drive to return to the world of science knew no limits. He went directly to the office of the chancellor of the University of Prague and announced that he wished to enroll the next day. It was unusual for the chancellor to deal directly with incoming students. When Chancellor Dr. Reithofer heard this request his reply was predictable.

"He wants to do what?"

"This young man wants to be admitted today."

"This is the middle of the semester! Tell him to come back in the fall at the beginning of the school year."

"I did that already. He will not listen to me. He insists on talking directly with you."

These people had never met anyone like Nikola Tesla. Despite the chancellor's busy schedule, he reluctantly agreed. It was a providential meeting. Nikola was able to convince Dr. Reithofer to allow him to take a graduate-level exam, with the provision that if he achieved a passing grade, the university would admit him.

He answered all questions perfectly, in the unheard of time of eight hours. Graduate students were normally given two full days to complete the exam. After having the heads of the physics, chemistry, and mathematics departments review the results, Dr. Reithofer agreed that they should consider the request that this

Tesla be admitted. They had not found a single error, not a misspelled word, not one cross-out in any of the eighty-seven pages of work.

Dr. Reithofer found Tesla pacing back and forth in the hallway. It was after midnight and he invited Tesla to meet with the distinguished professors, among them, the most learned men in Europe. He introduced Tesla to the group and for the first time in memory was unable to think of anything else to say. It was Professor Krausz, the head of the chemistry department, who broke the ice. "Young man, Nikola is it? I assume that this is your work we have been reviewing here?"

"Yes sir, I trust that you have found my test results satisfactory."

"Mr. Tesla, this is the most extraordinary work we have seen in our entire tenure here at the university. Is it true that you completed this entire test in just eight hours?"

"It was exactly seven hours and fifty-six minutes, sir."

"Were you told that these test questions are normally used as a final passage for our most gifted graduate students before we bestow the degree of doctorate?"

"No sir, I was not."

Next, the head of the physics department, Dr. Schulesko, spoke up. "Mr. Tesla, why have you asked to be enrolled at our university? Your knowledge of things scientific seems to be complete, and your analytical capabilities are beyond our ability to comprehend. What do you hope to learn here? I quite frankly feel that you should be teaching us, not the other way around."

"I wish to learn all there is to know about the new science of electricity. I have developed a theoretical concept for alternating current electricity, but there is much I have to do to reduce it to workable machinery. This university, with its vast library and faculty of learned men such as you gentlemen, can provide me with the environment I require."

Dr. Schulesko turned to the others. "It is my opinion that we should offer this young man a position in our graduate fellowship program and allow him to arrange his own course of study, with full access to any material or individual he deems necessary. I offer myself to be his sponsor and guide, and will review his study progress. This is a unique opportunity to help this gifted young man, and his work here will further advance the stellar reputation of the university."

Dr. Reithofer looked at the other professors, who nodded their agreement. "Consider it done, Dr. Schulesko. Mr. Tesla, when would you like to begin?"

"As I told you when we first met this morning, I want to enroll immediately. Tomorrow, actually later this morning would be ideal."

Thus began a two-year period of unprecedented growth. Before his first year was over Tesla had completed his dissertation on electricity and chosen the term "polyphase" to describe a method for generating AC electricity, which would ultimately be adopted worldwide. He was also exposed to humanitarian issues and as a result spent much of his career later in life striving to unburden mankind from unnecessary physical labor.

Two years later Tesla made the decision to move on, applying his knowledge and theories of electricity to the world of everyday. He was offered a full professorship and a handsome salary, as well as complete freedom to pursue research in any area of interest if he would remain at the university. He would have the services of bright young students to assist as he saw fit, opening vistas of opportunity to explore as many parallel concepts as his fertile mind could create.

Tesla turned down the offer. His mental capacity was superior to virtually anyone he had ever encountered. Because of this he felt burdened when working with or through others. When he was alone, he was unfettered—free to think, to create, to move at breakneck speed through the most complex of issues. But when he attempted to function with others, he had to operate at their slower more deliberate pace, a pace he found untenable. It wasn't an attitude of superiority, it was a simple statement of fact, but the long-term effect of this on his future success would prove to be disastrous. When he walked away from the offer, he also walked away from the opportunity to develop an ability to manage and lead people. Tesla did not appreciate that he could amplify his own abilities through the efforts of others. He was a perfectionist, preferring to do everything himself, thus being assured that everything was done correctly.

It was the first of many times in his incredible career that he would exhibit shortsightedness.

CHAPTER 15

Tesla Meets Edison—
Oil and Water Don't Mix

Tesla left Prague with the intention of traveling to Paris where interest was being shown for his concept of AC power generation. In his last months at the university he corresponded with leading engineers throughout Europe, attempting to find support for his "radical" approach to electrical power generation. He invariably found that most were building or planning to build DC generating plants. Try as he might, he had little success in persuading anyone that AC generation was superior for the efficient production and distribution of electrical power.

The reasons were twofold. In the first place, it was difficult to understand the theory of AC and its intricacies, but the most compelling reason could be attributed to the most famous inventor of the age, Thomas Edison. His reputation as the leading electrical technologist of the century was such that anything he promoted was pretty much the last word on the subject. Edison had a worldwide grip on the direction electrical power generation would take. But in Paris, Tesla had at least found a few people willing to listen.

Before he left for France, he made a short trip to visit his sister Christina and to meet her son. Viktor Gracac had been born shortly after Tesla began his studies in Prague, and he was intrigued to meet this latest addition to the family. Viktor (Viko) had already exhibited some of Nikola's traits, primarily his insatiable curiosity about everything. His physical resemblance to Nikola was uncanny, and Christina made the observation that Nikola looked just like Viko when he was two years old.

Tesla arrived in Paris, began to lecture on his concepts for AC power, and started to develop a few disciples. But finding investors willing to commit money was very slow going. He was a brilliant scientist and a foremost expert at the emerging science of electrical generation. He had no problem finding employment but his true goal was to introduce AC as the ultimate source of electrical power. He spent the next few years in an unsuccessful attempt to find disciples for his theories.

In 1883 fate knocked on Tesla's door when Charles Batchelor, Edison's foreman, arrived in Paris. Edison's European operations were having a difficult time getting a large new DC generator to work properly. Batchelor was about to give up when one of his French colleagues, Pierre Chales, suggested they talk to this young engineer, Nikola Tesla. With no other options, Batchelor agreed. He was quite surprised at Tesla's approach to the problem. Unlike Edison, Tesla did not start tearing the machine apart. He listened to the description of the problem, sat back, and closed his eyes. After a few minutes he asked for a paper and pen, and drew out the solution to the problem.

If he had not already tried every possible solution, Batchelor would have dismissed the paper just handed him. However, he had the machine taken apart and the changes made. Later that afternoon when the generator was tried again, it worked precisely as Tesla predicted.

The next morning a dapper young Tesla walked in and expressed no surprise at all that the machine had operated through the night with the problem solved. There had never been any question in his mind that his solution would work.

Batchelor had trouble understanding what he had just witnessed. Edison would most likely have figured out the answer, but only after days or weeks of around-the-clock experimenting with one thing or another until he stumbled on the correct answer. Tesla had listened to the symptoms, analyzed the problem entirely in his head, and correctly determined the course of action without so much as laying a hand on the generator.

He asked Tesla, "Would you like to come to America and work with Thomas Edison? After what I have witnessed here, I think you are just the man for the job."

They shook hands in agreement.

Batchelor then asked Tesla how much he wanted in compensation for helping with the generator problem. He was prepared to give Tesla any amount he wanted, but he was not at all prepared for Tesla's answer.

Tesla said, "You owe me nothing. Work such as this should be offered as a free gift from those like myself who have been blessed with extraordinary gifts of the mind. Such abilities are for the good of all."

This kind of reasoning would follow Tesla his entire life and was one of the ingrained beliefs that led to his obscurity.

Edison solved problems by experimentation. He simply kept trying things until he found something that worked. Tesla, on the other hand, would sit back, think, almost go into a trance, and then propose a simple elegant inventive solution that worked exactly as predicted.

No one can question Edison's success in creating new products by trial and error. He had 2,332 patents granted worldwide in his lifetime. Tesla had an impressive record of patents also, but his methodology of creation by careful analysis and thought stood in marked contrast to Edison's approach.

The problems of cooperation and collaboration boiled to the surface when the two tried to work together. The boisterous egotist Edison and the quiet, self-assured Tesla were cut from different cloth, never destined to be woven into a cohesive tapestry.

Tesla began working for Edison in 1884. At that time Edison was having problems with a new generator. It was the largest ever attempted. Edison was trying to "electrify" New York City. He was fighting insurmountable technical odds because of his choice of DC power distribution. He felt that all he had to do was use a bigger generator so he could shove more power into the wires that were already clogging the streets of lower Manhattan.

Tesla had the ultimate solution, his polyphase AC system. But at the time, Tesla was in such awe of Edison that he declined to offer an alternative as radical as switching from DC to AC.

Edison proposed a deal. He told Tesla that he would give him a fifty-thousand-dollar bonus if he could fix the generator. Tesla was thus motivated to solve the problem. He wanted to impress Edison, but his driving motive for the first time in his life was money. Fifty thousand dollars would give him the seed money he desperately needed to build an AC generating system and prove conclusively that his concepts were valid. He put in many sleepless days of analysis and after a few weeks had the generator working perfectly, with a few added new features never anticipated by Edison.

Edison was impressed. The generator was installed in Manhattan and its operation brought a minor improvement to the distribution of DC power. Typical of Edison, he claimed that the inventions and improvements were his— that Tesla was only *following his directions.*

Tesla waited for the fifty thousand dollars that never came. He was very reluctant to ask for money. However, earning eighteen dollars per week as a technician at the Edison factory was not what Tesla had in mind for himself. He got up the courage and demanded the fifty thousand dollars he had been promised. Edison laughed at him. "You stupid Europeans, you believe everything you are told—get back to work."

Tesla walked out on the spot, defeated but unfortunately none the wiser. This incident was a foretelling of Tesla's lifelong powerlessness to receive due recognition and compensation.

Tesla could have learned from Edison. He could have learned to see a project through to commercial success. He could have used Edison's contacts to develop his own relationships with the moneyed of his time, but he did not. Tesla was at first in awe of Edison. But as he became more and more familiar with him, he became very disillusioned with the "Wizard of Menlo Park." He watched him claim the ideas of others as his own, saw half-finished ideas become poor commercial products, and watched firsthand as Edison stuck stubbornly to his own ideas while being unable or unwilling to see the merit in the ideas of others, especially of Tesla. The most significant of these being Tesla's AC versus Edison's DC.

Edison often had ten or more significant developments going at the same time, facilitated by his large staff of mechanics and technicians. In contrast, Tesla was a one-man show, and as such he was never able to fully realize the reach of his many ideas and inventions.

Edison was dominated by his huge ego. His hatred for Tesla ran deep. In 1915, the Nobel committee planned to award Edison and Tesla the Nobel Prize for physics jointly for their work with electricity. Edison learned of this in advance and refused to share the prestigious award with Tesla. He denied Tesla an award that history would prove he richly deserved. The prize would have given Tesla's sagging reputation the major boost it needed. Edison knew this and made sure Tesla got nothing.

Other scientists blatantly passed off Tesla's inventions and developments as their own. One such man was Charles P. Steinmetz, who, after Tesla's fade into obscurity, was often referred to as the creator of AC power distribution. Steinmetz headed up the division of General Electric that competed head-on with Westinghouse. At one society meeting in the early 1920s, Steinmetz presented a paper in which he claimed that the mathematical basis for AC electrical generation was his own creation. When challenged by knowledgeable members of the audience that he was merely parroting Tesla's work of twenty years earlier, Steinmetz and the rest of the technical society simply ignored the protest.

Tesla was beyond brilliant but unwilling or unable to put himself first. He did not understand that to most people, the status quo is comfortable and change is often feared, or treated with indifference. When financial and business opportunities presented themselves to him, he created impossible situations and roadblocks. He was a scientific Mozart, a genius who died a pauper's death.

Nikola Tesla's genius and contributions went unrecognized until he was frozen in the ground.

BOOK 3

CHAPTER 16

Viktor Gracac, Nikola Tesla's Nephew

Viktor (Viko) Gracac, Nikola Tesla's nephew, was born February 12, 1876, to Christina Tesla and Branko Gracac. Shortly after Viko's first birthday, Branko and Christina moved to the village of Salonia. Three years later a daughter, Djouka, was born.

As soon as Viko could talk, it was clear to all that he was exceptionally bright. He had an insatiable curiosity about everything, asking questions constantly. By the time he was three he began to read the newspaper. Christina, who had practically raised Nikola after the death of her brother Dane, was constantly amazed at the similarities between Viko and Nikola. His behavior was nearly the same, and he resembled Nikola to the extent he could have been his son.

Christina saw another side of Viko that she found chillingly familiar. Like her mother Ana and her brother Nikola, Viko would experience bouts of depression and darkness. Christina first witnessed this when Viko was eight. An elderly neighbor, Mr. Francolin, was like a grandfather to the neighborhood children. Viko and his playmates went to his door one afternoon and found it ajar, with Mr. Francolin unconscious on the floor; he had suffered a fatal heart attack.

The town turned out as one for his funeral, honoring an old man who had brought joy and laughter to so many. The neighborhood children cried and sobbed at his funeral, but none more than Viko.

Viko could not get over the loss. He cried at night and often awakened screaming, as his nightmares relived the discovery of Mr. Francolin's body. He wouldn't eat, lost weight, and stayed in his room, often curled up on his bed rather than being outdoors playing in the fields. His father forced him to go outside and spend time in the sunshine, but Viko just sat listlessly in the shade of a tree.

This brought back the terrible memories of Christina's mother Ana after the death of Dane. She withdrew and became a shell of her former self and died much too young. Christina also recalled the deep depression she had seen in her brother Nikola, accompanied by episodes of deep trancelike sleep.

It was Viko's little sister Djouka, five years old, who drew him out and put him on the road to recovery. She pretended that he was a big doll and spoon-fed him. She made him play games with her, and slowly he began to go outside to be with his friends.

But a permanent change had occurred in Viko. He matured several years that summer. His mind took on a new level of brilliance as evidenced by his pursuit of learning at a new and faster pace. While Viko had been in the state of deep depression, something had obviously changed in his psyche, as if his mental capacity had doubled. After tucking him in to bed one night, Branko remarked to Christina, "I think there are going to be two famous members of this family in the near future, your brother Nikola, and our little boy, Viktor."

Viko had his uncle Nikola's intelligence and insatiable curiosity, often confounding his parents with deep penetrating observations and endless questions about the stars, the sea, almost anything that had to do with science.

His father saw to it that Viko put in his share of effort for the family business, a successful inn and tavern. Beginning with sweeping floors and washing dishes, Viko was shown no favoritism; he came to understand the reality of a working life and the value of everyone, regardless of fortune or position in life.

He completed his studies at the school in Salonia by the age of fourteen. He served as a teacher's assistant and tutor for two years, helping students three to four years older with their understanding of math and science. Shortly after his sixteenth birthday, and after several long discussions with his teachers, Branko and Christina agreed that Viko should attend a university.

Christina carried on a regular correspondence with her famous brother, Nikola, and had kept him informed of the amazing parallels between him and Viko. It was Nikola's recommendation that Viko attend the University of Prague, and he contacted the chancellor on Christina's behalf. They quickly agreed to allow this young prodigy and nephew of Nikola Tesla to begin at the start of the fall semester.

After a teary goodbye to his family, Viko stepped onto a train that would take him to destinations beyond his wildest imaginations. He arrived at a boardinghouse in Prague exhausted and just wanted to go to bed. Juliet Magas, his new landlady, would hear nothing of that. She sat him down at the kitchen table and placed a warm meal in front of him.

Juliet's young daughter Lilet sat next to Viko and prattled on about her friends and dolls, asking him endless questions: where was he from, did he have a sister, what did he like to do? Juliet tried, with little success, to quiet her down but Lilet prevailed, as usual, much to the delight of Viko. He found her to be just like his sister Djouka—a little pest that kept him in stitches with her antics and practical jokes.

Juliet introduced him to her other boarders: Karl, a second-year student, and Josef, like Viko, an entering freshman.

Juliet Magas, a young widow, had opened her home to university students, providing a comfortable place to stay and good home-cooked meals. Branko arranged for Viko to live with her during his first year at the university with the hope that the homelike environment would ease his transition into the larger world of advanced education.

Viko quickly became Juliet's favorite boarder. She found his youthful exuberance delightful. He was the son Juliet never had and was a playful older brother for her daughter Lilet, who was just one year younger than Viko's sister Djouka.

The living arrangement would have been perfect except for Josef, three years older and jealous of Viko. He was decidedly unfriendly toward the young interloper.

A week after moving in, Viko began his remarkable journey through the world of physics and engineering. Like all entering first-year students, he attended a lecture in the main auditorium where he received a warm welcome to the *most prestigious learning institute in Europe.* The distinguished chancellor of the university got Viko's attention with an unfortunately accurate prediction. He asked them to look at the students on either side of them. "At least one of you will be gone in a year—unable to maintain the effort that makes you worthy of the education you will be offered here."

Viko had already set his mind to the task and was prepared to put forth his best effort, and this lecture strengthened his resolve even more. He was determined to make his parents proud and to achieve his goal of going to America and working with his famous uncle, Nikola Tesla, the rising star of electrical generation.

A few days before Viko had left his hometown a letter had come from his uncle. Full of encouragement, the letter included advice on study and said Viko would be welcome to come to America whenever it could be arranged. That prized letter never left Viko's pocket.

At school in Salonia, he had known the friendship of all, teachers and students alike, even those older than him. However, when he arrived at the university, everyone was a stranger. No one knew about this young genius or why such a young, scrawny person was in their midst. His intellectual abilities played well in the classroom, but in the world of living, eating, and walking to and from class, he was alone, isolated, shunned by nearly everyone. Juliet became concerned for him as he grew more and more depressed. At first it was the same homesickness that most of her boarders experienced during their first weeks and months away from home, but when it did not subside she recognized it as something deeper.

One cold December afternoon Juliet heard sobbing coming from Viko's room. It was not yet two in the afternoon; he should have been at school. She went to his room and softly asked if something was wrong.

"Go away."

"Now Viko, Christmas is just around the corner, and in a few weeks you will see your family."

"They hate me; I never want to see them again!"

Assuming he meant his family, she scolded him. "Viko, what a terrible thing to say! Your mother and father love you and are looking forward to Christmas with you."

Viko screamed at her, "Those bastards in my class, I hate them!" He burst into deep sobs, collapsed onto the floor, and wept openly. She coaxed him to get on the bed, covered him with a warm blanket, and left him to get some rest.

Later that evening, she took Josef aside and asked if something had happened to Viko that day. The smirk that came across Josef's face and the silence that followed infuriated her. She repeated her question: "Josef, answer me. Did anything happen to Viko today?"

"Yeah, we taught that little punk a lesson."

A stinging slap across Josef's face wiped away his look of smug satisfaction. He hesitatingly told her of Viko's treatment by a group of older jealous bullies. They threw Viko's books and papers into the street and tore to bits the prized letter from his famous uncle. Josef was the ringleader.

Juliet was furious. "You miserable excuse for a human being! Get out of my sight. That boy in there is more man than you will ever hope to be. I want you out of this house as fast as you can find new lodging."

The next morning, Juliet went to the university. She was determined to do something to help Viko. He was the most extraordinary student she had ever met. He needed nurturing and guidance to achieve his full potential.

The first year after her husband was lost at sea, Juliet had found work at the university as a cleaning woman. She had had a brief involvement with Professor Aleksandar Stipcevic that went nowhere quickly. She was a bit apprehensive about seeing him again, but her concerns were dismissed as soon as they began to talk about Viko. Finding him in his office, she greeted him with a brief embrace, accepted the tea he offered her, and settled into the one chair not buried by books and paper.

"To what do I owe this pleasure, my dear?"

"Aleks, do you know of a student named Viktor Gracac?"

"Why of course, Juliet, whenever we have a prodigy like him at the university word gets around quickly. Why do you ask?"

"He is one of my boys, one of my boarders. I'm very worried about him."

"What is your concern? I hear he is a brilliant student, years ahead of his class, and is the nephew of Nikola Tesla. There must be something to heredity."

Juliet went on to explain her growing concerns about how he was treated the previous day, and her fear that without guidance he would return home.

"Juliet, you do understand that as young men, we all have to put up with bullies and taunts, and at times we must fight for ourselves."

"I understand that, Aleks. After all, I have three brothers and I saw enough of that as a young girl. But Viko is like a piece of rare crystal, beautiful and exotic, very fragile. He is young, surrounded by older boys, and inexperienced in dealing with them. I can give him a pleasant home, but he needs guidance and protection while in his classes, at least through his first year here. Can you think of anything that can be done?"

Aleks sat back and thought for a few moments. He had a good friend who was the newest member of the faculty in the physics department, Heinrich Lippmann. He had been a prodigy and, like Viko, a foreigner. If anyone could understand Viko's situation, it was Heinrich.

Aleks agreed to talk to Heinrich that evening, but under one condition. With a serious tone to his voice, he said, "Only if you will do something for me."

Juliet immediately became apprehensive. *She had nothing to offer in return, unless he was referring to...* Before her thoughts went any further, Aleks smiled, reached out, and touched her hand.

"All I am asking is that you join me next Saturday evening for dinner, and to attend the opera with me. I have two tickets for box seats. I was planning to take my mother, but she is quite ill and cannot attend."

Juliet hesitated to accept, nervous about what appeared to be the renewing of a romantic interest in her. She made a few feeble excuses about Lilet being left alone for the evening, but Aleks wouldn't take no for an answer. She gave in (not so reluctantly) and agreed to the date. She was secretly quite excited about the prospect of a little social life. Spending the evening with him would be a nice change from her daily chores of keeping up her boardinghouse and mothering a group of rambunctious university students.

As he had promised, Aleks talked to Heinrich about Viko Gracac and Juliet's concerns. Heinrich had two passions in life, teaching and physics. Now he had the opportunity to indulge in both with a very promising young apprentice. Heinrich also knew that behind Aleks' interest in helping Viko was an equally strong interest in getting close to Juliet once again, and he agreed to help in any way he could.

Over the next few days, the three of them put together a plan. Josef, the bully, found himself "invited" to move into university student housing—good riddance. A senior from the physics department, Damian Fenevesi, replaced him at Juliet's boardinghouse.

Three days later, Viko came home later than normal, and when asked where he had been, he explained to Juliet, "I had some personal business to tend to." Viko looked away when he said this, appearing to be secretive, or perhaps embarrassed. When she asked what he meant, he replied rather forcefully, "Juliet, please do not ask me any more about this, trust me."

Josef was found later that evening at the bottom of a flight of stairs in the back of a university building. He was unconscious but not badly hurt, just a painful bruise on the back of his head. Everyone assumed he had slipped on the ice on the top step. When news of this reached Juliet, she remembered Viko's lateness and his comment. Had he done this?

Viko was summoned to Aleks' office and introduced to Professor Heinrich Lippmann, who had been assigned to him as a special counselor and tutor, under the guise that Professor Lippmann would assist him through subjects at a faster pace than could be accomplished in a normal classroom.

The plan initiated by Juliet worked. It would be another few weeks before the depression completely left Viko and the nightmares subsided, but Juliet had successfully helped him to turn the direction of his life back onto the road toward success. Going home for the Christmas holiday was just the break he needed to knit closed the last fragments of the cloak of darkness that surrounded him. But Juliet, with her woman's intuition and her motherlike caring for Viko, noticed a change. He was a little less open, more serious, and at times more introspective than before. He normally never commented on the behavior of others, but now he was occasionally mentioning the need for retribution for those guilty of crimes.

Had the Mr. Hyde in Viko begun to reveal himself?

CHAPTER 17
Three Years Later (1895)

I
t was late winter in Prague, cold and blustery. Spring was just weeks away, but the weather had not yet warmed. This was of little consequence to Viko, who preferred to be in the lecture halls or the science laboratories of the university, listening with an insatiable mind to the secrets of science he had wondered about for so long. Viktor Gracac was in his element. He loved the university. The city was beautiful, with its historical buildings and museums. Juliet and Aleks had been married eight months earlier, and Juliet was in the third month of pregnancy.

Just nineteen years of age, Viko was in his final year of the engineering program and three to four years younger than many of his classmates. Final semester exams were only a week away, prompting Viko to work even harder than normal.

He received weekly letters from his mother keeping him abreast of town gossip and the latest antics of his sister Djouka, a very bright girl in her own right. As all mothers do, she closed her letters with the stern admonition that he get enough sleep and dress warmly. Occasionally there would be an added page from his father. Viko was not quite as faithful with his return letters, maybe one a month, but he did try. Juliet made certain to place letters to Viko on his pillow, as she knew of the happiness he felt as he read each one. He always brought them to her to read, or to relate some amusing story from home.

Viko dragged his tired body into the house, said a quick hello to Juliet and Aleks, and went to his room to catch a few moments' rest before supper. He found a letter waiting for him. A few minutes later, Juliet and Aleks heard Viko cry out in pain. Fearing he had hurt himself, they rushed to his room and found him holding the letter in his hands and shaking his head.

"No, this can't be." Viko held out the letter for them to see, unable to speak, his eyes pleading for help.

The letter was from Djouka. It was very short, just a few words printed painfully by a young hand. *A bad man stabbed Papa. He is dead. Momma is very sick, please come home.*

Juliet pulled Viko into her arms and held him as his tears flowed. After a few minutes of letting his grief pour out, Viko stood erect, patted Juliet on the back, and wiped the tears from his face.

"I must pack for home now. Aleks, would you be kind enough to speak to Heinrich for me? I will do my best to get back here soon, but right now my family needs me."

Aleks agreed.

Viko turned to Juliet. "You have been my second mother. I'm going to miss you. I promise I will write as soon as I can. I would like to leave most of my things here until I get back."

"Of course, Viko, we'll be waiting for your return, hopefully soon. Our prayers will be with you. Pack what you need, and let me make you something to eat while you travel."

Aleks made arrangements for a carriage to take Viko to the train station, and a few hours later Juliet, Lilet, and Aleks bid him a tearful goodbye as he stepped into the carriage. Little did they know it was the last time they would see him. The death of his father put his life on a new course, one that would take him to a country far away and change him and the world in ways he could not begin to imagine.

Juliet was troubled. After his initial shock at the news of his father's death, Viko had behaved in a calm, almost detached manner. She knew Viko as an expressive and volatile young man, not one who could easily flip from an extreme emotional shock to a quiet air of detached determination. He reacted to painful experiences with open crying and tears. During times of joy, he would get as excited as a baby with a new toy, and whenever he learned of some new scientific principle he would babble on about it for hours. However, today he had just learned his father was murdered, and after only a few minutes of shock he was composed and determined. This was not the Viko Juliet had come to know as a surrogate son.

She had just witnessed the further emergence of another side of Viko, one that surfaced during periods of extreme stress or emotional upheaval. She talked about this with Aleks, who had come to appreciate her finely tuned awareness of Viko's moods and unusual behavior. They agreed that Viko was a most unusual person, brilliant beyond measure, but increasingly unpredictable. Juliet knew there was more to this young man, and it troubled her.

CHAPTER 18
Death Enters Viko's Life

V iko's father, Branko Gracac, was an honest, hardworking businessman, a military veteran, a good husband, and a stern but loving father to Viko and his sister. Such was his reputation that he had easily won elections to the positions of mayor and town judge. When a criminal came before Branko for a hearing, he could be sure of a fair hearing, but if found guilty he received punishment so severe that committing a crime in the future was inconceivable. Organized to a fault, Branko found little difficulty in operating a very profitable and well-regarded tavern, as well as performing his civic duties as mayor and judge.

Branko walked around the village every morning greeting the villagers, talking to the housewives as they swept off their stoops, saying hello to his fellow shop owners, and stopping to swap the latest gossip and smoke his pipe over morning coffee at the pastry shop.

And so it was on this Tuesday spring morning in 1895, as he enjoyed his coffee and shared a joke with his chief constable, that a young boy came running into the shop hysterical, crying and pleading.

"Please help me, help my mother! He's hurting her. He has a knife. He's going to kill her."

The constable asked the boy to calm down and tell them what happened.

"A man came from the woods—he has a knife—momma is screaming for help, please come now."

Branko and the constable jumped up and followed the boy, running as fast as they could to keep up. As they got close to the house, they could hear the screams from the woman. "No, no don't. Oh God, please stop. I have no money, please stop."

Branko raced on ahead, his heart pounding as his military training took over in full measure. He and the boy crashed through the door of the house to see the woman bleeding from a slash across her face and a disheveled, filthy man holding a hunting knife.

The killer looked up with crazed eyes and grabbed the woman, pulling her in front of him with the knife to her throat, threatening to kill her if Branko took a step closer. He reeked of strong spirits and filth.

Branko thought only of saving the woman.

He lunged forward, reached for the man's arm, and pulled it away from the woman's throat, and with his other hand he grabbed the woman's wrist and pulled her roughly away from the would-be killer. Branko turned to see that she was okay and in that instant lost control of the killer, who raised the knife and plunged it into Branko's neck, severing his carotid artery. The small room exploded with the roar of a pistol as the constable, just seconds behind, fired two bullets into the killer's chest and turned to help Branko.

Branko was holding his neck. Blood spurted out between his fingers as his heart raced from exertion and adrenalin. The constable pressed a towel to his neck in an attempt to stem the flow of blood, but the wound was too serious, the bleeding too profuse, and Branko's life ebbed away in a pool of bright crimson as the constable held him.

Marta Bako, the woman Branko saved, stood for a moment in stunned silence and then let out a mournful cry.

— ◈ —

Viko's father had been murdered five days earlier. His mother was in severe shock. As he began the long trip home, he didn't know that he would never see the university again.

The town was draped with black banners; wreaths hung on doors, the mourning for his father everywhere. With heavy heart, Viko walked slowly to his house. His mother did not rush to greet him as she had always done. He went to the kitchen and found Djouka, just sixteen, sitting at the table with tears in her eyes. She ran to him, threw her arms around his neck, and sobbed. Viko felt the tears in his own eyes begin to form, and the two stood there holding each other, letting their grief pour out.

With Christina was the woman his father had saved, Marta Bako, pledging to stay by her side until she regained her strength. Christina was sleeping and heavily sedated. The town doctor had served in the army and was accustomed to horrible crimes and death, but he had never seen a wife so affected by the death of her husband. Part of her heart died with him. Not as a heart that pumps blood, but as the center of life-giving energy. For the next three weeks, she refused to eat, wouldn't get out of bed, and hardly acknowledged the presence of her son or daughter.

Christina's refusal of food was not done out of not wanting to eat—she simply didn't need to. Life was worthless, a barren plain without the man she loved. Her beautiful black hair became streaked with gray overnight. Her skin, once as smooth as that of a woman ten years younger, was wrinkled and lined with grief.

Three weeks later, to the day and time of her husband's death, Christina's life slipped from her, and for the first time since that tragic day she appeared at peace.

Christina's reaction to her husband's murder bore a striking resemblance to the reaction her own mother had when faced with the death, many years earlier, of her beloved son Dane. She became withdrawn, lost interest in her other children, especially Nikola, and died a young woman.

Viko and Djouka, hand in hand, watched as their aging grandfather, Milutin Tesla, repeated the final words and blessings over their mother, just weeks after intoning the same Scripture verses over the coffin that held their father.

After the burial, sitting side by side, they barely heard the words of friends, neighbors, and townspeople as they offered their sympathies and went on their ways. In front of Viko and Djouka, in side by side graves, lay the bodies of their mother and father—parents who just a few weeks earlier had been vibrant, very much alive, and looking forward to a long and comfortable life.

The woman Branko had saved, Marta Bako, stood by them. Despite her own meager subsistence, she gave freely of her time and comfort, especially to Djouka, who needed closeness and understanding as she blossomed into womanhood.

Viko, fighting depression and sadness, went to his father's tavern each day. He knew the day-to-day business well enough. For a while, the restaurant continued on as it had before, but without Branko's voice of authority, Viko was lost and confused. His future as a scientist was in serious doubt. How could he ever complete his studies with the responsibility of a sister to care for?

A few weeks later, two men approached him, claiming Branko borrowed heavily from them to start the tavern. Viko, with little experience of money handling, went to the town's banker inquiring if they were right. Not knowing that the banker was part of the fraud, and with no sense of the law, Viko was forced to sign a paper stating that the assets of the tavern belonged to them.

With no choice left, he accepted a job working for the charlatans who took the family tavern from him.

He dragged himself to work each day, performing the menial tasks of a janitor and dishwasher as the new "owners" of the tavern sat back, smirking and taking money that was rightfully his. His dreams, his future, the promise that had been in his hands at the university had evaporated before his eyes. His depression returned and became intense, but unlike before, it was giving him strength to fight back at the injustice of a God who could let this happen.

CHAPTER 19
Salvation

In early 1895, Nikola Tesla made one of his frequent trips to Europe. He was scheduled to give lectures for electrical engineers in England and France regarding his AC power developments. In planning the trip, Tesla included a few side trips: to call on his sister Christina in Salonia, to spend time in his hometown of Gospic, and to travel to Prague to visit his nephew Viko at the University.

It had been seventeen years since Tesla had been home to see his father or visit his sisters. Christina had been faithful in her promise to write often, and Nikola looked forward each month to her letters and the news, especially of the latest antics of Viko, who was sounding more and more like a shadow of Nikola's younger self.

He completed his work in France and boarded a train that would take him to Salonia and Christina's home—not realizing the tragic news that was waiting for him upon his arrival.

Meanwhile, Viko struggled to get through each day. The loss of his parents, the indifference and coldness of the town, and the loss of his future combined to produce a profound despair that consumed him. His life and its once great promise was dying a death of its own. His education had come to an end, and without money to proceed or someone to care for Djouka, he saw only a future as a waiter in a tavern that no longer belonged to his family.

On a Friday morning at the break of dawn, Viko trudged to the tavern to open the doors and clean for the coming day. As he wiped down the counters, he found a letter addressed to his father and postmarked in Paris. Judging from the date, it had been there for weeks and had been overlooked, shoved under the discarded wrappings from a wine delivery.

The letter was from his uncle Nikola, who was lecturing in Europe and planning a trip to visit family before his return to America. Nikola apparently didn't know that Branko had been murdered months earlier. No one had taken the time to let him know. According to the letter, Nikola would be arriving on Monday, just three days away! For the first time in weeks, Viko smiled. The sun began to shine for him once again. For the rest of the day and through the weekend Viko bounced through his work.

Shortly after noon on Monday, Nikola Tesla arrived. Viko and Djouka spent the afternoon relating the story of their parents' deaths. Together with Djouka and Viko, Nikola visited the gravesite and wept openly as he recalled the wonderful times he and his older sister had spent together. Christina had been like a mother to him, and her passing was as profound to him as the loss of his mother had been.

This changed everything for Tesla. Urgent business in Salonia would use up what little time he had left before he had to return to America. The story that these men could so easily take away the tavern from his sister's family was not at all credible to his keen sense of honesty and understanding of lawful procedures. Tesla's anger at the townspeople energized and intensified his natural beliefs in fairness for all.

He engaged a local attorney who quickly discovered that the tavern had been taken from his niece and nephew by fraud. The local authorities arrested the two men and the banker. The ownership of the tavern was returned to the rightful heirs, Viko and Djouka Gracac, and Tesla arranged for Marta Bako to manage it.

But what about the care of Viko and Djouka? Tesla knew he couldn't leave them as they were, virtual orphans in an indifferent village. He felt that his younger sister Milka would take in and care for Djouka, and he was willing to provide funds to send Viko back to the University of Prague.

With both of her parents gone, Djouka wanted to leave Salonia. Moving to Gospic and living with her aunt Milka was kind of exciting. She was ready to go.

But Viko had other ideas for himself. Would Uncle Nik take him to America and let him work with him? In Viko's mind, there was no greater educator than Nikola Tesla. No one had his uncle's mind. Where else could a student like Viko learn from a master? Working for Tesla in America would let him do real work on new inventions in this age of constantly evolving electrical miracles.

Nikola was hesitant. He didn't have the time to care for a young man and also carry out his important work. But Viko was insistent. He would work for nothing! He would sleep on the floor! He would sweep the floor! He had great original ideas himself, and he could help Uncle Nik in a way that no ordinary worker could.

Ultimately, Nikola acquiesced and agreed to take Viko to America with him. He canceled his plans to lecture at the University of Prague. He sent an apologetic letter to the chancellor citing urgent family business and made the necessary travel arrangements so that Viko could accompany him home. Viko was ecstatic.

While Nikola spent his nights in Salonia working on a new idea for electrical generation, Viko was at his side every moment. Nikola learned firsthand of Viko's drive, his intelligence, and his ability to think clearly through the most complex issues. He began to accept that this young man could be the asset he needed back in America, the missing link that could help him see his work come to fruition. And there was another important reason to bring Viko home with him: he could be trusted with Tesla's trade secrets, he was blood.

After a brief visit to Gospic and a tearful goodbye to Djouka, Nikola and Viko traveled to Paris where Nikola gave two lectures on his rotating magnetic field motors, extolling their efficiency and predicting that these motors, dubbed *induction motors*, would ultimately relieve mankind of backbreaking work. Viko was fascinated. He sat there in awe of his uncle. He had heard about him, of course, and his family often talked about his marvelous discoveries. But here he was, in the flesh, and Viko actually understood the concepts that his uncle could so clearly describe.

Viko believed in fate. Was this why his father was so cruelly murdered and his mother died of grief? Was it his destiny to work beside his uncle, making the world a better place? Was his family taken from him so that he, like his bachelor uncle, could work unencumbered to create the marvels that seemed to pour out of this age of discovery?

Both Nikola and Viko came from a family background of priests who preached the Word of God, who had guided others through a world of suffering, pain, and questioning. Was the life of scientific discovery not the same? Showing others that so much is possible, that life can be so much better, and that mankind can be lifted up to new levels of dignity? More time could be devoted to arts, science, and leisure, and less to the demeaning drudgery of work that reduces men to little more than trained animals, wearing a yoke, draining the life force from their exhausted bodies.

Viko had matured ten years in the span of a few months. A man emerged where once stood a youthful, exuberant university student. An irreversible change had occurred. The treatment he had endured after his father's death had erased any pretense he may have had about the integrity and trustworthiness of others. He was no longer a naïve young man but one controlled by something new, something hard, and unfortunately something darker.

He took a silent vow of loyalty to follow and support his uncle Nikola, setting aside his own life for that of this eminent genius.

BOOK 4

CHAPTER 20
Viko in America

Viko's first year in America rushed by so fast he barely had time to sit down and take in one new thing before the next began. He felt like he was constantly on the carousel at Coney Island. Gone was the naiveté of youth, replaced with the hardened reality of life. There were those who had shown him tremendous friendship and caring, Juliet and Aleks, Professor Lippmann, and of course Marta Bako, the woman his father had saved. They would not be forgotten, and he promised himself to somehow, at some time, return in some small measure the kindness they had unselfishly given him.

There were also those who had shown him hatred, jealousy, and downright dishonesty. They would not be forgotten either. He would single them out for retaliation, for revenge for the pain they had caused. A part of Viktor Gracac stored away the memory of his pain and hurt so he could summon it when needed to see justice done, the kind of justice that was delicious to think of, to contemplate and savor. From somewhere within, his dark side had moved closer to the surface, a protective shield he welcomed.

During the first few weeks after his departure from Salonia, Viko had vivid dreams reliving those terrible days. He welcomed sunlight because the terror of his dreams held no power during the day. As the weeks faded into months, the nightmares lost their intensity and finally disappeared. He became deeply involved in the work of Nikola Tesla, becoming his right-hand man in the process.

Tesla was struggling at the time. He had no lack of good ideas, but he was constantly in financial trouble. Time and again, one great invention after another was taken from him, at times through his own lack of business acumen, and at other times by attorneys and a court system that seemed to favor everyone but him.

He lost all ownership rights of the AC polyphase system he created and brought to commercial success through Westinghouse Corporation. Guglielmo Marconi, who was making a financial success out of wireless communication, copied Tesla's radio patents. To twist the knife in Tesla's heart, it was popularly heralded as the *Marconi wireless*.

His most recent undertaking demonstrated an ability to light lamps that were long tubes without wires (the forerunner of modern fluorescent lamps), the first of his attempts to convince others that electrical power could be distributed without wires, but no one was listening.

Tesla suspected there was a leak within his operation; someone, most likely Edison, had a paid informant who was conveying all pertinent technical data to him, and in turn Edison was passing it on to Marconi, or stealing it for himself. However it was occurring, it poisoned Tesla's attempts to raise funds.

Into his troubled world stepped Viko, a trustworthy blood relative. He was the person with whom Tesla could share his most valuable ideas and techniques. Viko did the legwork and gave him unconditional loyalty. Nikola Tesla had made a very good decision, not just as a family member, but also as a technical giant in need of help, as he struggled against the forces that seemed intent on preventing his success and the realization of his dreams.

Each day Tesla and Viko would take a carriage from the Waldorf-Astoria at 350 Fifth Avenue to Tesla's lab in lower Manhattan at 31 South Fifth Avenue, a practice that Tesla had followed every day for years. It did not take Viko long to conclude that such sumptuous accommodations as the Waldorf made little practical sense. Tesla was forever late meeting his rent, the Waldorf restaurant was ridiculously expensive, and furthermore, it was thirty-two blocks away from the lab, requiring an expensive carriage ride each way. Viko preferred the simplicity and warmth of an apartment or a house.

One night while dining at the Johnsons', Tesla's banker and close friends, Viko brought up the subject of the hotel. Viko had done some looking around the neighborhood near the laboratory and found a very nice apartment two blocks away on East Twelfth Street, for just fifteen dollars per month, and it included all utilities plus a doorman. He informed the Johnsons of this in advance, and that evening over dinner the three of them convinced Tesla that the move would be in his best interests. Most likely, Katherine Johnson's offer to assist them in setting up housekeeping took away any final objections.

As they gathered up their belongings and prepared to move out of the Waldorf, Viko reflected over the past five months to the day he took his first steps on American soil.

That first night in New York, they had gone directly to the Waldorf-Astoria Hotel. As they dined in the hotel's famous restaurant, Viko was wide-eyed as one after another famous guest came over to shake hands with Tesla, to welcome him home and ask what great new invention was around the corner—and a few actually asked for his autograph! He knew that his uncle was famous, but people treated him like a celebrity. He half expected someone to bend down and kiss his uncle's ring. And of course each person, after greeting Nikola, turned to the handsome young man across from him and asked the obvious question, "Is this your son?"

Nikola was quick to point out that, no, this was Viktor Gracac, his late sister's son who had come to New York to live and work with him.

Viko was surprised, as he had been many times over the past few weeks, to see how little Tesla ate. He hardly ate enough to maintain his gaunt frame, choosing small portions of the blandest food on the menu as if the action of digesting excessive food would overburden his fertile mind. His choices in menu items were puzzling, especially considering that the delicacies on the Waldorf menu were the best in the city. This was just one of many oddities and idiosyncrasies of Nikola Tesla that would puzzle Viko as time went on.

They fell into a natural working arrangement; Tesla was the idea man, the one who dreamed big dreams, whose avid mind took leaps beyond the bounds of ordinary mortals. And Viko became the responsible one, sorting through the constant outflow of Tesla's creativity. Nikola enjoyed being the one whose name was in the papers, speaking at events where his demonstrations of high-voltage electricity were better than any circus show. The unnoticed man in the background was Viko, quietly and effectively being the man behind the man, the one keeping the wheels turning and the operation in full swing as Tesla ranged far and wide, in spirit and his travels.

Tesla introduced Viko to George Westinghouse, taking him along when he visited the Westinghouse manufacturing facilities in New Jersey. Westinghouse was building the generators, motors, transformers, and distribution systems that were the core of Tesla's polyphase AC electrical power. It became commonplace for Viko to make the trip alone to assist the engineers and mechanics when problems arose with the newer and larger generators and motors that were constantly being developed. The older engineers at Westinghouse were initially skeptical about the twenty-one-year-old wonder boy, but they quickly developed respect for his talent and ingenuity. More than once, he studied a problem they were having and with uncanny accuracy recommended a change that solved the problem quickly and economically.

In no small measure, Viko's quiet, understated personality had much to do with his success. In addition to his brilliance, he was without pretense or guile. Unlike Tesla, who often came across as aloof and insular, Viko was friendly, respectful, always referring to older men as *Mister* or *Sir*. When he found errors in others' work, he presented his solutions without ever referring to "mistakes" or blame on the part of others, but simply as suggestions, *perhaps another approach*. He brought others into the implementation of repairs and redesigns, ensuring that credit went to everyone. Viko had a natural ability to draw out the very finest in others, and they came to see him as a leader they wished to follow, an unusual ability for a young man working with men twice his age.

Unfortunately, Viko became aware of another side of Nikola Tesla. Tesla had little appreciation for the value of his work. Viko saw value, wealth, and sources of income at Westinghouse, at the generators at Niagara Falls, in Tesla's ingenious induction motors that were rapidly becoming the workhorses of industry. However, Tesla constantly struggled because of a lack of funds. Tesla had assigned most of his patents, especially the lucrative ones, to the likes of J.P. Morgan and George Westinghouse, usually in return for an empty promise or, worse, as compensation for work that Tesla failed to complete on unrelated tasks.

The seriousness of this came home to Viko while having lunch with Thomas Allen, George Westinghouse's electrical foreman. He asked Viko why Tesla never presented a bill to Westinghouse for the services they were providing, such as the help that Viko was offering to Westinghouse. Viko had no answer; that part of the business was foreign to him except for the bits and pieces of conversations he picked up around the office.

Viko never thought to ask about such a thing as payment arrangements. He had supposed there was an agreement, a fee for such work, but beyond that he had never inquired about it.

One evening, when they had a rare night off and were dining at the Johnsons' home in Manhattan, Viko asked Nikola why he was not billing for his consulting and assistance time. Viko was actually a little reluctant to bring it up, fearing Nikola would tell him that his time wasn't worth much—but the answer he got made him drop his fork.

"It is beneath me, and it should be beneath you, to charge for simply helping others to solve their problems," his uncle Nikola said. "I do not lower myself—I have too much self-respect to put myself in the same category as the likes of Edison, whose ego and buffoonery puts him on the front pages and results in his ridiculous charges. Why, I understand that he charges as much as twenty-five dollars an hour for his time. Our work, Viko, is for the good of humanity, and it is a gift. Just think of all the good we are doing, the burdens we are lifting from the common man, the free time we are giving to everyone to pursue music, art, family. That is enough compensation for the truly gifted."

Viko just stared at him.

This was not new ground for Robert Johnson, who was at his wits' end trying to get Tesla to understand the financial side of business. Nikola Tesla was a man hounded daily by suppliers demanding overdue payments, a man who gave away inventions worth fortunes to raise a few measly dollars, whose mind was brilliant beyond measure, but whose financial wherewithal was so lacking as to be laughable.

For the first time since they had worked and lived together, Viko got angry.

"My God, Uncle Nik, if Edison is worth twenty-five, you are easily worth fifty dollars per hour. How can you be so naïve? Are you stupid?"

Stupid blurted out in the emotion of the moment. Tesla had only been called stupid once before—by Edison when he refused to pay Tesla the fifty thousand dollars he had promised him for fixing a dynamo.

If the Johnsons' dining room was quiet before, now it was like a mausoleum. It was as if Tesla suddenly turned to stone. His features hardened and his eyes bored into Viko with a look that chilled Viko to the core. Time stood still. Tesla was practically catatonic, no sound or movement save a shaking in his hands. He pushed his chair back and as if in a trance removed his napkin from his lap, neatly folded it and placed it next to his plate, and got up, turning to leave.

Viko was petrified. He had never seen his uncle like this. What had he done? His eyes darted back and forth between Robert and Katherine.

"I, I, I'm sorry, Uncle Nik, I didn't mean it, I'm so sorry."

Tesla continued toward the door.

This behavior was not new to Robert and Katherine. They had both seen him become trancelike in the past, usually when something of a critical nature was said to him. It triggered something deep within. Katherine looked pleadingly at Robert, her eyes begging him to do something. Robert got up, crossed the room, and put his hand on Tesla's shoulder. Tesla stopped and turned, looking in Robert's direction, but his eyes seemed not to see.

"Nik, please stop; come sit back down. It was an innocent remark! My God, Viko wasn't trying to hurt you. Now come be sensible and sit back down with us."

Tesla seemed to understand but he continued to stand and look straight ahead, like someone who had just awakened from a dream. Katherine walked up to him, stood on his other side, and held his hand in hers.

They led him back to the table. Robert helped him with his chair and Katherine offered him his wineglass. Tesla took a sip, savored it for a moment, looked over at Viko, and smiled.

"What wonderful friends I have. I don't know what I would do without all of you."

The dinner continued as if nothing had happened.

The next morning, Viko traveled downtown and went to the American Citizens Bank where Robert Johnson greeted him and invited him into his office. "I imagine you're here to talk about last night?"

Viko nodded.

"Katherine and I have seen this happen before. The first time we saw this was about four years ago. He invited us to his workshop to demonstrate his new lamps and had also invited his good friend Samuel Clemens for the evening.

"Nikola was holding one of his lamps. It glowed with the most unusual blue color, and there were no wires at all connected to it. It was amazing! He began to describe his ideas about wireless power distribution, and it was obvious to us poor mortals that it worked! He suddenly stopped talking and moving. He just stood there, his eyes like those of a blind man. Samuel shrugged his shoulders in our direction and frowned, as if to say *what's this?*

"At first we thought the electricity was flowing through his body and somehow affected his speech or his muscles. We took him by his shoulders and gently guided him to a divan in the corner. Katherine brought him a glass of water. He was cold and clammy. Samuel was about to run off to find a doctor when Nikola coughed, looked around at all of us, and smiled. He got up, went to his desk, and wrote and drew electrical drawings with such speed that the pen was a blur. He looked up and said, 'Just a thought I had, wanted to get it down while it was fresh.' And then the evening continued as if nothing had happened."

Viko didn't realize it, but this was exactly the behavior he himself had exhibited in the past when at the university.

During his next trip to the Westinghouse plant in New Jersey, Thomas Allen again questioned Viko regarding the invoices. Tesla was broke as usual and Viko decided that a small fib would not be out of order. "I was going to bring that up today. We will be submitting a statement for a small payment."

"Small? No indeed, I have been authorized to give you a check for all the work that the two of you have done for us."

He handed Viko a check, signed by George Westinghouse, for $42,863—a fortune in 1902. Viko held it in his hand and just stared, first at the check, then at Allen. Viko was not quite sure what to do or say, but he was not about to give it back.

Sheepishly he said, "George is most generous. I'm sure that my uncle will be pleased."

As Viko headed back to the city that night, he was full of anxiety. In one hand, literally, he had the answer to all the financial problems his uncle was having, but on the other hand, he held the memory of his uncle's admonition that he would not lower himself to accept money like this. And that exacerbated his fear that Tesla would have another of his strange attacks. He decided that before he did anything else he would talk with Robert Johnson.

They met two days later at the bank offices.

"Viko, what brings you here today?"

"This is why I am here."

He handed Robert the envelope containing the check. Robert put on his reading glasses to make sure his eyes were not playing tricks on him and then let out a long slow whistle. He sat back. "Care to explain this to me?"

Viko recounted the events of the past few weeks, and of Westinghouse insisting he take the money to Tesla. He feared that telling Tesla would provoke another reaction.

"He needs this money, but I don't know what to do with it. I came to you because you would know how to talk to my uncle. I don't want a repeat of the other night."

"I agree with you, Viko. It is baffling to me how someone with your uncle's intelligence and grasp of the scientific world can be so impractical regarding money. His work is worth a fortune. I think he sees it somewhat like being paid in the same manner that an attorney is paid, and he has quite a degree of contempt for the legal profession, which he views as nothing more than a bunch of vultures. Let me think about this overnight. You were right in coming to me. If it is acceptable to you, I will keep this check in the bank vault for safekeeping."

The next day, sitting at a quiet table in a nearby restaurant, Viko and Robert had just ordered lunch and were sipping their beer. "Well, what do you propose we do?" asked Viko.

"I have an idea regarding the money. But first I must warn you that what I am about to suggest is not quite in keeping with proper accounting practices, but I consider this to be an extraordinary situation, one calling for an extraordinary solution. I propose that you, Viko, become the de facto head of accounting of the Tesla Electric Company. You and I are the only ones who will know about this.

"I further propose that we set up a trust account into which we will deposit the check, and when we feel it is appropriate I will see to it that funds from the account are transferred into the Tesla account. I am going to convince him to let you handle the finances. I am not quite sure how, but Katherine is close to him and I can use her influence to convince him that it is a good idea. What do you think?"

Viko asked several clarifying questions. He worried about Tesla going to Westinghouse and angrily confronting him over his paying money directly to Viko. He was unsure of what to do.

Robert asked him a single question. "Do you think that your uncle deserves this money?"

"Yes, of course."

"Then let's move ahead and worry about problems with your uncle, if and when they occur. The check is made out to the Tesla Electric Company. It must be endorsed before we can deposit it. At present, and until we put you in charge of finances, there is only one signature that we can accept, *Nikola Tesla*. I am going to ask you to do something that I have never done myself, and I have never asked anyone to do before. I have seen your handwriting. It is indistinguishable from your uncle's. Will you sign the check, using your uncle's name?"

The question troubled Viko—*does the end justify the means? Is a solution to the consistent, acute financial crisis worth a potentially illegal act, regardless of its potential positive effect?*

"Robert, let me sleep on this. I see the good in your proposal. It holds Uncle Nik's interests at the core, but I'm troubled by signing his name."

"I know this is a huge decision for you. Think it over carefully, and please contact me if you have any questions."

Viko chose to walk thirty blocks to lower Manhattan and the Tesla Electric Company. He needed to think, and the fresh air would help. To sign or not to sign? What a dilemma.

He arrived at 31 South Fifth Avenue as confused as when he left the restaurant. But when he walked in the door, the scene before him made up his mind on the spot.

Tesla was in a shouting match with three men. Viko recognized Abe Cohen, the proprietor of the largest hardware supply in New York. Cohen and Tesla were nose to nose, screaming and gesticulating with their arms. The two in the background were large and burly and not there to have a nice chat.

Cohen shouted, "Pay the bill now! I have had enough of your promises. You have until tomorrow morning. The bill is $1,585. I want cash, and I want it no later than noon. Do you understand me? Do I need to have these men show you how serious I am? Charlie, how about a few broken fingers? Maybe a good kick in the balls? Maybe both?"

No one noticed that Viko had entered the room.

As the man called Charlie stepped toward Tesla, Viko quietly reached to his right, picked up an iron bar, and pushed one of Tesla's fluorescent lamps onto the floor. The sudden crash, followed by the sound of imploding glass, caused everyone to spin around. Viko held the thirty-pound iron bar as he had seen baseball players hold their bats.

The two men began to move toward him. Viko raised the iron bar and calmly said, "I have served in the Serbian army; I have killed men with a bayonet. Step away from Mr. Tesla."

Even Tesla showed signs of fear, not of the two apes that were about to work him over, but of Viko. Was this the young man he worked with day and night? There was something behind the voice—an edge that spelled danger. The thugs nervously glanced at each other trying to decide how to rush him, neither one willing to go first. Cohen broke the silence. "Okay boys, I think we've made our point. It's time to leave."

"Not so fast," said Viko. "What's this all about?" Abe, who knew Viko, tried to tell him that it was none of his affair. However, Viko insisted. He took a practice swing with the iron bar, and the look on his face caused everyone to back up a bit.

Abe explained about the past-due bill and the countless promises from Tesla. Viko glanced at his uncle, who was relieved that he wasn't going to be nursing a broken hand or a very painful set of testicles, but was obviously very embarrassed that Viko had had to learn about their precarious financial condition in this way.

Viko told Cohen that he would have the money by noon the next day. Tesla started to say something, but an angry look from Viko made him think better of it. Viko repeated, "You have my word; your money will arrive by midday at the latest."

Looking a little skeptical, Cohen and his "persuaders" left. Viko put down the iron bar. His hands began to shake. Slowly he shook his head. "How long has this been going on?"

"I owe you a debt of gratitude. Those men were going to hurt me; did you see how unreasonable Abe was with me? Why, he was demanding—"

"You owe me a *huge* debt of gratitude! I should have let them twist off a couple of your fingers or give you a good kick in the privates. How can you be so blind? Listen, Uncle, I care about you. You are a genius, but you have to stop living in your dream world that surrounds you like a cocoon. You are not a king to whom your subjects owe a living. This place has to run like a business, not like some kind of grand experiment. I look around and I see failure. I see piles of worthless paper, paper containing the greatest advances of the last hundred years, and yet because of this fantasy world you live in they result in nothing for you, but result in millions for those to whom you constantly owe money. You give away everything for a handful of change.

"From this moment, I am going to handle the finances around here. Do not question me. Do not get involved except to let me know how much you need and what it's for. I will decide the rest. Do you understand me?"

Tesla just sat down, stunned. He stammered a bit, tried to speak. "I, I don't know what to say."

Viko said again, "Do you understand me?"

Tesla nodded hesitantly. "Yes, I understand. But may I ask where you intend to get the money to pay him by tomorrow? We only have about three hundred dollars."

"As I said, do not ask. Consider it done. I want to see all the financial records of the company."

As they strolled later that day down to a nearby park to watch the seabirds and look out over the water, Viko felt an inner strength he had not felt before.

That night over dinner, the tension of the afternoon dissipated, Nikola reflected, "You were very intimidating today. When did you serve in the army, and did you really kill people?"

"Was I that convincing? I was never in the army, and I have never been able to deliberately hurt anyone, but when I saw those men about to attack you, something in me snapped. When I worked in my father's tavern I had to learn to deal with an occasional drunk. One day a man from the village, completely drunk, came in demanding wine. He grabbed an empty bottle, broke it off, and threatened to slice my face open. He rushed at me. I stepped aside and he fell, swearing and cursing as I had never heard before. I grabbed a chair and swung with all my might—it knocked him out!

"When I saw those men coming after you, I relived those moments, and something in me told me that I must defend you regardless of any danger to me."

The next morning a smiling Viko walked into Robert Johnson's bank. "Shake hands with the new finance officer of the Tesla Electric Company!"

Robert said, "Excellent! Let's get to my office. I have an idea as to how we can do this without Nikola finding out."

"No need to do that, my uncle agrees to it all."

"Excuse me, but how?"

They sat in Robert's office drinking their morning coffee. Robert listened as Viko told of his return to the office and the events that unfolded there.

"He doesn't know about the Westinghouse check, and he doesn't need to know. I can sign my own name to the check. Let's get on with it. I need to get money to Abe Cohen before his goons come back and turn my uncle into a eunuch!"

It took Viko a month to straighten out the financial mess that Tesla had accumulated over the previous twelve years. Every time Viko got things under control, a new creditor would surface and he had to once again deal with another angry supplier. He found that Tesla had not invoiced legitimate deliveries, and he was able to bring in another $65,386 to the account.

When all was settled, Viko paid all creditors, old hotel bills, restaurant bills, attorney's fees, patent filing fees, and back pay to the workers. It totaled $32,594, leaving a healthy balance in the accounts of the Tesla Electric Company. For the first time in a long time, Tesla was solvent, no longer hounded by creditors, and the change in him was remarkable. His health improved, his step quickened, and his creativity reached new heights.

CHAPTER 21

January 1903—
Viktor Gracac Becomes Viktor Tesla

Nikola Tesla was forty-seven years old and knew that he would never marry; his life had no time for that kind of commitment. His hermitlike existence in the confines of the lab never gave him the chance to meet anyone of the opposite sex. Despite this, Tesla had a desire to be a father, if even of an adopted son.

As he and Viko worked together, the thought often crossed his mind, but he was reluctant to bring it up. Would Viko think it an insult if he asked him to be his adopted son? The physical resemblance between Nikola and Viko was uncanny. It was common for first time visitors to refer to Viko as *Viko Tesla*. Viko never corrected them. The misunderstanding gave Tesla a swell of pride. He wanted to be a father, and Viko would be the perfect son.

Viko's twenty-seventh birthday would be in a few weeks, February 12, 1903. Tesla planned to use the occasion to ask Viko if he would consider changing his last name to Tesla. With Katherine's help, he planned a surprise birthday party.

The twelfth arrived on a particularly cold and windy day, and Viko wanted nothing more than to go home to their apartment and sit in front of a warm fireplace. When Tesla told him the Johnsons had invited them for dinner he protested, "Since when do we get invited to the Johnsons' on a Thursday? You go. Tell them I'm sick."

Nikola had invited all Tesla Electric employees; they needed to leave work early to attend. He had to get Viko out of the way. "Viko, I forgot to mention that Robert is bringing a banker home tonight. He wants to talk to us about investing in the electric rifle I've been working on. You must be there! You know how bad I am when it comes to money details. That's your department. You need to get home and take a bath; you smell like Edison."

Hearing this, Viko knew he needed to be involved. He reached for his coat, gathered it about himself, and headed out the door. He was mildly exasperated at his uncle, thinking to himself, *When, if ever, will this man learn a little organization, and when will he think to let me know about these things in advance? Brains and common sense do not always exist side by side.*

An hour and a half later a very cold Viko Gracac and Nikola Tesla stepped out of a carriage and hurried to the Johnsons' front door as the wind whipped down the street and did its best to blow their hats away. Katherine opened the door. "You two look like Eskimos!"

Viko grumbled, "Could we just get inside? I'm freezing." They hung up their coats and went into the library where a warm fire burned in the fireplace. Viko started to ask about the banker. But before he could get the question out he heard a very loud "Surprise!" and turned to face all of his friends, fellow workers, and even a few engineers along with Thomas Allen from Westinghouse. The Johnsons' young children were there, done up in their finest. Viko's face turned a bright shade of crimson; he was embarrassed to be the center of attention.

After a sumptuous meal, everyone went into the library for cake and coffee. The Johnsons' maid wheeled in a teacart with a beautiful cake and twenty-seven brightly burning candles. Viko took a deep breath and with a huge exhalation of air extinguished each candle to the great delight of the crowd.

After the applause died down, Robert said, "Well, Viko, what do you think of the cake and its decorations?"

Viko had been so preoccupied that he had not read the inscription on the cake: "Happy Birthday Viktor Tesla."

He started to say that his name was wrong, but he looked at his uncle who was shaking his head slowly.

"No, Viko," Tesla said, his voice cracking with emotion. "The cake is correct. Since everyone already thinks you are my son, I think it is time we make it official—consider yourself adopted."

Viko had been an orphan for years, ever since those terrible days in Salonia. He had been forced to take on the burdens of adulthood almost overnight. Nikola Tesla was a close relative, his uncle, and for him to consider Viko a son was an affirmation beyond anything Viko could have imagined. From that day forward, Viko ceased to call himself Viko Gracac and proudly began to use the surname *Tesla*. In his mind, Uncle Nik would always be his uncle, and his memories of his parents would never fade away, but he had a renewed sense that he belonged someplace, no longer isolated, but part of a family again.

CHAPTER 22
Nikola Tesla and the Johnsons

Nikola Tesla and the Johnsons had been close friends for many years. Robert was the president of American Citizens Bank of New York, a small but very successful bank navigating the early waters of financing new business ventures. He and Katherine had been married for four years when Robert first met Tesla, a struggling scientist with a brain better suited for the technical world than for the financial world. Tesla had just left his employment with Edison and was striking out on his own.

When choosing those he would support, Robert looked for integrity, honesty, and expertise in their chosen field. Tesla possessed those qualities in abundance, but with a financial naiveté that was almost frightening. Tesla was so assured of his technical prowess that he deemed business matters irrelevant.

Their first meeting was accidental. Tesla was on his way to see John Astor when he inadvertently walked into American Citizens Bank. Robert politely said, "Sir, I think that you are in the wrong bank, but may I help?"

Tesla's reply took him back a bit, and coming from a lesser person would have been laughable, but Tesla had such an air of confidence that Robert asked him to repeat what he had said. Tesla repeated: "You can help me only if you are willing to invest in the greatest motor developments yet to be introduced. I am going to revolutionize factory production techniques."

Robert found him intriguing. Their relationship grew, and Robert became his most trusted confidant on business matters. He introduced Tesla to financiers, reviewed contracts for him, advised him on legal matters, and helped him find a trustworthy patent attorney. In the course of their many meetings, Tesla met Katherine Johnson while having lunch with Robert. The warm feelings were mutual; Tesla's brilliance put Robert in awe, and his European charm and manners delighted Katherine.

He visited their home at least weekly for family dinners that were better than the famous restaurants he loved to frequent. Katherine learned of the dishes he had enjoyed as a boy, researched European recipes, and directed their cook to prepare meals especially for Tesla.

Robert and Katherine Johnson became his American family. Tesla was so involved in his work that he developed few close friendships, yet he was drawn to both of them. Katherine was one of the few women he valued as a friend, and at times her compassion for him filled in gaps that had been left open when his mother died.

Robert was invaluable as a source of financial advice, but he found Tesla's strange attitude toward accepting money counter to intelligent business operations. Had it not been for the entrance of Viko into the picture, that part of their friendship would be very strained indeed.

BOOK 5

CHAPTER 23
1904—J.P. Morgan and
the Fluorescent Lamp

After months of experimentation, Tesla and Viko reached a satisfactory level of reliable performance with the "Tesla lamp" (the forerunner of the modern fluorescent lamp). Tesla arranged for publications throughout the country to report on this new, wonderful cool source of indoor light. It attracted one of the richest men in America, and arguably the single most influential person as regards United States financial policy. J. Pierpont Morgan had such control over monetary policy that he forced President Howard Taft to support his plan for circumventing a major financial crisis in 1909. His business acumen, as well as his reputation for ruthlessness, was second to none. He epitomized the term *Robber Baron.*

Among Morgan's achievements was the formation of the General Electric Company, which he created by combining the Edison General Electric Company with the Thomson-Houston Electric Company.

One of Morgan's most extensive business developments was the formation of the IMM, the International Mercantile Marine. This led to his financial control of White Star Line and its manager, J. Bruce Ismay. He provided the majority of the funds to build *Titanic.*

When Morgan expressed interest in the new Tesla lamp, it represented not only a huge opportunity for Nikola Tesla, it also was a blow to Edison, whose hatred for Tesla was legendary. Edison was furious. Tesla's AC was clearly superior, but Edison refused to accept it and did everything possible to discredit him.

Robert Johnson was approached by Morgan's representative and set up a meeting between Morgan, Viko, and Nikola for a Tuesday afternoon at Tesla Electric. Robert warned Viko and Nikola, "He wants to see the lighting. This could be the break you have been waiting for, but be careful with him. He did not acquire a personal worth of eighty million dollars by giving money away. He will come in and seem to be willing to help, but before you know it he will own everything of yours."

The next Monday morning, as Nikola and Viko were putting plans together for the meeting with Morgan, they received an urgent message. A generator at Niagara Falls had gone down in the extreme cold and the remaining generators were unable to make up for the loss. Sections of the city of Buffalo were without power. Thomas Allen of Westinghouse needed someone there immediately. With Morgan about to arrive, the message could not have come at a more inopportune time.

Viko had supervised the Niagara installation. He spoke up immediately. "I should go." He quickly gathered his notes, ran home, packed a few things, and caught the next train to Niagara Falls. His last words to Nikola were, "Go ahead with the demonstration, but remember what Robert said: Morgan is not to be trusted. Do not strike a deal with him until I get back."

Morgan presented an unusual caricature. He was a short squat figure of a man and suffered from rhinophyma, a condition that caused his nose to swell to huge proportions resembling the red rubber nose that a clown might wear.

Pierpont, as Morgan preferred to be called, visited Tesla's facility as planned and was thoroughly taken with Tesla's amazing new lamp, mesmerized as it glowed with soft pure light while remaining cool to the touch. Morgan and Tesla talked throughout the afternoon and into the evening, discussing in detail a plan to manufacture the lamps with Morgan agreeing to provide all funding. He was quite aware of Tesla's genius and the power of his inventions regarding electrical generation and distribution. He was reaping returns from the private investments he had with Westinghouse. To be involved in the manufacturing of this new lamp was simply icing on the cake.

Morgan owned a large unused warehouse in the Bronx with two hundred thousand square feet of manufacturing space and offices. He offered an incredible deal. "I will provide all financing. You will receive a 51 percent interest in the business, which gives you controlling interest. I think such a generous offer is fitting for a venture with this kind of promise. The business will be named the Tesla Electric Lamp Company. Will you assign the patents to a manufacturing company, assuming of course that you are properly compensated?"

Conveniently setting aside the fact that he and Viko had agreed that Viko would handle all financial matters and agreements, Tesla reverted to the same twisted logic that had plagued him for years. "I do not expect compensation for my patents; I am willing to accept income as a royalty from the sale of the lamps." With that statement, Tesla turned down an offer worth hundreds of thousands of dollars. He continued, "As regards the percentage, I will accept no more than 49 percent ownership. It is you who should have control, not I."

Morgan was taken aback. He had just put forth a dream offer. Tesla could realize huge profits from this and remain in control. "Are you sure of that position? My advice is that you discuss this with your banker friend Johnson, or your nephew Viktor."

"No, these are my lamps. I will make this decision, and I will take no more than 49 percent and no compensation for the patents."

As Morgan put on his hat, his parting words to Tesla were, "Nikola, you are the strangest man I have ever met."

Three days later, Tesla was at the Johnsons' for dinner. Robert asked, "How was the meeting with Morgan? Is he interested?"

Smiling like a Cheshire cat, Tesla replied, "Interested? He certainly is. Tomorrow we sign a contract."

"What does Viko think of the deal?"

"He knows nothing of it. I'll tell him when he gets back from Niagara Falls."

Robert was stunned. Tesla had no one to advise him on contract terms. His predilection to sign away valuable patents and concepts was legendary. Once again he was going to sabotage himself.

Robert excused himself and raced to his office. He had to contact Viko. Robert knew that Viko would not let Tesla be taken advantage of. Such a deal could not be signed without Viko's approval, a fact conveniently or naïvely overlooked by Tesla, but unknown to Morgan. He rushed to the bank. Locking himself inside, he sat in front of the telegraph set and tapped out an urgent message:

COME TO NEW YORK URGENT UNCLE NIK IS IN TROUBLE

The telegram didn't reach Viko until late the next afternoon. He came back to New York as fast as possible. He and Robert went directly to Tesla's facility. But it was too late. Tesla, giving everything to Morgan, including all future patents for improvements, had signed an ironclad contract. Viko collapsed into a chair. His desire to help Tesla seemed to evaporate. Why try? It was an impossible situation—Tesla was on a permanent course of self-destruction. He had just given up control to a notorious despot.

Robert heaved a deep sigh. "All right, Nik, give us the contract. Let's see how much damage has been done."

It took Robert and Viko two days to read and digest the entire contract, and when they were finished they realized it was worse than they could have imagined. Not only had Tesla given Morgan operational control, he signed over the rights to all of the lamp patents and all future patents pertaining to illumination, lamp design, and power distribution to lighting. Morgan's attorneys had thought of everything.

Robert arranged a meeting with Morgan. He went right to the heart of the matter, explaining that any contracts involving funding of the Tesla Electric Company, or its patents, needed joint approval from both Tesla and Viko.

That's as far as he got.

Morgan raised his hand, as if to say "Just a minute," and turned to his attorneys, who obviously had been prepared for this. The contract was between Nikola Tesla and J.P. Morgan as individuals; there was no mention of the Tesla Electric Company. Morgan, taking advantage of Tesla's naiveté and childlike excitement about having his lamps manufactured, had created a contract that demonstrated once again why he was one of the richest men in America. He looked out for just one person, J.P. Morgan.

A thorough review of the contract by Robert Johnson's attorney confirmed their worst fears. As Robert and Viko watched, he asked Tesla, "Why would you agree to something like this? Just a few more days and we could have rewritten this to give you ownership of your patents with conditional assignment to Morgan, much more in your favor. Why didn't you let someone see this before signing, at least your good friend Johnson here?"

Without saying a word Tesla slowly got up and put on his coat. At the door, he turned and said, "What's done is done."

After Tesla left, Robert asked, "Is there any chance of overturning this contract in court?"

"Possibly," the attorney responded, "but Morgan will tie this up for years. He will drive you into bankruptcy and sue Tesla for not producing the lamps."

The attorney continued: "Let me tell you a story about Morgan. I was a young attorney, just out of law school, when I first heard it. I dismissed it out of hand. A senior partner took me aside and assured me that it is true.

"During the Civil War, Morgan financed a scheme, the Hall Carbine Affair. He arranged the purchase of several thousand defective rifles that were being liquidated by the government at a cost of three dollars and fifty cents each. He then sold them back to the government, supposedly repaired, at twenty-two dollars each. The carbines were not repaired, had never even left the government warehouse where they were stored. The scheme existed only on paper. Morgan netted a ninety-two-thousand-dollar profit. The guns, which could misfire, killing or maiming a soldier, were put back into service. Morgan professed complete innocence of the defect in the weapons, a claim that only the most naïve of the day could swallow. There was never an investigation."

The lawyer paused. "Do you want my advice, Viko? Find a way to be cooperative with Morgan and proceed with the production plans. You and your uncle will realize a substantial income for a long time. It is not as good as it could have been, but an envious position nonetheless."

The following Monday, Viko went to Morgan's office alone. "Mr. Morgan, I came here this morning to ask you not to exploit my uncle. I will do all I can to see that the lamps are manufactured properly. Also, I assure you of something else: if you attempt to harm my uncle in any way, you will have to contend with me. My family means more to me than any amount of money or possessions."

Morgan said, "Please be assured, Viko, that I am serious about manufacturing your uncle's lamps. These new lamps will be in demand everywhere, and I intend to sell millions of them. I have no desire to harm your famous uncle in any way."

They shook hands and parted.

Morgan had not expected a threat from such a little person. He smiled. He feared no man and quickly dismissed Viko's warning.

Morgan made few mistakes. But he had just committed his biggest one. Viko, a mild-mannered Serbian immigrant, would one day bring Morgan's largest business venture to its knees.

Viko left New York to return to Niagara Falls, his work there not yet completed. With well-founded apprehension, he left the work of getting lamp production underway in the hands of Nikola Tesla. He could not begin to imagine the catastrophic mess that would be waiting for him upon his return to New York weeks later.

As part of the agreement, Tesla sent a small crew to Morgan's office to install fluorescent lamps. Morgan wanted firsthand experience with the lamps, and to demonstrate them to raise additional funds as the need for larger manufacturing facilities developed. But Morgan always had more than one reason for his actions.

As soon as the installation was complete, Morgan invited another famous inventor to see the lamps, Thomas Edison. Morgan considered Edison to be a vulgar, unkempt, smelly, loudmouthed braggart. He never enjoyed visits from Edison, but he endured them, unable to ignore the millions he was reaping from Edison's electrical work.

Edison arrived in his usual rumpled black suit, his hair disheveled and his hands stained with filth from whatever he had worked on the night before. He slapped Morgan on the back, leaving a blotched stain on his shoulder. "Good to see you, JP. Why did you call me? Got some new way to print money?" He paused, looked around. "What is this lighting you have here?

Morgan explained to Edison about his dealings with Tesla. After a slew of colorful outbursts from Edison, punctuated by a few loud farts, Morgan managed to get him to sit down and listen. "I had these lamps installed so that you can look them over. Tesla's patent applications and copies of his notes for future improvements are in my filing cabinets, yours to review. Set aside that famous dislike you have for Tesla. I want your honest evaluation. I do not trust him. He is so naïve as to be childish. I fear that a mass-producible lamp will never see the light of day with him running things. I plan to move all production to Schenectady as soon as possible. I want him out of the picture.

"Curtis (Mark Curtis was Morgan's personal bodyguard and the director of his security operations) will arrange security at the Bronx plant. We will explain to Tesla that we need guards on duty at night. You or anyone you choose will have access to the building. Give their names to me or Curtis."

As Edison got up to leave, Morgan's final words were, "Do not let your temper get in the way. This is too important."

Edison hated Tesla and everything he ever did.

Morgan stared at the door Edison had left ajar and spoke to his secretary. "Tell me, Miss Harbaugh, do you think that Edison would understand the message if I sent him a bathtub, a large supply of soap, and instructions for their use?"

The normally staid and humorless secretary burst out laughing. "Well, it certainly wouldn't hurt to try! Would you like me to open a window and air this place out?"

CHAPTER 24
The Lamp Fiasco Begins

Tesla received the first installment of funds and immediately set out to renovate the Bronx facility. Unfortunately, his ability to plan for production was diametrically at odds with his ability to manage the work required. He changed his mind constantly and made the workers redo their work every time he got a new idea. He insisted on making every decision, no matter how small. Workers were idle most of the time as they waited for him to make up his mind. His lack of punctuality exacerbated the situation. He typically arrived for work in the late afternoon and then expected everyone to put in twelve to sixteen hours, working well into the night.

Tesla was brilliant beyond measure; his mind was simply too creative to be confined by mundane construction details. He had already moved on. The lamps were an old idea. His brilliant intellect was consumed with his quest to create a world where wireless power would be available to all. Two months were wasted with frustrating starting and stopping, and the devastation inflicted on the production preparations was nearly fatal.

Morgan's worst fears were becoming reality. He monitored expenses and saw daily reports containing nothing but bad news. Had he made a huge mistake? Edison and his crew pored over the patent applications and dissected

Tesla's lamps, to no avail. Edison's massive ego and his hatred for Tesla were obstructing progress. In his typical bull-in-the-china-shop methodology, he insisted upon achieving DC operation, impossible for a practical fluorescent lamp, with the predictable result that each attempt at making the lamps resulted in failure.

Viko returned from Niagara Falls, only to find that Tesla was planning to leave town for Colorado. As he arrived at the apartment after his ten-week absence, he was surprised to see several packed trunks and two suitcases in the hallway near the front door. Totally exhausted from weeks of nonstop, sleep-deprived work, he went to bed. The questions in his mind would wait until the next day.

As sunlight filtered in through the curtains and the sounds of Saturday Manhattan traffic sneaked in through the open window, Viko unfurled from the position he had been in all night. Though the comfort of his own bed was welcome, his body seemed to remember every night he had slept on the floor or in an uncomfortable cot at the Adams plant in Niagara. After washing up and putting on a clean shirt, he wandered into the kitchen where Tesla had put a pot of coffee on the stove.

Tesla asked about the situation at Niagara, and they spent the next several hours discussing the technical issues involved and the solution that Viko had implemented. Tesla nodded in approval.

As the coffee restored some semblance of clarity to his sleep-deprived brain, Viko returned to the conversation they had started the night before.

"Exactly why are you going to Colorado? How do you expect me to carry on without you? You have a responsibility to be here."

"Viko, the lamps will come later. Don't you see that the lamps are only a demonstration, a glimpse through a window into the future, a future where everyone on earth will have access to wireless electrical power? Where everyone can light their lamps, run their homes, power their factories—all without wires. Viko, the lamps were just my way of opening the door. Morgan will see that, and he will thank me."

Viko could do little more than shake his head. Here before him was a perfect demonstration of Tesla's inability to see the devastating effects he had on those who put trust and faith in him. He expected everyone to understand as he did. He didn't understand that true success did not come from multitudes of imaginative ideas; it came from the hard practical work of seeing things through to a conclusion. He was incapable of understanding the world of business and commerce and the practicalities involved.

Tesla continued, "I have been waiting for you to return. Now that you are here you can take over for me. The plans are all drawn up; you just have to follow them."

And with that, Tesla returned to his final packing details.

Viko spent the rest of the weekend recovering from the arduous two months he had spent at Niagara. He got up early on Monday morning and went to the Bronx to get a firsthand view of the progress made, and the remaining work now dumped in his lap.

His first surprise when he arrived was that he couldn't get inside the building. A guard, not recognizing Viko, refused to let him enter. A rather loud argument ensued. Henry Abbott, Tesla's foreman, came out to see what was going on. Finding Viko, he ran over, grabbed his hand, and nearly shook it off.

"Finally you're here. This place is a mess. I have a mutiny on my hands."

The bewildered guard looked on for a few minutes. "Who is this?"

"This is Viko Tesla. For God's sake, get out of the way and let him in."

Viko was greeted enthusiastically. Most of the workers knew him and respected his abilities. Shouts of "Thank God you're here," "We've missed you," and, most surprising, "Does this mean Tesla won't be coming back?" rose from the crowd.

Viko turned to Henry. "What's this all about, and why the comment about my uncle?"

The group became quiet and a voice from the back said, "If Tesla never comes back it will be too soon," followed by murmured approvals.

Henry Abbott asked everybody to take a break, and he and Viko went off to a quiet corner. He told Viko of the chaos that had reigned for the past two months.

Viko learned of the constant changes, work having been completed and then torn out three or more times. He learned of everyone waiting while Tesla would sit for hours on end, trancelike. Even the smallest decisions needed Tesla's personal consent.

Viko listened impassively. He was genuinely saddened to hear how his uncle was affecting those around him. He was shocked at the lack of progress toward outfitting the facility. Having someone like Tesla in charge of the "trivial" matters relating to outfitting a production plant was a gross error. It was akin to swatting a fly with a defective sledgehammer.

This was a déjà vu moment for Viko. Missed deadlines, disgruntled employees, and failed opportunities. This time, however, a new dimension was added to the picture, planned and orchestrated by J.P. Morgan. If the venture continued to head down this path, the damage to Tesla's reputation would be irreparable. Morgan would shut down every venture, every financial plan, and cut Tesla off. Tesla would be hard pressed to find employment as a janitor.

Henry said, "Viko, I don't think it's too late. I will not attempt to minimize our problems here. Morgan keeps sending that damned Curtis around, asking questions and looking over our shoulders. If you show us what to do, these people will follow you. Viko, I will work day and night. You know you can count on me."

Viko saw the looks on the faces of the twenty-three workers anxiously waiting, wondering what they should do next. Those eyes were looking to him for direction. He searched for an answer, looking for some input, anything at all to convince him that the monumental task awaiting him was worth the personal investment he would have to make. Perhaps this was why he was brought to America, to be the one to do the work left in the wake of his uncle's creations.

Something dark within him flashed. He would be the part of Nikola Tesla that was missing. He jumped up on a box, called out to the group to gather around.

"Are you ready to get this place up and running?"

A resounding "Yes!" came from everyone.

"Let's start. Get busy! Clean up this mess. By noon, you will get your marching orders. If Nikola Tesla shows up, send him to me. Ignore anything he tells you. Now get off your lazy asses and get moving!"

Before noon arrived, Viko had divided the men into groups, each with a leader, and he chose one man to be his assistant—a runner to handle the many messages that would be required within the building and with outside factories, chemical supply houses, and mills.

Work settled into a routine. The building was noticeably cleaner. A makeshift bulletin board contained lists of jobs for each group. Viko and Henry roamed freely among the workers, lending a hand, offering advice, and made themselves visible and available to all.

A few minutes after four-thirty, Nikola Tesla walked in. Viko was busy going over a drawing and didn't notice Tesla's arrival until Henry elbowed him in the ribs and pointed toward the door. Tesla saw that people were leaving for the day, and he raised his hand. "Everyone get back here. I have several new ideas that I want to try tonight."

One of the workers said, "Mr. Tesla, you are to talk to Viko, not to us."

Tesla was becoming red in the face just as Viko shouted out, "Why, Uncle, so nice of you to grace us with your presence. These men have put in a day's work and are going home to their suppers."

Tesla started to speak, but all that came out was sputtering as the entire group of workers filed past him out the door.

"Viko, what is the meaning of this? Get them back here!"

"I will do nothing of the sort. You will demand nothing from me, now or at any time. Come over here and sit down."

Before Tesla could utter a word, Viko took him by the arm and sat him down at a makeshift desk.

"Last night you told me you are leaving for Colorado and that I was to take over here. I have begun to set this place straight, and you will not interfere. If you want or need to try a new idea, you can tell me about it. I will decide if it is important. If you try to stop me, I'll go to Morgan and disclose that you are using his money for other purposes. If you want my help, this is the way it is going to be!"

Tesla had never seen Viko so in control, so ready to carry out the threat he had just laid before him. Inside he was seething that his judgment was in question and his authority usurped. But implied was the truth that with Viko in charge, he could make his trip to Colorado, conduct his experiments, and make (in his mind at least) another contribution to the world of electricity.

They sat and talked for several hours, and as Viko questioned Tesla regarding details of lamp production, Henry Abbott took pages of notes.

Tesla had established an account at American Citizens Bank in the name of the Tesla Electric Lamp Company. Morgan deposited funds into the account as needed. Tesla arranged for Viko to have access to the funds. Viko signed documents, approved by Morgan, allowing him to write checks against the funds. Tesla reluctantly agreed to stay away from the Bronx building unless invited, thus putting full responsibility for the success or failure of the venture on Viko's shoulders.

CHAPTER 25
Treachery and Deceit

By the time four weeks passed, Viko had made miraculous progress in readying the building for production. If progress remained steady, they would process their first lamps in two months' time. Morgan knew that Viko was running the show, and the reports from Curtis brought good news every week.

Viko was usually the first one to arrive at the building. March 8, 1905, was an important milestone date. The first deliveries of chemicals would arrive. He went to his desk to get the bills of lading kept in his upper left drawer. They were missing.

As soon as Henry Abbott arrived Viko asked him, "Did I leave those chemical lists with you?"

"No, I haven't seen them at all."

They looked around their small office and on top of a filing cabinet found a folder containing a list of suppliers. It was also out of place, and inside were the missing bills of lading for the chemicals.

Viko was a creature of habit. Neither he nor Henry would have left out an important file, nor would they mix up important paperwork.

Viko closed the office door. "Who's been in here besides us?"

Something was definitely amiss. The most troubling aspect was that there was a guard on duty outside the only unlocked door. Was an employee going through sensitive files? Could it have been the guard?

From that moment on, the desk and the filing cabinet remained locked whenever they were not in the office, and the office door was locked after hours. Later that day when Mark Curtis came by, Viko told him of the apparent breach of the files.

Curtis's report to Morgan that week reported the discovery by Viko that there might be a security breach, and he concluded, "Tell that clown Edison that his people need to be more careful."

Six weeks later, after herculean effort on everyone's part, the first production line was ready. The work was not without its personal toll on Viko. He was no stranger to hard work and long hours, but for the first time in a long time, he began to look forward to weekends so that he could get some extra sleep.

Late on a Friday afternoon, Viko said goodbye to the last of the men and returned to the office. He had hours of paperwork to do before he could leave. As he sat there in front of the piles of paper, his eyes got heavy; he leaned back in his chair and closed his eyes. After all, resting a few minutes couldn't hurt.

He awakened several hours later to the sound of something falling, followed by cursing. "Get this damned box off my leg. Dammit Batchelor, will you try to be a little more careful!"

Did the voice say "Batchelor"? Viko glanced at the clock on the wall in front of him, a quarter to twelve. He had been asleep for four hours. Who was in the building?

He carefully got up from his chair and looked around the corner and down the hall. He could not hear all they were saying, but he heard enough to make his instincts razor sharp. He heard Morgan's name. They seemed to be looking over the latest installation progress.

He quietly worked his way through the dimly lit building, hiding behind boxes and machinery until he was just twenty feet from three men who were standing and talking.

One of the men said, "Listen, Edison, when are you going to admit that Tesla knows things about these lamps that are not in the patents. If you could get past your bullheadedness, you two could learn to cooperate."

"I will never cooperate with that son-of-a-bitch. If you bring that bastard's name up again, you can get the hell out of my sight—forever. Morgan wants nothing to do with him! Why the hell do you think he arranged for us to get in here? He wanted this place shut down, but ever since that young Viko, or whatever he calls himself, has taken over, he's not so sure."

The third man spoke up. "Look, Edison, you've had five months to duplicate the lamp, and all you have are hollow glass tubes that turn black. Viko is going to make a prototype run within the next ten days, and if these lamps work Morgan will have to continue to back Tesla. He doesn't want to do that. I've arranged for you and your men to get in here at night for months, and you haven't been able to make one good lamp. Batchelor is right. Tesla is a smarter man than you give him credit for."

Before Edison could lash out with another string of profanity, Batchelor spoke up. "Curtis, we know this, but we're convinced that the patent applications are incomplete, Tesla has left something out."

Curtis?

Was it *Mark Curtis's* voice?

Viko took a chance and lifted his head just enough to see the three men. He could clearly see Charles Batchelor and Mark Curtis, and facing away from him was Edison. He fought his urge to get up and confront them, but his cold calculating side remained in control. It was more important to listen and learn as much as possible. He needed to understand the extent of Morgan's deceit. Was there another breach of security? Were any of their workers spying for Edison during the day?

Viko listened carefully to the conversation.

Batchelor said, "If they're about to make the first run of lamps, let them. Talk to Anderson and make sure he is familiar with each step. We need daily reports from now on, and considering how much I pay him he had better damned well follow through. As soon as they produce the first few lamps, we come back in here and see for ourselves. Once we know how they do it, we take over the building and move the assembly line out of here to Schenectady."

Edison put his arm around Batchelor. "I knew there was a reason I liked you. That son-of-a-bitch Tesla will never know what hit him."

Viko quietly got up and made his way back to his office. One name kept running through his mind: Anderson—Kenneth Anderson, a new hire, brought to Viko's attention by none other than Morgan's man, Mark Curtis.

Curtis was responsible for the safety and security of Morgan's varied and scattered business interests as well as serving as Morgan's personal bodyguard. Viko never really questioned why someone who had a rather prestigious position with J.P. Morgan would take such an interest in a small part of Morgan's ventures. If the true extent of his duties had been known, Viko would have been shocked to learn that this man had perpetrated some heinous acts of violence against hapless steel factory workers who had the temerity to try to form a union.

Kenneth Anderson was an expert in handling glass. The fact that he was recently an employee of Edison's Menlo Park facility was carefully hidden. Because of a fat bonus provided by Morgan, he was more than willing to become an employee of the Tesla Electric Lamp Company, gather inside information, and pass it on to Edison. The idea of putting a mole inside the plant started in Morgan's mind after he became convinced that Edison was not going to be able to reproduce the Tesla lamp without inside help.

They would plant a good person inside the building, one who could learn the process and gain the confidence of the other workers. Once the line was operational, they would move it to Schenectady and run production from there.

Returning to his apartment in Manhattan at three in the morning, Viko located some red wine and drank straight from the bottle.

Despite his fatigue, sleep was impossible. He paced back and forth, stopping only long enough to take another slug of wine, finally heaving the empty bottle against a far wall. He watched it shatter, imagining it was Morgan's head exploding. The veins in Viko's neck stood out like the lines in a relief map of the world, pulsing violently with each beat of his pounding heart. Were he not young and in good physical condition, he would likely have been dead on the floor from a stroke or heart attack. The ability to think rationally escaped him. Nothing in his life—the loss of his parents, his depression at the university, or the rejection of the townspeople in Salonia—had prepared him for this.

He never fully trusted Morgan. But this outright intent to steal Tesla's property, this was beyond his ability to comprehend. It had all been a deliberate plan to steal the lamps. Morgan proved himself worse than a common thief, worse than even his own reputation for ruthlessness. In Viko's mind, there was no forgiving this deliberate act by the pathetic little man with a clown's nose.

One thought circulated through Viko's mind. There would be no more attempts at negotiation, no further efforts to make a success of the lamps as proof of Tesla's superior technology, no asking the advice of people like Robert Johnson and especially not Nikola Tesla. No, this time it would be him, Viko Tesla, who would exact a measure of revenge on this despot, this worm of a human being, this fat man in his plush office with his fat cigars and fancy Brazilian coffee. Morgan would rue the day he ever heard the name "Viko Tesla."

The bottle of wine dulled his senses. His body was screaming for sleep. He fell into the nearest chair, and as the first light of dawn crept through the window, he drifted into a troubled sleep.

In his nightmare, demons surrounded and taunted him. They wore faces of hatred. Men who had stolen his father's tavern, the man who had killed his father, Josef, the student who mocked him at the university—they repeatedly tore up letter after letter from his uncle Nikola, laughing and poking at him. In the distance he saw his mother and father, Juliet, Professor Lipmann, all watching, unable to help. A grotesque face belonging to Morgan floated back and forth, directing the others like puppets: "*Hit him, poke him, taunt him.*" Viko screamed for help. No one came to his aid. The last to turn away was the face of his uncle Nikola, repeating quietly, "*You must help yourself; we cannot help you.*"

The bright light was hurting his eyes. He turned away and his head hit against something hard. Viko opened his eyes. He was on the floor in bright sunlight, curled up in a fetal position, trying to protect himself.

Soaking wet from sweating, he realized he had also pissed in his pants. He got up, staggered toward the bathroom, and filled the tub with the hottest water he could stand. The time was half past three in the afternoon. He had slept most of the day.

As he soaked in the hot water, he recalled the conversation he had overheard the previous evening, knew that the era of the Tesla Electric Lamp Company was about to end, and began a mental list of the irreversible steps he had to take.

Viko knew the final secret of successful lamp operation. There was a tiny, key step that made it all work, a step Tesla deliberately left out of his patent filings, having learned the hard way that filing a US patent in 1904 was simply a way of conveying the most complex and clever secrets to anyone who wished to copy them.

One step in the preparation of the phosphor materials was the ultimate secret to the longevity of the lamp, one ingredient so common in the world and yet so unexpected that only the analytical mind of Tesla would have realized its importance. If this step, this added catalyst, was omitted, the lamps turned black within hours, sometimes in minutes, rendering them inoperative. Edison did not understand this step. With his bullish approach to problem solving, he never would. Viko didn't keep the chemical at the plant for fear of discovery. He kept it in a kitchen cabinet in their apartment, sitting among all the kitchen spices, hidden as well as it would be at Fort Knox.

It was his original plan, as the first lamps were being coated, to explain this all-important step to a few key employees, and one of those had been the traitor Anderson.

CHAPTER 26
Justice

The following Monday morning Viko arrived at the plant and greeted the ever-present Mark Curtis with a friendly handshake. "We'll make our first lamps this week. We are as ready as we can be!"

"That's great news, Viko. This will make Morgan very happy."

"Mark, the news he gets this week will be among the most important he has ever received."

Viko checked the financial balance: just over twenty-eight thousand dollars in the account. He waited until Henry arrived, explained that he had some business to tend to, and went to the bank. He withdrew twenty-five thousand dollars, issued as two thousand in cash and the balance in three cashier's checks—two at eight thousand dollars and one at seven thousand dollars. The remaining three thousand dollars in the account would meet the week's payroll—the last he would issue. He then stopped at three small independent banks, opening new accounts in the name of Viktor Gracac, and deposited the three cashier's checks.

He arrived back at the plant just after lunch and had the spy, Kenneth Anderson, brought into the office. "This week you are going to earn your keep. We are going to make the first lamps. I want you to stay close, as I have much to teach you."

Sensing something unusual, Henry asked, "Why just him? I don't understand. Why not teach others as well?"

"I have my reasons. Trust me."

There was something different about Viko, not as pleasant or forthcoming, somehow secretive.

By Monday evening, Edison and Morgan knew of the eminent launch of the first lamp production. At Edison's Menlo Park headquarters that same day, another failed attempt at making a lamp occurred with the same result of blackened lamps shortly after being turned on. "That son-of-a-bitch has left out a detail!" Edison spewed. "That has got to be it. With Anderson in there we are finally going to get the answer. He will let us know at noon on Thursday if they are on schedule. Plan to go over there Thursday night; we need to see for ourselves. I can't wait to get that bastard Tesla out of the way."

On Wednesday afternoon, Viko called together five men, large strapping farm boys, all more than six feet tall. They were men he knew well. They met in the office with Viko and Henry. Viko closed the door, got a bottle of whiskey out of a drawer, poured seven shots, and offered a toast. "Boys, to Nikola Tesla, the genius who has made it possible for us to work here."

There was agreement all around, and the group relaxed as Viko asked them to sit down.

"You all know that you can trust me. I am asking each of you to swear to me right now that what I am about to tell you will not leave this room, that you will tell no one, not your friends, not your family, and especially not anyone who works here or guards this building. I want a show of hands, do you agree?"

It was unanimous, but a few started to ask questions, especially Henry.

Viko continued: "Let me explain. I think that what I have to say will answer all your questions. We have a spy. Someone has been in this building gathering information and taking it to Edison. Henry and I have suspected it for some time, and last Friday I found positive proof that it's happening. I've asked you all here to help me catch them in the act and to take them to the authorities. I don't trust the police to do this, and you will understand why when we have caught them. You men are big and tough, not afraid of a fight, and I trust you to keep this to yourselves."

Viko outlined his plan.

He was quite certain that Edison and his cronies would be so curious that they would come to the plant Thursday evening after Anderson told them the lamps worked.

At quitting time on Thursday, they were to leave just as they did every day. Viko and Henry would meet them in the back alley at ten o'clock where Viko had changed the outer lock. They would steal into the building and take up positions where they could block any attempts at escape, and on signal from Viko (a blast on the plant's time clock whistle) they would surround the thieves and detain them.

"Any questions?" Viko asked.

Henry had the final word. "Everyone here has worked for Tesla Electric for several years. Do you remember what it was like before Viko? Remember the weeks without pay, putting up with Tesla and his moods and tantrums? But this man, Viko, has turned it all around. Tesla is respected because of him. We owe our livelihood to him. Viko, we are with you. Let's stop this bastard who is trying to discredit Nikola Tesla with one hand and steal his secrets with the other."

"There is one more thing." Viko opened the top desk drawer and took out five envelopes and passed them out. Each contained one hundred dollars in cash. Considering that the average weekly pay in those days was about six dollars, this was a fortune. "This is not an attempt to pay you for your help tomorrow night; it is simply my expression of gratitude for your loyalty and willingness to put yourselves in harm's way for my family."

When they were alone, Viko handed Henry Abbott an envelope containing five hundred dollars. He was overwhelmed at receiving several months' pay in one lump sum. "That, my friend, is for your unwavering support and friendship. Now let's get home. Tomorrow should be an interesting day."

Viko waited until everyone left the building. He walked over to the production line where everything was in readiness. Fifty glass tubes lay there in their naked beauty. He took a covered beaker from a nearby cabinet. It was filled with the phosphorescent chemicals that glow with soft light when activated by electricity. Viko withdrew two small vials from his pocket, one containing a dilute hydrochloric acid solution and the other mercury, or as it was commonly called, quicksilver. He placed the half-filled hydrochloric vial next to the beaker of chemicals. He removed the cover from the phosphorescent chemicals and poured the mercury over them. Who would suspect that mercury was the secret ingredient? And who would ever suspect that mild hydrochloric acid, mixed in with the lamp chemicals, would create a mixture so hot as to melt through the bench top?

The following morning there was excitement in the air. Most of the workers arrived early, and even those not involved with actual production were hard at work when Viko and Henry arrived. Anderson was standing at the coating machines and noticed the presence of the hydrochloric acid. He asked Viko why it was there. Viko replied, "I must have left that out last night." He took Anderson aside. "I should have known that someone with your education would have noticed. You might as well know now, *that* is the secret ingredient, the thing that makes the lamps work. Without it, the electric field within the glass destroys the chemicals, causing them to turn black."

Doing his best to suppress his glee at finally learning the secret, Anderson nodded in serious agreement. Viko continued, "The acid needs several hours to permeate the mixture. I added it last night before going home."

One by one the glass tubes were inserted into a tumbling machine that coated the inside surfaces with the pure white phosphor chemicals. The tubes were flame sealed and a huge vacuum pump began to withdraw the air. At three-thirty in the afternoon, Anderson carried the first tube to Viko waiting at the test station. Viko connected the wires protruding from its ends and then called the entire production crew to gather.

Anderson turned the large knob on the voltage control transformer. For a few seconds, nothing happened. And then, starting as a small sputter at one end, the lamp came to life, giving off a warm glow that got brighter and brighter until it stabilized in a blaze of sunlight-like illumination.

A roar of approval went up. Hearing the noise from the guard shack, Curtis came running in. Seeing the lamp, he glanced at Anderson for just a moment in silent recognition.

Viko noticed this. Anderson's next move didn't surprise Viko in the least. He announced that he needed to leave early. His mother was arriving in town and he needed to meet her at Grand Central Station. Anderson left the building, followed immediately by Curtis.

As six o'clock approached, the workers began to drift away as the novelty of the lamps waned. Viko and Henry locked up the offices and took some of the workers to a local pub for a congratulatory round of beer. By nine o'clock everyone had left to go home for the evening except Viko, Henry, and the five chosen workmen. No one noticed that they only had one beer each, being careful not to dull themselves or to become overly tired.

Viko and Henry went back toward the factory and slipped unnoticed into the alley that ran behind the building. They quietly went inside to wait for the other men.

Anderson had gone directly to his apartment a few blocks from the lamp factory. He called Edison's offices in Menlo Park. Charles Batchelor answered the phone.

"I need to speak to Edison right now!"

"He isn't here. Who is this?"

"This is Ken Anderson. I have an important message for Edison."

Batchelor explained that Edison had an emergency at the GE plant in Schenectady. He wasn't expected back for a week. Anderson went on to describe what had happened that day, that he had learned the secret of lamp fabrication, and that several new lamps were operating perfectly.

Batchelor couldn't leave. He was in charge whenever Edison was away. He sent Francis Jameson, Edison's chief chemist, in his place. Batchelor arranged for Jameson to be taken directly to Anderson's apartment. After seeing him off he went back to his office and put in a call to Edison—they were beginning to see the light at the end of the tunnel, or so they thought.

CHAPTER 27
Caught in the Act

M ark Curtis cursed as he struggled against the ropes and handcuffs. They leaned him up against a wooden crate and bound his legs to stop him from kicking out at them. "You little pissant, do you think this is going to accomplish anything? I work for Morgan, you son-of-a-bitch. Let me up!"

Viko stood in front of him, holding Curtis's pistol. "Some guard you turned out to be, you piece of shit."

Viko wanted to kick him in the face, but doing physical harm was not part of his plan.

Anderson for his part was in shock and had pissed his pants. He was held from behind by two of the workers. Jameson the chemist, the most innocent of all, was staring down at the floor as his arms were being bound behind him, showing remorse if not outright contrition for being a part of this theft. He was talking, and despite Curtis's shouts to him to keep quiet, was explaining to Viko that he tried to talk them out of their plans to steal the trade secret. "Just because Morgan said we could was no excuse. Edison's success has gone to his head. He thinks he's God, can take whatever he wants."

The takedown had gone much easier than Viko envisioned. The perpetrators were caught completely by surprise.

Earlier That Night:

It was silent as a tomb in the building when Viko let the men inside. Using hand signals, he sent them to conceal themselves in the shadows, placed so that all paths to the front door were blocked.

Jameson arrived at ten-forty-five at the apartment where Anderson and Curtis were waiting. Anderson assured them that the lamps were working perfectly, and more importantly, he knew the "secret."

Jameson was relieved; finally they could tell Morgan they could make lamps and that Tesla could be shunted aside. But he was concerned about the night visit to the plant. He felt there was no need for it. But it was Curtis, operating on direct orders from Morgan, who had insisted they go into the plant and take the chemicals out that very night.

As soon as they opened the door of the plant, they could see the lamps in a corner, giving off a soft white light. They were so enamored by the prospect of finally seeing the elusive lamps in full bloom that they never considered that they were walking into a trap.

Jameson reached down and touched one of the lamps. Feeling its cool surface, he gently lifted it, looking it over as one might examine a fine carving or sculpture. Anderson and Curtis, while not as fascinated as Jameson, were curious too and were looking down at the lamp when a deafening blast from the building's air horn shattered the silence.

Jameson jumped; the lamp fell from his hands, hit the corner of the wooden bench, and shattered in a shower of sparks. The high-voltage electricity, freed from the confines of the vacuum, arced out and gave him a nasty shock.

The report from the shattering glass was like a gunshot, loud enough to be heard above the shrieking air horn. Anderson started to run toward the door but after taking just a few steps ran headlong into Curtis, knocking him hard onto his back. Curtis's head bounced on the concrete floor as Anderson tumbled down onto him. Two of Viko's men rushed around the corner; one grabbed Anderson and forced him onto his back while the other rolled

Curtis onto his stomach and pinned him to the floor with a knee against his spine.

Two more men rushed over, one carrying enough rope to tie everyone securely, and the other to ensure that the thrashing Curtis did not get up. They found a pair of handcuffs in Curtis's back pocket and locked his wrists together before turning him over and sitting him up.

It was over.

The Tesla fluorescent lamp would not see production status for at least another twenty years. The secret to making them work was forever locked in Viko and Tesla's brains, never to be divulged.

Viko knew this would not put a stop to Morgan, but his only desire was to exact some revenge, a small satisfaction that he, the *little pissant*, had thwarted them.

When Morgan arrived at his office on Fifth Avenue that Friday morning, he was surprised to find Viko waiting for him. Viko had two packages, each with a bright ribbon. One of the boxes was quite large and heavy. With Viko were two barrel-chested men who carried the large box into the vestibule of his office. Viko kept the small box tucked under his arm.

Something about Viko caused Morgan to be wary. Perhaps it was in the way Viko's eyes never left him, watching with an intensity that made Morgan take pause. Where was Curtis this morning? He expected him to be at the office early, and right now his presence would have been comforting.

"How are we this morning, JP? Did you get a good night's rest? I have some gifts for you."

Viko's men opened the large box—sitting there in the soft packing material were two pristine fluorescent lamps.

"I thought you would like these for souvenirs, the first two operational lamps made by the plant."

Viko placed them on Morgan's desk. His men walked out the door, closed it, and locked it from the outside. They prevented anyone from entering. Morgan's internal alarms went off. "What is going on here? What are those men doing?"

The look on Viko's face turned to one of contempt. "I want to be alone with you while I give you this second present."

He opened the small box and lifted out Mark Curtis' pistol. Morgan staggered backwards, bumped against his chair, and fell into it as his breath became a series of short gasps.

"Wha-what are you doing, why do you have that gun?"

Viko held the pistol in his hand and held it out for Morgan to see.

"Recognize this?"

Morgan's eyes darted from the gun to Viko's face and back again. Beads of sweat formed and started to run down his face. A scuffle could be heard in Morgan's outer office. Morgan wanted to shout out for help, but the steady gaze from Viko's eyes and the gun in his hand made him think better of it.

"I asked you a question, JP, do you recognize this gun?"

Morgan looked closely at the gun and shook his head. Viko tossed the gun into Morgan's lap. "Take a look at the initials on the grips."

Morgan grabbed the gun from his lap, aimed it at Viko, and pulled the trigger, hearing nothing but the hollow sound of the firing pin echoing into empty chambers.

Viko laughed. "You are so damned predictable. Did you think I would come here and shoot you? Now do as I ask and look at the initials on the grip!"

Morgan looked down and saw "MC" carved neatly in each side of the grip. He was holding Curtis's gun. He looked up. Viko tossed a small set of keys onto Morgan's desk.

"Your bulldog is locked up inside the plant along with your spy Anderson and Edison's man Jameson. They were caught breaking and entering last night. They're probably quite sore and numb from being tied up all night. You might want to get over there and let them loose. You miserable excuse for a human being. I know all about the plans to take the lamps, about Anderson the spy, Curtis's weekly reports to you, the disclosure of the patents to Edison."

Viko would have continued venting except for the ruckus that was getting louder by the minute outside Morgan's door. He didn't want the police called.

Morgan's heart rate returned to normal only after taking a weekend of doctor-ordered bed rest. The sedatives left him in a weakened state. Despite his wealth, Morgan suffered from ill health all his life, and his confrontation with Viko left him a nervous wreck.

Several days later, Morgan, Curtis, and a few of Curtis's most trusted men along with three of Edison's people arrived at the locked and chained doors of the former Tesla Electric Lamp Company. Anderson was going to explain the finishing process to the rest of Edison's men. It was very unlike Morgan to be so far from his comfortable office, but the situation with the lamps had deteriorated into such a mess that he demanded to see with his own eyes exactly how this was done. He trusted no one. He was seriously considering shutting the entire thing down despite the fact that he would be writing off nearly two hundred fifty thousand dollars in investments in buildings and equipment both here and in Schenectady. He questioned why he needed or wanted the aggravation that pestered him whenever he became involved in anything related to the name *Tesla*.

The prototype lamps burned brightly. They were truly amazing, unquestionably the future of lighting. They marked the end of the domination of electrical lighting by the Edison carbon filament lamp. Tesla's superior intellect, his ability to think well beyond the constraints of even the most brilliant of human minds, was on exhibit before them. Morgan slowly shook his head in wonder, expressing silently his admiration for the mind that created this light.

As the others from Menlo Park gathered around and prepared to take notes, Anderson got down a sensitive scale to verify the weights of the chemicals. Anderson repeatedly told them that the mixture was critical, that improper amounts, even in a small error, could have negative effects on brightness and longevity. As Morgan watched Anderson he judged correctly that he was simply showing off, using his unique position to its fullest advantage.

"And now, gentlemen, this is the secret ingredient." Anderson held out the stoppered bottle labeled "30% HCL," *dilute hydrochloric acid.*

Seeing this, Jameson the chemist spoke up. "Are you certain of this? It seems implausible that Tesla would have added acid to this mix of chemicals. There are compounds in that mixture that will liberate oxygen and heat. It could be dangerous."

Anderson turned to him, quite annoyed that his moment of glory was being dimmed. "Listen, dammit, you have struggled for months and gotten nowhere. I have seen this exact process and am repeating precisely what I have seen. Would it be asking too much for you to remain there as a silent observer?"

Anderson was not being truthful. He had never seen anyone add acid to the mix—he should have listened to Jameson.

"Anderson is right," Morgan said. "You have been completely inept at this. Let the young man continue."

Chagrined, but knowing full well that the acid was a dangerous ingredient, Jameson stepped back; in fact, he stepped quite a ways back, about twenty feet. His colleague from Edison's electrical department joined him.

Anderson held the small bottle of acid for all to see and then let the acid drip slowly into the mixture of chemicals. The acid soaked into the tinder dry powder. Small bubbles of pure oxygen appeared at the liquid surface, followed immediately by a blazing bright white light accompanied by a loud hissing caused by the escaping gasses. The heat generated by the releasing oxygen (just as the chemist predicted) ignited the magnesium powder. It burned at a temperature in excess of three thousand degrees, immediately melting the glass container. As the chemicals melted and burned their way into the wooden bench top, trapped moisture in the wood turned into superheated steam causing an explosion that threw the bench backwards and spread the burning chemicals and glass onto the shocked onlookers and over the surrounding area. The entire reaction took place in less than two seconds.

Morgan lifted his hand to shield his face and turned to the side to look away. This move saved his eyes from the hot powders that ignited the wool overcoat he was wearing. The intense heat felled him like an oak, down to the floor and flat on his back. Jameson, who had been standing behind Morgan, rushed to his aid, got him onto his feet, and helped him toward the door. He spun Morgan around and ripped the burning coat off, throwing it to the side over Morgan's objection to having his expensive coat treated in such a manner. When they were outside Morgan learned that the quick action saved him from serious burns.

Curtis caught the full blast of burning powder in the face. Fortunately his glasses kept him from losing his eyes. Tiny, painful burns covered his forehead, nose, and cheeks. The burns would heal eventually but leave permanent acnelike scars.

Anderson was not so lucky.

The exploding mixture peppered Anderson's face with burning specks of volatile chemicals. His eyes were wide with surprise as the chemical reaction followed its violent course. He was blinded, blown back against a crate, and knocked unconscious. His clothes were on fire as Curtis dragged him out of the building to safety. Anderson lost all vision in his right eye and his left eye was severely damaged. He was unable to see anything clearly for the rest of his life. His burning clothes left first- and second-degree burns over his chest and abdomen.

Everyone escaped, but the building was a total loss. The initial explosion spread burning chemicals over a wide area, igniting wooden crates. The tinder-dry excelsior packing material in the boxes exploded into flames, and the expansion of the air caused by the fire's heat threw the burning excelsior out like the flames from a Roman candle. Explosions occurred as containers of chemicals burned, spreading more flames and noxious gasses throughout the building. The heat caused the concrete floor to crack, and huge vertical iron beams softened and sagged.

The fire department arrived twenty minutes after the fire began but could do little more than stand back and watch the building collapse into itself.

Morgan and Curtis sat in the safety of Morgan's Packard a block from the fire and watched in silence as the fire department put water on the embers and knocked down those few hot spots that still had active flames. Even from a distance they could feel the intense heat and the ground shake as explosions rocked the area. Morgan turned to Curtis and studied his damaged face. He tapped his chauffeur on the shoulder. "George, let's get this man to a doctor."

BOOK 6

CHAPTER 28
1904—Colorado Springs, Colorado

Nikola Tesla reread the newspaper account in utter astonishment. He was having trouble believing that the story Viko just told him was the truth and not a fictional tale of deceit, failure, and retribution, a Shakespearean tragedy unfolding in twentieth-century America. He could not deny, however, the cover page of the *New York Times* that described in dramatic terms the terrible fire of unknown origin that destroyed the better part of a Bronx block of industrial buildings fourteen days earlier. The devastation was total. The building's owner, industrialist J.P. Morgan, could not be reached for comment. His office released a short statement confirming that Mr. Morgan was on an extended visit to a health spa in Geneva, Switzerland.

An accompanying story described the severe injuries suffered by Mr. Kenneth Anderson. A *Times* reporter managed to get into the hospital room where Anderson was recovering from severe burns. He reported that Anderson's eyes were covered in bandages, and he found him to be quite willing to discuss his injuries. Anderson claimed to be an employee of Edison Laboratories in Menlo Park, New Jersey. The next day the reporter learned Anderson had been moved to a private undisclosed location. Inquiries placed at the Menlo Park headquarters of Edison Labs received a terse "No comment."

After letting Nikola absorb the news, Viko said, "Morgan had no intention of letting you produce lamps. As soon as you brought him the first working lamp he was going to toss you aside. Everything that Robert Johnson predicted when you signed those papers happened just as he said. When are you going to learn that this world is a treacherous place? How is it that you trust your property, the products of your incredible mind, to these thieves that have only their own greedy interests at heart?"

The questions elicited no reply from Tesla, nor did Viko expect they would. The questions he was asking had no answers. The mystery of Tesla was locked somewhere within the most creative mind of the twentieth century, hidden from everyone, most likely even Tesla himself.

Tesla looked off in the distance as if trying to find something else, anything at all, to take his mind away from the moment.

They avoided each other for several days. Tesla buried himself in his work while Viko used the time to recover from the trauma of the previous month. Viko found a local livery stable, rented a gentle horse, and spent his days exploring the countryside and the spectacular scenery.

He was sleeping soundly for the first time in years, no longer burdened with the issues that confronted him in New York. Perhaps it was the country air, or maybe the altitude, or most likely it was the effect of finally taking a vacation after years of nonstop activity and tension.

Ten days after arriving, Viko finally decided that enough was enough, and after rising early one morning he knocked on Tesla's door and invited him to breakfast. Viko spoke first. "So you're angry with me. Can we get past this? There is a lot that we can still do together, and quite frankly I'm beginning to miss you."

A smile came across Tesla's face. He shrugged his shoulders in resignation. "Yes, I agree that we need to get past this, but you must realize that I am having difficulty understanding the actions you took. You could have gone to the police. You could have obtained a lawyer. There were other more civil ways to deal with Morgan."

Viko sighed. "Can we put this behind us and move on? I am interested in your work out here. May I come in and work with you for a few weeks before

I return to New York? Perhaps I can lend some insight into the forces you are struggling against."

Tesla reached across the table, offering his handshake to Viko. "The past is the past. The slate is clean. I can really use your help here. Let's eat and get to work."

CHAPTER 29
Reconciliation and Discovery

Nikola Tesla was the father and original creator of practical radio communication, making nearly all of the basic discoveries that led to wireless communication by the turn of the century.

Tesla believed that wireless power distribution was simply an extension of wireless communication, much the same way that telegraph wires and AC transmission lines were simply different versions of the same electrical interconnections. He came to Colorado because of the extreme electrical discharges that occurred there. He believed this environment would be the ideal testing ground for his attempts to launch and retrieve airborne electrical power. He never did realize his dream, but in the process of trying he discovered a unique method of wireless communication.

One afternoon Viko was about fifteen miles away driving a horse-drawn cart that contained receiving coils and measuring equipment. He stood in front of the coil jotting down numbers registered by the meters when he heard a voice that sounded a great deal like Tesla's asking for a pen and paper. Viko was alone—there was no one else for miles. He turned to see who was speaking when the voice he heard spoke again, saying "Thank you."

Was he hallucinating?

He looked back at the meters as the voice spoke once more: "I hope Viko is getting the readings. We have to shut this down in five more minutes."

One of the meters was perceptibly moving as the voice was speaking. When the voice stopped, the meter stopped. Viko put his ear against the coil, and after another minute he distinctly heard the voice of Tesla call out, "Ten minutes has passed; turn off the power." The meter emitted a distinct clicking sound and its reading fell to zero.

Viko and Nikola were alone in the transmitter building the following Saturday. Viko asked him to sit down for a few minutes and go over the measurements he had taken a few days before.

"There is something else here. I think that you'll be interested. Take a look."

Tesla frowned as he read what appeared to be a transcription of a conversation. "I don't understand. What is this?"

"That, dear uncle, is your voice. I heard it distinctly while I was fifteen miles away monitoring the transmission. Your transmitter is sending your voice out with the transmission of power."

Tesla reread the words. He had total recall, able to remember the tiniest of details even from years ago. He thought for a few seconds and remembered that these were indeed the words he used while they were testing the transmitter.

They decided to do a quick test to determine what was happening.

The "quick test" turned into a weekend of discovery as they studied the effect, learned how to make it stronger and weaker, and finally late on Sunday evening made an amazing discovery.

The ramifications of their findings were overwhelming. Here, in a dusty barn on the outskirts of a small town in the shadows of the majestic Rocky Mountains, was the basic blueprint that would direct and shape communication for decades. They agreed that they would discuss this with no one. Curious to learn as much as possible about the phenomena before Viko traveled back to New York, they conducted long-distance tests. To their amazement, reception remained excellent at distances up to one hundred twenty miles from the transmitter, over all kinds of terrain, including deep into the bottom of distant canyons.

Viko and Nikola Tesla had discovered the basic principle of frequency modulation, or as it is more popularly known, FM radio.

Armed with blueprints and schematics of the wireless power transmitter and the receiving coil apparatus, Viko bid farewell to his uncle. He boarded the train that would take him to Chicago and his long trek home.

CHAPTER 30

May 1909—Financial Salvation

V iko was hard at work completing the design and construction of two transceivers embodying the discovery made in Colorado. The work was daunting and made even more difficult by the lack of funds and the constant distracting demands on his time. Fulfillment of commitments to Westinghouse used up most of his daylight hours and those of his men at Tesla Electric. It was their only source of income.

Tesla spent the entire year in Colorado constantly fighting the immense technical challenges he faced attempting to prove that his concept of wireless power distribution would work. Only after nearly destroying a power generating station in the Rocky Mountains for a second time during one of his more aggressive attempts did he finally wear out his welcome. He rebuilt the damaged generators for the power company, closed up shop, and returned home to Manhattan.

Tesla's return to New York took a great deal of pressure off Viko. His insights into the FM wireless concept were a great help as they struggled to overcome one technical hurdle after another. It was rough going as Viko and Nikola spent their daylight hours addressing existing commitments and all night working on wireless voice communication. Their major obstacle continued to be a lack of funds. They went to Robert Johnson for help but quickly found that all possible sources of investment funds to them were blocked. Robert was convinced that Morgan's tentacles extended into every financial institution in New York, perhaps the entire country, and Morgan's hatred for Tesla ran deep.

A courier delivered a letter from Robert Johnson.

My Dear Nikola:

I trust that you are well, not working more than your usual 18 hours a day. Please do not discuss the contents of this letter with anyone, even Viko whom you trust with everything, until we meet.

Late yesterday, I opened a new account (a very large account for that matter) for a gentleman previously unknown to me. He is from Great Britain and is heir to a very large coal mining fortune. He has traveled to America in search of investment opportunities. While processing his paperwork and arranging for the international funds transfer he told me about the Marconi wireless on the ship and how fascinated he was with it.

I was quick to inform him that Marconi is a sham and a charlatan, and that he has stolen all of his ideas from an American inventor. At that he perked up and asked for more information. I haven't disclosed your name to him but I did tell him enough to whet his appetite. It is his intention to invest in shipbuilding, and after seeing the Marconi wireless he sees the tremendous importance of ship-to-shore communications.

This could be a major breakthrough for you Nik. I cannot stress enough the importance of meeting with him, and soon, especially to talk to him before he goes to Marconi. Let us know when you will be available for dinner at our home in Manhattan.

Remaining your true and faithful friend,

Robert Johnson

Two days earlier, Robert had been at his desk when his secretary knocked and announced that a gentleman from Great Britain was in the reception area to see him about a financial matter. His name was Harold Wittington. Robert's first reaction was one of annoyance at having his lunch hour interrupted, but that changed quickly when she added, "He was attempting to deposit one million five hundred thousand in British currency with a teller on the bank floor and was directed here to speak with you."

"One million five hundred thousand in British pound sterling? Are you certain of that, Miss Simmons?"

"I know, sir, it sounds ridiculously large, but that is what I was told."

Wittington was scanning that morning's copy of the *Wall Street Journal* when Robert came out to greet him. He immediately extended his hand and said, "Harold Wittington here. I do hope I'm not disturbing you. I didn't suspect that there would be any difficulty in opening an account, but the young man downstairs seemed quite flustered."

"Mr. Wittington, good morning. I am Robert Johnson, president of the bank. I assure you that there is no problem. Mr. Atkinson was not so much confused as he was overwhelmed. Accounts of this size are handled exclusively by me. You will qualify for a much higher interest than the average depositor. I am flattered and honored that you have chosen my bank. Let's go into my office and discuss your banking needs."

Wittington explained his situation. His family's involvement in coal mining spanned over a hundred years; he was the third generation to be in charge of the business. He wanted to find solid investments outside of the field of mining, and having read about the explosive growth in American manufacturing, he came here to seek opportunities.

Robert found Harold Wittington to be friendly, gregarious, and quite down to earth. *Harry* was without affectation and showed a genuine interest in all things American, never once looking down his British nose at the funny mannerisms of speech. The afternoon turned into early evening as they went through the steps to arrange the deposit and the conversions of British pound sterling into the dollar value of US bank notes.

Wittington had become fascinated with the Marconi wireless aboard the ship as it sailed to New York. He recognized its huge potential for communication and was planning to seek out the New York office of Marconi and discuss investment possibilities.

His choice of Robert's bank was an incredible stroke of fortune for Nikola Tesla. Robert immediately recognized that this could be the answer to Tesla's financial problems. Here was a man of means, one who saw potential and could use his means to exploit that potential. This might be the solution to the unending problems of funding and the effective American blockade that Morgan built around Tesla.

Robert asked, "Harry, would you like to meet the real inventor of wireless?"

"Do you know Marconi?"

"Marconi is nothing but a thief. He has stolen the work of a true genius. There is another man in whom you should invest."

"Why, who is he? Of course I would like to meet him!"

"I'll give you his name in due time. He has a well-earned distrust of investors in America, a distrust as intense as his hatred of lawyers. These people have stripped him of everything, even his ability to earn a simple living. Let me talk to him. I will arrange for the two of you to meet at my home here in Manhattan. Can you give me two days to arrange a meeting?"

It was an eventful and beneficial day for Robert and Harold. They had established a working relationship based on trust and cooperation. He agreed to wait a few days. There was a lot of sightseeing to do in New York.

Robert needed to spend time alone with Tesla before he introduced him to Wittington. He was going to try to put an end to his predilection to give away everything when negotiating with investors. He intended to cajole, plead, threaten, beg, whatever, to open Tesla's eyes and help him achieve the recognition and wealth he deserved.

It was nearly impossible for Nikola to believe that he was ever in the wrong. He considered himself to be a giant intellect among inferiors. His leaps of technology left everyone years behind. He was not incorrect in his assessment, but those "inferiors" had a big advantage over him: they lived in the world of here and now, living with the daily consequences of their successes and failures. When Tesla failed to complete something and left people, promises, and money hanging, it was (in his mind at least) because he was moving on to a more important idea, but the consequences of those abandonments cut him off from those he depended upon for support.

Robert knew he would have to work very hard, walking a tightrope between winning Tesla to his argument or having him storm out of the house, furious at being treated like a naughty schoolboy. Viko was not invited. Robert felt it was important that he not make Tesla feel like he was under attack.

To their surprise, Tesla was actually on time. Robert had originally planned to wait until after dinner, but since Tesla was early and dinner was not ready, Robert began, proceeding carefully. Robert, Katherine, and Nikola sat in the library with glasses of wine.

Robert began, "Nik, are you aware of why you are unable to raise investment funds?"

"No, I don't understand at all. I offer the most significant electrical developments, but no one is interested."

"Nik, they turn you down because you are not dependable. You are the greatest inventor of the present day. Your ideas are the most far-reaching of anyone alive, but you cannot be counted upon to complete what you start. You have a history of walking away from your commitments."

Tesla became very quiet. His demeanor took on a look of confusion and anger. His breathing was slow and steady. He stared into Robert's eyes for what seemed an eternity. He could not understand how Robert, his most supportive champion, could say such a thing. About to shout out in self-defense, he stopped as similar words that Viko had so often spoken to him echoed through his mind. His shoulders sagged; the fatigue of the weeks of struggle flooded over him and he fell back into his chair, buried his face in his hands, and sobbed uncontrollably.

Robert nodded to Katherine and together they helped Tesla settle down. Katherine spoke softly to him, "Nik, please Nik, you know that we care for you. We think of you as family. Please listen to Robert. He wants to help you. That's all he is trying to do."

Tesla's muscles relaxed. He rested his head back on the cushion and stared at the ceiling for a few moments. Then, looking at Robert and Katherine standing before him, he said in a quiet voice, "You two are the only true friends I have in this city and, except for Viko, the only family I have left. Go ahead, Robert, I need to hear what you have to say, no matter how painful."

At that moment, they were interrupted by Ginny, their maid, who was awkwardly standing in the doorway. "Dinner is ready, but I can keep it warm, Mum."

To their surprise, Tesla spoke up. "I'm famished. Let's enjoy another wonderful meal together."

As they walked to the dining room Katherine and Robert exchanged glances and shrugged their shoulders; one could never predict the events of an evening that included Nikola Tesla as company. At dinner one would not have known that anything of a discordant nature occurred between them. Conversation was light and friendly. Once again, Tesla showed the unusual ability of compartmentalizing his emotions.

After dinner Tesla and Robert went to the library where Robert poured brandy. "Have you ever heard of Harold Wittington?" Robert asked.

He explained that Harold had been at the bank the previous day and that they had quite a discussion. He went on to explain Wittington's fascination with wireless communication and how he saw the tremendous commercial potential for it. But Wittington saw it as unreliable. There were too many periods at sea when the wireless operator could not communicate with anyone. If only these problems could be solved, the potential for communication, for entertainment, for military use was limitless.

Robert feared that if Tesla operated true to form, he would accept a partnership with Wittington, agree to finalize the development of the FM wireless, and after a few months, or maybe less, would be distracted by some new revolutionary idea. The wireless would be left in the eraser dust of his drafting table. The key to success was to make sure that Viko was in charge. They agreed that they would meet Wittington the following evening and that Viko would be there not just as an observer but as an integral partner in the undertaking.

— ◇ —

Tesla, with an apprehensive Viko in tow, arrived at the Johnsons' house at precisely eight o'clock the next evening. Viko usually enjoyed the Johnsons' company and hospitality, but this evening an investor would be present. He was decidedly uncomfortable with that prospect, feeling a little like he was walking into a lion's den. Katherine was radiant as always and greeted Tesla and Viko with a warm handshake. "Robert and Mr. Wittington are in the library, and Harold is most anxious to meet both of you."

As they entered the library, Robert rose from his chair, took Tesla gently by the arm, and announced, "Nikola and Viko, I present Mr. Harold Wittington; Harold, Nikola Tesla and his nephew and adopted son, Viktor."

Upon hearing the name *Tesla*, Wittington jumped up and grasped Tesla's hand in both of his. "The great Nikola Tesla of AC power fame?"

Blushing slightly, Tesla nodded in acknowledgment. Wittington reached out and with an equally enthusiastic grasp of Viko's hand said, "Please call me Harry; I find Harold much too formal. This is indeed a pleasure! My goodness, the great Tesla. What a jolly good pleasure this is, three thousand miles from home, invited into the home of Robert Johnson and his lovely wife Katherine, and then meeting Nikola Tesla."

At dinner, Wittington regaled them with stories of growing up in England, of traveling by ship to America, and of his family's involvement in coal mining in Great Britain. He went on about meeting the royal family, the theater life in London, the rain and fog; "I prefer New York weather."

Later in the evening, as they sat in the easy comfort of the library, Wittington turned to a serious business mood. He explained that his initial intention was to contact Marconi, but Robert had suggested a better idea, and thus they were together for this discussion. He didn't know that the "mystery" inventor was none other than Nikola Tesla. He asked Tesla to relate his work with wireless and his relationship with Marconi.

Tesla began, detailing his early work on wireless communication, begun fifteen years earlier. He became quite animated and somewhat agitated as he told of Marconi's theft of his ideas. Then he spoke of his latest development. "Working together, Viko and I have taken the next step in wireless communication, and we desperately need financing to complete our work. I assume that is why we are here this evening."

Robert and Harold nodded agreement.

Tesla then wisely added, "Before we proceed I must have your understanding that this is absolutely confidential and will not leave this room."

Harold replied, "Nikola, I am a man of my word, and anything you say to me is kept in strictest confidence. You have my assurance that whatever is discussed in this room stays in this room."

Tesla went on. "While conducting experiments in Colorado, my nephew made a most interesting discovery. Viko, since you are deeply involved in this, go ahead and tell Harry what you found."

Viko was flabbergasted that Tesla would ask him to do this. "Me—you want me to explain this?"

"Of course, you understand it completely and your enthusiasm for it is contagious."

Viko took a sip of his drink for a little liquid confidence and launched into the meat of the concept. "We have created wireless voice communication. Think of the telephone that Bell has invented without wires! We think that this can easily communicate across the Atlantic. It will revolutionize wireless communication and will kick Marconi right in the backside and out of the picture."

Wittington said, "My goodness, this is so much better than I could have dreamed. When I was traveling at sea, there were a number of times that I thought of Margie, my dear wife at home, and how I missed her smile and how lovely it would have been to hear her voice. How much better than a telegram sent by wireless. And the potential for this, why this is amazing! Mr. Tesla, will you consider letting me provide financing for this improved wireless of yours?"

Tesla looked to Viko for approval and then replied, "Assuming we can come to an acceptable agreement, of course. I look forward to the opportunity."

Robert suggested they meet at ten the next morning—everyone agreed.

Viko and Tesla walked into the bank ten minutes early and were pleased to see that Wittington was already there. He took little sleep that night. He had worked straight through, completing the basic outline of a business arrangement.

Three days and little sleep later, a contract was passed around the table, signed and witnessed, and followed by handshakes all around. Nikola and Viko Tesla were in business. The New Tesla Wireless Company was a reality, and funded with an initial investment of two hundred thousand dollars. Nikola and Viko owned 60 percent of the stock.

They were back in business. Viko was president. His future looked bright, and for the first time in a long time he was optimistic about the future. Unfortunately, fate had other plans.

Two weeks later Viko accompanied Harold to the docks on the west side of Manhattan. Harold had investments in the Leyland shipping line and had arranged for Viko to travel in the future at no cost while they tested the new wireless system. He took Viko aboard to meet Captain Lord.

The name of the ship was the *Californian*.

CHAPTER 31
The Seagoing Experiments

E ight months later, January 1910, at two o'clock on a Sunday morning, Viko, Nikola, and foreman Henry Abbott stood at a workbench at the New Tesla Wireless Company. Before them were two transceivers that had just been through several weeks of testing. It was time to take one to sea.

Viko and Henry had tested them in and around New York by building one into a steamer trunk and carrying it around in a carriage. As Viko was driven around the city and beyond, he and Tesla enjoyed an ongoing dialogue as Tesla relaxed in the comfort of the laboratory. The system worked flawlessly, even producing excellent clarity in the confines of a subway tunnel under the streets of New York. Viko traveled eighty miles north to the small city of Poughkeepsie, surrounded by huge granite hills, and could find no location where he lost communication. The system was exceeding all of their expectations.

The *Californian* would be sailing in a week. Viko would be on board under the guise that he was the new wireless operator. Captain Lord knew his true identity but was only told he was going to be testing new code for the Marconi wireless. The true nature of the mysterious transceivers remained a closely held secret.

The trip from New York to Great Britain went smoothly. Viko wandered the *Californian* without restriction, spending time on the bridge fascinated by the workings of the ship.

At night he would power up the transceiver in the steamer trunk and communicate with Tesla back in New York. Viko would send Tesla the location of the ship, latitude and longitude, the time, and weather information. When Tesla replied, Viko would note the quality of reception, noise and static, and strength of the signal he received. Tesla would do the same for Viko's signal, and then after just a few minutes of talking, they would sign off.

The communication from Tesla to Viko never failed. While docked in London, they could communicate across the entire North Atlantic. This was an unheard of distance for wireless at the time. They were in voice contact across the entire span of ocean with relatively small wireless sets, clearly and consistently. Tesla had done it again. He established transatlantic two-way wireless voice communication far superior to anything Marconi or anyone else could or would claim for several more years.

The return trip eight days later went just as well, except for a few days of a full-blown North Atlantic storm. The ship was buffeted by heavy rain, high seas, and a spectacular thunderstorm. The *Californian* showed herself to be a solid steamship, constantly steaming west despite the heavy seas. Viko and Tesla were able to maintain clear voice communication at all times, with only slight interference from the lightning that forked through the skies for hours on end. During one particularly rough day, as the ship rolled and dipped through heavy waves, Captain Lord assured a nervous Viko, "Not to worry, Viko, storms at sea are part of the business, and the *Californian* can handle anything. I hope your stomach can take it."

Viko, for his part, was impressed with the crew and the captain and even more so with the ship as it pitched into the waves and rolled from side to side. Despite the rough sea, everyone on the bridge remained calm and in control, as they continued westward at a steady twelve knots.

The Marconi wireless was so overloaded with static during the storm as to be completely out of commission. But the FM system that Viko had stumbled onto that providential afternoon in Colorado was proving to be a perfect medium for communication, regardless of weather conditions.

Back in New York, Viko bid farewell to Captain Lord and was met by Tesla. The two of them talked into the night about the trip, the results, and the outstanding performance of their new wireless. It appeared that nothing could stop them now. Armed with positive solid results, they held the future of wireless communication within their grasp.

Before going to bed, Viko sent a short cablegram to Harold Wittington saying simply, "Outstanding success, we are in business."

CHAPTER 32

Titanic and the New Wireless

T wo months later, March 1910, Viko made his second trip to Great Britain aboard the *Californian*. Wittington had cabled Viko that an opportunity had come up, and he requested that he come to England as soon as possible.

Harold had seen to it that Viko had the grandest time possible during his first visit. They went to the finest restaurants, saw a musical in London's theater district, and had a private tour of Buckingham Palace. Viko had a wonderful time. This was a life he could get used to, and one that he fully expected to enjoy with the promising success that the new wireless would provide for him.

As he disembarked the *Californian*, he was greeted by Wittington, who was smiling like a schoolboy greeting his parents after a long absence.

No sooner had they arrived at Wittington's London home than Wittington rushed him into his study and began to explain.

He had recently learned of a new venture being put together by J.P. Morgan. International Mercantile Marine (IMM) was making headlines. Morgan was stepping into the world of international shipping, and his reputation as a ruthless competitor was shaking the foundations of the European-dominated control of the seas. Viko stiffened at the mention of Morgan's name. His dislike for the man could not be hidden.

Harold went on to explain that the White Star Line was in trouble due to competition from German shipping companies. Morgan had proposed the creation of an international trust, a business form he had used to quash competition in mining, railroads, and steel production in the States. Due to the weakened state of White Star, J. Bruce Ismay, its chairman, had been forced to sell controlling interest to Morgan.

White Star was in the process of building three huge ships, rumored to be more advanced than any commercial steamship yet put to sea: the *Titanic*, *Olympic*, and *Britannic*. Once completed by Harland and Wolff, these ships would set a standard that few shipyards could equal. And since White Star had an exclusive arrangement with Harland and Wolff, they were ensured that no one else would have such ships in the foreseeable future. Many thought that this time Morgan bit off a little too much, that his past success further inflated his opinion of himself, and that IMM would be his undoing. Wittington knew better; Morgan was many things, but he was no fool. If he said that he could do it, Wittington would take it to the bank.

Always looking for opportunity, Wittington outlined a plan. "Viko, these ships are going to make worldwide headlines. What do you say we take advantage of that?"

Viko's revulsion to the name Morgan made him shocked to hear this. "That bloodsucker, how can he or anything he touches be of help to us? I want to see that bastard on the street, penniless."

"Now Viko, there is a business opportunity here, and to exploit it might just be the best revenge." Viko reconsidered; perhaps he should listen and learn. Now was the time to watch a master at work.

The sailing date for the ships was to be in the spring of 1912. It seemed to Wittington that properly planned and presented, these ships could be outfitted with Tesla's new wireless. With all the publicity, the use of Tesla's new wireless would be included in headlines worldwide. It was exactly what was needed to elevate Tesla to the status he richly deserved.

Wittington explained to Viko that he could deal with White Star and convince them to use the new wireless. He was acquainted with J. Bruce Ismay through the Maritime Commission, was aware of his massive ego, and knew that if the new wireless would make Ismay look better, Ismay would insist on it.

Titanic was to be the showcase vessel—the jewel of the White Star Line—and the ship would set a new standard of seagoing luxury. That would be the ideal place to showcase their new wireless.

CHAPTER 33

May 1910, New York

V iko rushed to Nikola with the cablegram in his shaking hands. Wittington had actually pulled it off! Harland and Wolff wanted a demonstration of the new Tesla wireless. At Wittington's request, Edward Harland had arranged for Viko to visit the shipyard in Belfast to show the engineering group, headed by Thomas Andrews, this new wireless marvel.

As with most successful business relationships in Great Britain at the time, the meeting had been arranged more because of who Wittington was, rather than what he had to offer. Wittington and Harland attended the same prep school and graduated from the same university, although at different times. They were also members of the same clubs. Such social connections meant everything in Great Britain.

Wittington had been careful not to reveal too much about the new wireless, including its originator. No need to give Marconi another chance to steal Tesla blind.

It was the chance of a lifetime. What better endorsement could they have than to be able to say the *Titanic* builders chose a Tesla design over a Marconi design? When the passengers on *Titanic*, the topmost of the upper crust of society, used the wireless to send messages, told their influential friends about it,

193

and expected it when they traveled, the demand for it would spread like wildfire. There would be no stopping Tesla this time.

Using the remainder of the initial investment that Wittington provided, Viko and his crew worked through the hot summer months and into the fall building two additional wireless sets. His plan was to first demonstrate a short-distance wireless link between the shipyards in Belfast and Wittington's London office and then demonstrate a transatlantic link back to New York to Tesla's laboratory. To prove that the link was actually going all the way to New York from Ireland, Viko would ask Harland to compose a secret message that would be sent to Tesla by transatlantic cable just minutes before the demonstration. When Tesla read back the message, there would be ironclad proof of transatlantic voice communication.

Viko arrived in Belfast for the providential meeting with Harland and Wolff on October 16, 1910, eighteen months prior to the completion of *Titanic*.

As prearranged at Wittington's request, a private room with appropriate electrical power and easy access to the roof had been provided by Harland and Wolff. Viko set up the antenna, verified that the equipment had made the trip without damage, and announced that he was ready for the demonstration. He was careful not to use his adopted name *Tesla*; rather he was using his family name, *Gracac*.

The demonstration was scheduled for the following morning. Before he left for the evening, Viko installed heavy-duty padlocks on the three access doors to the demonstration room, explaining as he did so, "I trust that you understand this is a necessary precaution. Sometimes the walls have eyes and ears."

Viko had gone to extremes, but he had reason to be overly cautious. Patent applications had yet to be filed for the new technology, and he was taking no chances. Nothing would be disclosed until they were on the verge of their initial sale. Nikola Tesla was certain that the US Patent Office had leaks. He had lost all faith in the secrecy aspects of patents during the application process. Why trust anyone else?

Prior to turning in for the night, Viko sent a cablegram to Tesla, informing him to expect a telegram from Harland and Wolff with a secret message. Viko explained that the demonstration was to be conducted in the morning, and that it would be shortly after five a.m. in New York when Tesla would be contacted.

Viko arrived at nine-thirty the next morning and found the two mechanics and a rather disturbed Thomas Andrews waiting for him. "I am insulted that you felt it necessary to lock the door. We have twenty-four-hour security here and you were assured of complete confidentiality."

Viko did not apologize. "These precautions are an expression of the value we place on this wireless development. If you still feel wronged after the demonstration, then I will offer a sincere apology."

Viko went about turning on the equipment. Andrews studied the machinery before him. The two transceivers were smaller than a small steamer trunk. There was no transmit key and no headphones. His first reaction was that it appeared to be much too small. He had seen Marconi sets take up entire rooms with a wall of complex wiring, dials, and knobs. His inquiries about these anomalies were answered by nothing but a wink and a gleam in the eye of Viko, as if to say, *that is part of our secret.*

At ten a.m., four of Andrews's top designers and Mr. Edward Harland entered the room. Harland inquired of Andrews, "Tom, what do you think of this new wireless?"

"I am as much in the dark as you are. Viko calls them transceivers. To be honest, the claim that they can communicate across the sea seems preposterous. But I am here to observe and learn."

At that Harland turned to Viko. "Well, young man, this is your show."

Viko said, "What you are about to witness will amaze you. These two devices represent the future of wireless communication. They will speak for themselves."

He picked up the handheld device (microphone) on the transceiver labeled "Wittington."

"Harold, my good man, are you there?" To the amazement of all, the voice of Harold Wittington spoke plainly and clearly from the speaker: "Of course, is my dear friend Edward there with you?"

Viko gave the microphone to Harland, showing him how to press the button when speaking. Harland hesitated a moment and said, "Harry? Is that really you? Where are you?"

"I am in my office in London."

Harland was speechless. He had never seen or heard of such a device, and he didn't know what to say.

Wittington asked, "Well, Eddie, cat got your tongue?"

"Why didn't you tell me about this; it is amazing! I am having trouble believing my ears!"

"Now tell me, Eddie, would you have believed me if I told you about this? Would you really have believed that this is possible?"

Edward Harland had to admit he would not have; he would have been doubtful that such a thing could be done in 1910.

Thomas Andrews asked if he might use it. He held the microphone in his hand and looked it over as one might expect of an engineer. He pressed the button and spoke over the miles to Wittington.

"This is Thomas Andrews. Who is responsible for this? Is this Marconi's newest wireless?"

"Let me assure you, Mr. Andrews, Marconi knows nothing of this. He is little more than a thief. Why do you think Viko has taken such precautions? Would you like to speak with the two inventors of this marvelous new wireless?"

"Are they there with you at your office?"

"One of them is standing before you, Viktor Gracac. The other, the world's greatest inventor, is in New York City. Viko, please introduce him to our distinguished guests. I will stand by at this end."

At that, Viko took the microphone from Andrews. He turned off the first transceiver and operated a control that applied power to the second transceiver, the one labeled "AMERICA."

"What are you doing?" asked Andrews.

"Well, do you want to speak to him?"

"But he is in New York."

Viko picked up the second microphone. "Uncle Nik, how is the weather in New York at five this morning?"

With just a slight hissing sound in the background, the baritone voice of Nikola Tesla came through with excellent clarity: "A slight wind is blowing, and it's a chilly sixty-eight degrees outside."

"Gentlemen, let me introduce you to the creator of all wireless, Mr. Nikola Tesla."

There was complete silence in the room. The name *Tesla* was well known in Great Britain as the inventor of polyphase AC electricity, but his work with wireless was practically unknown. Such was the veil of deception that Marconi had pulled over everyone's eyes.

Viko handed the microphone to Thomas Andrews.

Andrews stammered a bit and said, "I can believe that we have spoken with Harold Wittington 300 miles from here. But you are at least three thousand miles away. How is such a bloody thing possible?"

Tesla said, "That will be explained at an appropriate time in the future. Did you send a secret message via cablegram to your office in New York to be delivered to the following address, 31 South Fifth Avenue?"

Harland took the microphone from Andrews, introduced himself, and replied, "I did. Viko here suggested we do it to remove any doubts regarding this new invention of yours."

"Well, a Mr. Findley, who claims to be from the New York office of Harland and Wolff, is standing here with me with a sealed envelope that I have yet to open. Here, I will let him speak directly to you."

Findley spoke into the microphone. "Mr. Harland, is that you? Why didn't you let us know that you were traveling to New York? We would have been prepared for your arrival. Why have I been summoned from my bed at three in the morning to deliver a cablegram to Mr. Tesla?"

Harland was momentarily speechless. Here was proof that he was communicating across the Atlantic Ocean. "I am in our office building in Belfast, Ireland. Let me assure you that I am not in New York."

Tesla read the secret message: *"Mary had a little lamb whose fleece was white as snow, and everywhere that Mary went the lamb was sure to go."* Tesla chuckled. "My, my, I'm sure the doctors were most surprised at such a delivery," at which the entire room of people in Belfast burst out laughing.

Thomas Andrews and his engineers were spellbound. They wanted to know more and the questions came like the staccato of machine gun fire. How did it work? When would it be available? Was it thoroughly tested? After nearly two hours, a very tired Nikola Tesla begged that they say goodbye as it was seven o'clock in the morning in New York and he had been up for nearly two days. They agreed to a meeting the following day to arrange to put this new wireless on *Titanic*.

As Harland was leaving, he proposed a question to Viko. "What would be involved in equipping all of our ships currently under construction, as well as ground stations in both Ireland and New York with this new device? We will need about twenty units in six months' time."

Viko was speechless. He was not sure how to reply, never expecting such an overwhelmingly positive outcome. After regaining his composure, he replied, "Sir, I am humbled that you think so highly of these machines. I'm at a loss for words. Let me discuss this with Mr. Wittington and Mr. Tesla, and I will be prepared to talk tomorrow."

Viko and Thomas Andrews went to a nearby pub for lunch to discuss the technical details of installing the new wireless. Andrews agreed to provide Viko with full access to the electrical system planned for *Titanic* and her sister ships.

A meeting was held the next day with Harland, Wittington, Viko, and Andrews in attendance. They discussed contract details, essentially confirming that all pending orders with Marconi Wireless would be canceled, and immediate orders would be placed with the New Tesla Wireless Company for twenty transceivers, four for ground-based installation and sixteen for use on ships. They agreed that Viko would make recommendations to the ship designers regarding the electrical requirements and any accompanying changes needed to the electrical systems of the ships.

Wittington would immediately transmit the orders to New York via cablegram while Viko went over the ships' electrical plans with the electricians. Viko was going to be in Ireland a bit longer than planned. Tesla was in New York to handle things until Viko returned, with production soon to be underway.

Or so they thought.

This was the biggest development in wireless communication to date, and it was not a baby step, it was a giant leap forward. Those few in the demonstration room of Harland and Wolff that historic day when Nikola Tesla said hello from across the ocean knew they had just witnessed the future. With its success came possibilities hard to contemplate in 1910. This invention could revolutionize worldwide communication.

Tragically, none of this was to be. Forces commanding far-reaching power, driven by greed, fear, and hatred, would throw insurmountable roadblocks in their way.

Weeks dragged by. Technical meetings were testing Viko's considerable patience. He was getting his first glimpse into the world of large company politics populated by influential managers whose primary goal seemed to be protecting their own turf and whose vision did not extend much beyond the tips of their noses. Decisions that would have been made at Tesla Electric in minutes took an entire afternoon at Harland and Wolff as arguments erupted, sensitive egos had to be assuaged, and consensus decisions that were mostly poor compromises were hammered out.

The electricians at Harland and Wolff were twice Viko's age and had been designing ships and their electrical wiring longer than he had been alive, but the designs were primitive at best. Being as diplomatic as possible, and acting the part of an apprentice observing the work of masters, he asked questions that led others to see the errors in their work. Slowly he gained their confidence, and they found themselves listening to the advice of this rather remarkable young man.

Thomas Andrews was impressed with Viko's insightfulness and skill as a manipulator. He asked him a favor. "Would you mind spending some time with me tonight after hours to take a close look at the layout of *Titanic's* electrical system, in private, where you will not be inhibited by the presence of these men? There are aspects of it that concern me, and I would appreciate your input."

Bruce Ismay had set a ridiculously early sailing date for *Titanic's* first voyage and everyone was rushing about, at times haphazardly, not having adequate time to fully consider a problem before being forced to move on. Andrews made the decision that Edison DC generators would be the source of electricity, not because of any compelling advantage they possessed, but simply because he could use most of the wiring details from earlier ship designs and did not have to be bothered with new designs and the bitching and complaining he inevitably heard from Ismay about "unnecessary details."

Mundane details did not bother Ismay. His only concerns revolved around the luxury that could be provided and the earliest possible sailing date. Andrews was constantly fighting a losing battle for more time to ensure safety and reliability.

Later that evening, as they sat in the quiet corner of a local pub, Andrews once again asked Viko for his honest evaluation of the electrical design from an "outside" person. Viko did not have to hold back or worry about being diplomatic. He was given the opportunity to be totally honest.

"There are many things that concern me about the ship. First of all, there is no redundancy in the electrical system. It ultimately controls the steering of the ship. This seems terribly shortsighted."

Viko continued. "There is but a single boiler dedicated to providing steam for electrical generation. The generators are Edison DC dynamos that require constant maintenance to be reliable. What are you going to do in the middle of the ocean when that boiler goes down? AC generators from Westinghouse would be smaller, more reliable, and you could use AC power throughout the ship rather than DC."

Andrews responded, "You are very insightful for a young man. You have just expressed several of the fears and concerns I have had since these plans were first drawn up. This is not how it started. I specified to the designers that there were to be three boilers available for the electrical generators, a primary and two backup systems. I also requested that a thorough study be done regarding using Westinghouse AC rather than Edison DC.

"One of the crosses I have to bear as the chief designer is putting up with the White Star Line and its director, Bruce Ismay. He knows nothing of ship design or the inner workings of vessels."

Andrews went on, "In the early days of the project, he insisted on a weekly review of our progress. The subject of one of the reviews was a detailed discussion of the steam engines that will be powering the ship. During that discussion he learned that two of the small boilers could be diverted in an emergency to provide steam for the electrical generators. The total power that this was to use would have been about two thousand horsepower, a pittance compared to the full capacity of the main engines of fifty-nine thousand horsepower. When Ismay heard 'two thousand horsepower,' he went berserk and screamed at everyone, *'You cannot take two thousand horsepower for electricity, absolutely not! That power needs to go to the main engines.'*

"It was a terrible display of temper. Unfortunately, I lost my temper and kicked him out of the meeting. It was only a few hours before I was hauled on the carpet. Ismay had gone directly to the top and threatened to pull all three ships unless I apologized and acquiesced to his demands.

"I did my best to make Harland understand the foolishness of Ismay's demand, but Harland was adamant. At that point, I suggested to Harland that he find another chief designer, got up, and turned to leave. I was fully prepared to resign my position.

"Harland put his hand on my shoulder and asked me to calm down and reconsider. Then he turned to Ismay and asked him to step outside and leave us alone, RIGHT NOW. I watched Ismay turn a dark shade of red as he got up and stormed out of the room.

"Harland and I sat down in the corner of his office. He explained to me that he was backed into a corner. He considered Ismay nothing more than a pompous ass, a man who got where he was only because of the premature death of his father. And then he explained the cold hard facts to me. *'Unfortunately, Thomas, you are going to have to change the electrical systems as he requests and then do everything in your considerable talent to minimize risk as a result of this.'*

"I was left with two choices: leave a job that was my whole life or acquiesce to this shortsighted demand. I told Harland that I would do it under one condition. He would get Ismay out of my hair, permanently. The next day Morgan contacted Ismay, telling him to sail to New York immediately. That night I took the entire design team to a pub and proceeded to get thoroughly snockered. We happily toasted Ismay's departure from our lives. But, as you can see, we dropped backups to the electrical system. Welcome, Viko, to the world of influence, power, and money. Makes for some very poor decisions doesn't it?"

Viko just sat there quietly listening to Andrews. Had he not known of the tribulations Tesla had been through in his dealings with the likes of Edison and Morgan, he would not have believed it. How could a few shortsighted men manipulate and control the destinies of innocent, unknowing multitudes?

Viko suggested they use Westinghouse AC generators rather than Edison DC dynamos. He was able to demonstrate that the AC generators would work with most of the other electrical equipment on board, except that the motors would have to be switched to Westinghouse AC induction motors.

The next day, Andrews informed his designers and engineers that they were to make the necessary changes immediately. Orders to the Consolidated Edison Company were put on hold, and Westinghouse received orders for AC generators and induction motors for all three ships.

Viko remained at the shipyards for two more weeks then made a short trip back to London to report the progress to Wittington. Exhausted and much looking forward to a few days' rest at sea, he boarded the *Californian* for his trip back to New York.

CHAPTER 34
Another Tesla Failure

N
o one greeted Viko when he arrived in New York. He had sent his last cablegram from London seven days earlier and was quite specific about Tesla meeting him at the west-side docks.

Viko found an empty carriage near the pier, loaded up his luggage, and headed off to the company, arriving there in the early afternoon of a cold December day in 1910.

When he walked through the door, it looked packed up and ready to be relocated. Wooden boxes of all sizes were stacked along one wall, and tufts of excelsior packing material, looking like a beige snowstorm, were everywhere. None of the workmen were around.

Where were the new transceivers? Viko didn't expect to see them completed, but he did expect to see chassis fabrication and glasswork underway.

He found Tesla, bent over his desk, obviously engrossed in writing a letter.

"Viko, it's good to see you. How have you been? How was the trip?" Tesla got up and embraced Viko in a warm greeting. "I have much to tell you."

Thoroughly confused at this point, Viko sat down, not quite sure what his uncle was about to say. Several times during his stay in Ireland he wrote Tesla, and cabled, keeping him informed of the activities at the shipyards. Each time he ended his messages with the same question, "How are the new transceiver sets coming along?"

He expected to return to New York to a flurry of activity, finding new employees busily building and wiring the new transceiver chassis. Wittington had provided the funds, so everything should have been happening, leading to a day when the world would learn of voice communication, used on none other than *Titanic* herself. Viko savored the thought of the success and recognition this moment would bring.

"Uncle Nik, where are the workers? Where are the new transceivers?"

Tesla sat there. He paused for dramatic effect and said in hushed tones, "I have done it, Viko. I have finally figured out the secret I have been seeking these past many months."

At first Viko thought Tesla meant some type of improvement for the transceivers.

"What secret are you talking about? Do we have time to include it? We have less than six months to meet the delivery of the first four transceivers?"

"Delivery schedule? Six months? What are you talking about? No one but I myself know of this. There is no schedule. I am talking about wireless power."

Viko stared in total shock. It all hit him at once. All this time, Nikola Tesla had ignored work on the new wireless sets ordered by Harland and Wolff! He had gone off in another new direction, abandoning yet another of his own huge technological leaps and those who were depending on him to deliver it.

Viko used every ounce of self-control he could muster, forced himself to relax, took a deep breath, and looked right into Tesla's eyes. "Uncle Nik, what is going on here? Why all the boxes? Please tell me where the new transceivers are."

Tesla began, "Viko, I am leaving tomorrow for Colorado. I have finally realized and proven that the secrets to wireless AC power distribution can be found in the mysteries of lightning electrical discharges, their origin, and in controlling them. The boxes you see contain materials and equipment that will prove I am right. Do you realize what this means, Viko?"

Viko held up his hand. "Just a moment. Answer my question. Where are the new transceivers? What have you done with the order from Wittington?"

The look on Tesla's face answered Viko's question, just as he feared—nothing at all had been done.

Tesla then confirmed, "Viko, don't you understand? Harold will understand. I am using his money for much better purposes. When he learns of the success I have in Colorado he will be ecstatic!"

Viko shot out of his chair, sending it crashing backward to the floor. "You are using his money? But it is for the transceivers! What have you done? What about the faith that has been put in us by Harland and Wolff? Do you realize that the future of communication is teetering on a brink you have brought about, and you are ignoring it?"

Tesla tried again, "But Viko, you are young, you do not understand, let me explain."

"No, you let me explain! What kind of stupid old fool are you? How can you possibly be so blind? You cannot use other people's money like this! You cannot abandon your responsibilities. No wonder the likes of Morgan will have nothing to do with you! You are no more than a thief. You are the most brilliant idiot I have ever known. I cannot leave you to follow through on anything! I have just convinced the world's largest shipyard to use your new wireless; I even convinced them to redo the complete electrical systems on these ships to use AC power, your AC power for God's sake! I come back and you have abandoned yet another opportunity of a lifetime?"

Viko was about to continue but he stopped his tirade. His emotions were on an explosive edge and he feared that if he continued he might actually do physical harm to Tesla. He threw up his arms in disgust, took a few steps toward the door, and looked back at the pathetic little man before him.

"Go ahead, get out of here! Pursue your idiotic dreams. The rest of us will make these transceivers, and stay away, very far away."

Viko stormed out, leaving a bewildered Tesla to stare after him in shock.

— ◇ —

Tesla was gone, off on another wild goose chase to Colorado.

Despite his initial feelings of abandonment and the flashbacks to the failed fluorescent lamp project, Viko managed to pull himself out of an onrushing darkened mood and took stock of the situation.

His first order of business was to find out how much damage Tesla had wreaked on their financial condition. Early the next morning he went to see Robert at the bank. Robert was delighted to see him. As they sat down in Robert's office he inquired about the details of the trip.

After a very brief description of the success he had in Great Britain and a promise to fill in all the details later that night at dinner, Viko explained that Tesla was on a train for Colorado, that he managed to do it again, escape from reality. Viko needed to determine the financial condition of Tesla Electric.

Robert knew that Tesla used funds from the account in the past month, all related to "wireless." Robert assumed that the expenses were going toward the manufacturing of the transceivers. Tesla used a little over twenty-three thousand in the past month, leaving the account with a balance of twenty-nine thousand, eight hundred dollars.

Viko and Wittington had determined that the total amount needed to finance the expansion, hire new people, and arrange for the purchase of raw materials would be just over forty-five thousand. Wittington made a deposit of fifty thousand, giving them a small cushion with which to cover contingencies. Now there was not enough money. For a few moments, Viko and Robert sat there in silence. Once again Tesla abandoned a project that was a sure path to success to move on to yet another idea, possibly brilliant, possibly world changing, but as yet incomplete, and in so doing betrayed the trust and faith of his friends and business partners alike.

There was no saving this man from himself.

Robert spoke first. "Can you do this by yourself? I will do what I can on the financial side, but I need to know that you can make this happen. Can you get these transceivers built on time?"

"Yes, I can do it, and I'm starting right now!"

They shook hands and parted as Robert reminded him, "See you tonight, eight o'clock sharp, and I'm certain Katherine will want to know all about your escapades in Ireland and England."

Viko went back to Tesla Electric. The place was deserted except for Henry Abbott, Tesla's foreman.

Viko was troubled to learn that everyone had walked out two weeks earlier. Tesla had not shown up for a third week, no one had been paid, and there was nothing to do. Henry was sent out with instructions to round up everyone he could find and get them to come in at three o'clock that afternoon for a meeting.

Viko went to Tesla's rolltop desk and found a huge stack of unopened mail and a few cablegrams. Underneath the bills and assorted mail was the original cable from Wittington, its seal unbroken. It contained the order from Harland and Wolff for twenty transceivers.

This was going to be even harder than he imagined.

At the three o'clock meeting, with most of the employees present, Viko explained about the new program. The following morning they would be on a twelve-hour day, six-day-per-week schedule. He announced a 6 percent raise for everyone. He figured out the back pay they were owed with a promise to have cash for them the following morning.

He sent Henry to the bank with a letter explaining his need for cash to pay back wages and asked Robert to have it for him that night at dinner. He proceeded to put together lists of the work to be done, as the road ahead seemed to get longer and longer.

What have I gotten myself into echoed through his brain like the melody of a song trapped in his head.

Dinner at the Johnsons' was a welcome relief. Robert had the money for him and announced that there would be no talk of business. It was a marvelous evening. Viko relaxed for the first time since his return; he had wonderful stories to relate about being in England and Ireland, about the fabulous ships being built at Harland and Wolff, and the incredible hospitality shown him by Harold Wittington.

CHAPTER 35
Bad News from Great Britain

W eeks passed in a blur of activity. Equipment was coming together. Everyone was putting in extra effort under the encouragement and leadership of Viko. There was harmony in the group that had been missing for a long time. Using the transceivers that Viko had brought to Europe for the demonstration, the men quickly learned how to put together this new device and constantly marveled at the ingenuity that went into it.

It was shortly after ten o'clock, Tuesday, March 22, 1911, when Robert Johnson rushed in looking for Viko.

They went into a corner of the building where they could be alone. "I've just received terrible news from England. Harold has passed away."

"Harold, dead? He was in wonderful health when I saw him a few months ago. What happened?"

"It was his heart. There is a history of heart problems in his family. His wife Margie is beside herself with grief. He dropped over at his office yesterday. By the time they could summon a doctor he was gone; it was terribly sudden."

Robert paused. "This spells major trouble for the New Tesla Wireless Company. No one but Harold himself knew of his investments with you. He kept it a complete secret in order to protect Tesla from his enemies. He feared that Morgan would learn of his support for Tesla.

"There will be no more funds coming into the company. I went over the accounts this morning. There is a little less than ten thousand dollars left. I am looking into some assistance to help out, but you must proceed with extreme caution."

The delivery date for the first transceivers was getting close. Due to his careful management and the herculean efforts of a few dedicated employees, they managed to make up for the six weeks lost by Tesla's inactivity—and now this terrible news!

Viko and Robert went for a walk. They considered going back to Harland and Wolff and asking for an advance payment, but they feared this would get back to Morgan. Viko estimated that with eighty-five hundred more he could complete the delivery of the first four transceivers, meet the delivery deadline, and the cash flow they generated would allow them to continue forward.

Robert made a personal loan rather than trust the New York financial world for even a dime of funds. Morgan had eyes everywhere. The news of any loans connected to Tesla would reach him at the speed of the nearest telephone.

M organ was quite surprised when his secretary came into his office and announced that Edison was in his waiting room ranting about changes to *Titanic's* electrical purchases.

Edison stormed into Morgan's office. "Have you seen what those bastards at Harland and Wolff are doing with those God-forsaken ships? They've decided against my dynamos and are putting in AC power equipment from that bastard Westinghouse. I can't believe it! The equipment was nearly finished and ready to ship when we received notification to cancel the order. They put the orders on hold months ago, and now have cancelled the damned things. I sent Batchelor in there, and after nosing around he found that they had switched to AC power. That son-of-a-bitch Tesla must have had something to do with it."

"Now Thomas, please calm down before you have a heart attack. You know very well that after all the problems I've had with Tesla, I will allow nothing of his anywhere near the *Titanic*. Give me a few days to sort this out. I suggest that you continue with the work to complete the original order."

Morgan wasted no time. He sent for J. Bruce Ismay at the New York offices of IMM, and then he sent a cablegram to Belfast demanding a complete explanation of what was happening, and referenced Edison's accusations. When Ismay arrived, Morgan sent him to Belfast with instructions to immediately send him back a cable with a full report of the changes being made.

Ismay smiled as he left Morgan's office. Harland and Andrews would rue the day they arranged for his exile to New York. Oh yes, he knew they were responsible for whisking him away from overseeing the progress on *Titanic*. Who did they think they were to have him banished!

Thomas Andrews and Edward Harland braced themselves for Ismay's arrival. The stream of cables from Morgan was occupying all of their time, as they faced the very real threat from Morgan that he would pull funding. And now Ismay was returning. He had the personality of an anvil and a voice like the sound of fingernails on a blackboard.

Harland and Wolff Shipyards had an exclusive contract to build all ships for White Star Line. Morgan suggested that they better explain themselves if they wanted to remain in that enviable position.

Andrews felt there was a way out of their dilemma. "When we tell Ismay about the new wireless and voice communication across the Atlantic, he cannot help but relent. He will see this as another marvel of modern luxury for the passengers, and that will appeal to his sense of extravagance. We need to make him see this as his idea."

That made Harland relax somewhat, but a part of him still remained apprehensive.

Harland and Andrews did not understand the extent of the hatred that Morgan held for Tesla and anything related to him, and that in some measure was justified. Burned so many times by Tesla, Morgan would allow nothing of his near the ships. He would go to any lengths to prevent such a thing from happening.

Ismay arrived. He stormed into Harland's office. Pulling himself up to his full six-foot-two-inch height, he said, "I have been sent here by J.P. Morgan himself to find out exactly what you two think you're up to. Have you any idea how much you have upset him?" And as his voice rose to its usual nasally pitch he screamed, "What is the meaning of your removing the Edison equipment from the *Titanic*? Have you lost your minds?"

Harland, who had the ability to soothe an angry lion, crossed the room and extended his hand to Ismay, who was both amazed and infuriated that his tirade seemed to have no effect whatsoever on either Harland or Andrews. "It is good to have you back; I trust that you enjoyed a pleasant crossing?"

"Cut the bullshit, you know very well why I'm here; I have been given the directive by none other than Morgan himself to get this ship back on track."

"But you do not understand, Bruce. Give Thomas here a chance to show you. We have something for *Titanic* that will make the name *White Star Line* more famous than you can imagine. It will be in every headline of every newspaper in London and New York, and of course your name will be prominent in all the articles as the head of the IMM."

Andrews had always been in awe of Harland's ability to cajole, soothe, and kiss ass, but this was nothing less than masterful. And it had the intended effect. The color in Ismay's face returned. He began to breathe normally, thinking that maybe he had better listen.

"You have five minutes. What is so damned important that you have allowed it to upset Morgan?"

Andrews told Ismay of a device that would allow his passengers to talk directly to their families and businesses half a world away while they were in the middle of the Atlantic. "Think of it, voice communication, just like a telephone. No Marconi wireless forms to fill out, no limit on the number of words. *Titanic* will be the first ship, in fact the first installation anywhere of this marvelous device. The word will spread that *Titanic*, the greatest ship ever, the flagship of the *White Star Line*, under the leadership of *J. Bruce Ismay*, is a marvel of modern invention. People will stand in line for the chance to sail on *Titanic*. The German competition that you are fighting won't know what hit them."

"What has this got to do with Edison, and why have his orders been canceled?"

Andrews explained the advantages of AC over DC, and that the new wireless required AC as a source of power.

Perhaps he needed to listen to what Andrews and Harland were trying to tell him, that these were indeed the best decisions for *Titanic*. After all, if this would give his passengers more comfort, more luxury, all at no extra cost to Morgan, why not? But in reality, it was the thought that his name would be prominent in more newspapers that was the convincing argument.

Ismay relaxed. The tension that had consumed him since being sent by Morgan ebbed. He asked for tea.

Harland explained that Ismay's friend, Harold Wittington, invested in a new company in America that invented this new amazing wireless. Ismay knew Wittington and was aware of his business acumen, but considered him a coal man. "What was he doing with a wireless company, in New York City no less?"

Harland told of the entire experience of the demonstration, the communication across the sea with Nikola Tesla, and the tremendous opportunity that lay before them.

Ismay felt relieved by all he had just heard. He asked for a stenographer, and using his most diplomatic and carefully chosen words, dictated at length to Morgan about the new wireless from Nikola Tesla and explained the reason behind the electrical changes to *Titanic*. He praised the help given them by Viko Tesla.

With a five-hour time difference between Belfast and New York, the cablegram marked "URGENT, DELIVER IMMEDIATELY" was dutifully delivered to the offices of Morgan at three o'clock in the morning. It was not until nearly ten o'clock the next morning, when Morgan took a break from a meeting, that his secretary, Miss Harbaugh, handed him the cablegram. She apologized profusely that a cablegram marked "URGENT" wasn't delivered to him at his residence in Manhattan regardless of the time of day.

Morgan demanded to know who delayed the cablegram. Then he stormed into his office, slammed the door, and tore open the cablegram.

For the reaction that came from Morgan, the cable may well have contained just one word: "**TESLA**." When he read the name, he let out a bellow that could be heard several offices away.

"NO! NO! NO! NOT POSSIBLE! THIS WILL NOT HAPPEN!"

Fearing that someone was attacking him in his office, his secretary rushed in to find Morgan staring down at his desk in a rage, which even for Morgan was extreme.

"Sir, sir, are you all right?"

His eyes bulged and his face was red. His normally huge nose seemed to have swollen to larger proportions. The shirt around his neck was restricting his breathing. Having seen Morgan's temper before, Miss Harbaugh was frightened. Morgan slumped down into his chair. Fearing he would throw her out of the office, she began to back away.

"Come in and close the door. Contact the Harland and Wolff office on Sixth Avenue, and tell the manager to get over here immediately. After you have done that, send Curtis in to see me."

In a short time, Harold Findley from the offices of Harland and Wolff was in his office. With them was Mark Curtis. Morgan asked Findley to describe what he had witnessed in the offices of Tesla Electric. "What is this new wireless?"

"I was told that it was confidential and to be kept a secret."

Morgan stabbed forcefully at the cablegram. "This is from J. Bruce Ismay. I'm sure you know who he is. He has told me that they're planning to use this new device on the *Titanic*. I have a major financial investment in *Titanic*, and since Mr. Ismay of White Star has already told me about this, I think you are quite free to discuss it with me."

Findley explained what he had seen. Morgan asked for a few clarifications, took a few notes, and thanked Findley for his time.

Tesla had never fulfilled his promises to Morgan. This time it had gone too far. This was not the lamp fiasco that ended in a disastrous fire, it was not his latest motor development that was abandoned, nor the harebrained babble about wireless electricity. This was a huge ship, the world was watching, people were waiting. The future of International Mercantile Marine rested on this.

The world's newspapers were questioning the wisdom of this investment. They were actually questioning *J. Pierpont Morgan*, the man who twice in the last six years saved the United States from financial chaos. *Morgan*, who demonstrated investment acumen and a business ruthlessness that made the most hard-shell industrialists take pause and admire him. In Morgan's mind, Tesla involved in any way at all spelled doom to the *Titanic* schedule. He foresaw delays, failure, and ridicule.

Morgan's Folly, the world would say.

Morgan decided then and there that Tesla needed to be stopped—permanently. In the privacy of his office, he huddled quietly with Curtis.

After Curtis left, Morgan sat alone for a few minutes and forced himself to relax. He splashed cool water on his face, lit a fresh cigar, and returned to his railroad meeting, apologizing for his lengthy absence. There was a noticeable lightness to his step; he seemed to be smiling to himself, as if he were entertaining a pleasant private thought.

Later that afternoon Morgan sent a letter by courier to Edison, assuring him that any inclusion of Tesla's AC power into *Titanic* had been an error on the part of the ship's designers. Edison could rest assured that all had been "corrected" to the original plans and, very shortly, all the orders for his equipment would be restored.

CHAPTER 37

Disaster

The pounding awakened Viko from a sound sleep. It had been months since he had enough rest, and this night was like all the others. Arriving back at his apartment after one o'clock in the morning, Viko had collapsed on his bed and fallen instantly asleep fully clothed.

Nothing was going smoothly. Tesla was off in Colorado playing with lightning bolts, chasing his dream of wireless power distribution, while Viko was struggling to turn one of Tesla's most far-reaching inventions into its first practical production design.

But what was the noise? Who was pounding on his door at this hour? Viko turned on the light; it was two-thirty in the morning. He had gotten less than two hours' sleep and some idiot was trying to wake him up. As he shook the cobwebs from his brain, he heard the shouting voice, and one word found its way into his consciousness. He bolted from the bed and rushed down the stairs to the door.

"Viko—there's a fire!"

He threw open the door to find his foreman, Henry Abbott, soaking wet and covered with soot. "There's a fire, the whole place is engulfed, and the fire department is on its way."

As Viko and Abbott arrived back at Tesla Electric, they found a crowd gathering, the first fire engine arriving, and a police officer standing by. Viko's first thoughts were that they had to get the partially finished wireless sets out of the building so they could salvage their work. He found the fire chief and told him of the rear entrance. Running down the side of the building with two firemen and Henry Abbott, Viko was in the lead as they rounded the corner next to the back door.

He stopped, staring straight ahead.

He shouted to Henry to go back and get the policeman. Accompanied by one of the firemen, he walked up the steps to the back door. It was wide open; the sturdy lock was obviously smashed and hanging by its hasp. Lying on the steps was one of the transceiver chassis, its metal bent, the glass tubes shattered.

Viko pointed out the broken lock and the chassis lying on the ground to the policeman. "This was a burglary, an attempt to steal our property!"

In the meantime, the two firemen entered the building to judge the fire's progress. Luckily, the fire stayed in the front of the building, but looking around inside at the section not yet engulfed by flame, they were surprised by what they saw. Furniture was tipped over, cabinets were on their side, and contents of drawers were emptied on the floor. Viko and the policeman briefly went inside when the firemen summoned them. To Viko's complete horror, not one wireless transceiver was to be found. All four of the chassis were gone. The one he saw outside was most likely dropped as the arsonists left in haste. One of the firemen approached carrying a metal can with no top. The unmistakable odor of kerosene reeked from within.

"Did you use kerosene in your operation here?"

Viko answered with a firm "No."

As Viko stood there in utter disbelief, a ceiling beam not more than fifteen feet away fell with a tremendous crash, nearly knocking him to the floor. The firemen grabbed him as they ran out of the building.

"Get out of here before it all comes down."

Viko had the presence of mind to take the kerosene can with him, important evidence of the crime committed.

They could do no more. Viko and Henry made their way down the alley to the front of the building and watched from across the street as the firemen struggled against the flames, doing their best to prevent the fire from spreading to the adjacent buildings.

It was a total loss. Nothing was left of the building save its brick façade and front steps. Everything inside was gone, the papers, the drawings, the many inventions of Tesla, all gone. But the biggest loss was the wireless transceivers; gone was the future of communications, stolen away by unknown enemies of Tesla. They were in ruin with nothing to deliver to Harland and Wolff.

Simultaneously, three thousand miles away, two curious things happened at Harland and Wolff Shipyards. Two cablegrams, one from Consolidated Edison and the other from Marconi Wireless Ltd., were received. The cablegrams thanked them for reinstating their equipment onto *Titanic*. The Marconi wireless and the Edison dynamo were put back into the plans, and they were very appreciative that Andrews had reversed his earlier decision. The cablegrams were addressed to Harland, who immediately sent for Thomas Andrews inquiring as to what was happening, why the change?

Andrews had left the office early that day to attend a play in London with his wife, and it was not until the next day that he was informed of the cablegrams. However, by that time, another more troubling message arrived from Viko. It told briefly of the fire and the total loss. They could not deliver, there was nothing left.

The following day, after being summoned by Harland and queried about the change of plans, Andrews gathered his design managers. With Harland next to him he asked, "Which one of you authorized the change in the electrical system and the wireless?" Everyone looked puzzled.

Sean O'Reilly, the principal engineer in charge of the ship's electrical system, spoke up. "Sir, there has been no change that I am aware of. Certainly nothing has come from my office, and I wouldn't authorize such a change without direction from you."

Questioning everyone in the room revealed nothing. It was abundantly clear that someone, somewhere, was in control, and it had to be someone in a high position of authority. The coincidental timing of the fire in New York was simply too much to be overlooked.

By noon the fire was fully extinguished. An exhausted, dazed Viko began to sort through the rubble looking for anything to salvage. Everywhere he looked was destruction: glass from the lamps was melted, metal legs that once held wooden bench tops sagged and drooped, the fish tank by a window lay shattered on the floor, its occupants long gone. The machinery used to fabricate and turn motor parts lay buried under the collapsed roof. Melted tar ran down into precision gear mechanisms, eliminating all hope that any form of recovery was possible.

Although he was physically and mentally exhausted, Viko found sleep impossible. He spent the next few days trying to piece together what had happened. He wandered the streets. He spent an evening with Robert and Katherine, whose kindness and friendship were invaluable. His mind kept going back to those terrible days fifteen years earlier and the tragic death of his parents. Once again he felt like that same helpless orphan who had been so cruelly treated.

Three nights after the fire he found his way to a small pub on 38th Street, a few blocks from the ruined offices of the New Tesla Wireless Company. It was a place he knew well, having spent a good many evenings there with the men he worked with, relaxing and telling jokes after a long day's work.

Gus, the bartender, reached a huge hand across the bar and engulfed Viko's hand in a welcoming handshake. "Viko, my lad, how good it is to see you. I hear that you have had a fire, saints above. Thank the Lord no one was hurt."

Viko gave him a tired smile, muttered a weak thank you, and asked for a pint.

"And where would your mates be tonight? Looks like you could use a friend."

Like most bartenders, Gus was a good listener. There were few others in the pub, and Viko found it comforting to be able to release some of the tension that had filled his body like a steel coil for the past three days. The Guinness was thick and delicious, its chocolaty rich taste warm in his throat. He was always fascinated by the way the foam would rise up within the glass, a light brown swarm of cloudiness that reminded him of gathering clouds before a refreshing rain. Soon he was on his second pint, the bar had filled up with regular patrons, and he found himself swapping jokes with Gus and had everyone at the bar laughing along with him. He felt better than he had in days.

Just after ten o'clock, three men wandered in and proceeded to a table in the back, hollering at Gus for service as they passed by. One of the men was limping quite badly and his right hand was wrapped in a large dressing, a bandage of sorts. He was obviously injured, and considering how he limped it was a serious injury.

Every fifteen minutes or so, the three men shouted for more drinks. They were beginning to get a little too rough, even for an Irish pub in New York City in 1911. Gus was a big man and not at all hesitant to evict people from his bar when they began to get out of hand. All it took was one look at his six-foot-four frame, his rugby player's body, and the nastiest tough guy usually complied apologetically with Gus's request to quiet down.

Gus, while serving their fifth round, said, "Boys, I'm glad that you have chosen me pub this evening, and I value your patronage, but if you don't calm down a wee bit, you're going to find yourselves in the street."

They heard the message clearly: "Calm down or get the hell out."

The one who seemed to be the leader of the group was quite apologetic. Speaking with a heavy Italian accent he explained, "We were getting a bit out of hand, weren't we boys?" They all nodded their heads and muttered grunts of apology. "You see, Gus, we were just trying to make poor Alphonse here feel a bit better. He is not feeling well, what with his burned hand and injured leg causing him so much pain."

Gus was a kind person at heart. He said to the one called Alphonse, "My goodness, man, what happened to you?"

"Oh, it's nothing actually, just a stupid mistake."

At that, the leader retorted, "Stupid mistake my ass! That stupid mistake got you five hundred dollars. How many of us could make that kind of money for one night's work?"

"Yeah, but look what it got me." He winced in pain, "My hand is burned to the bone, and I shattered my kneecap. If I had known how dangerous it was going to be I wouldn't have said yes for twice that amount. That *bastardo* simply said, 'I have another job for you and your boys, and you will each get five hundred.' Who turns down that kind of money? He never mentioned the fire until we agreed. We thought it was just another union bust."

Alphonse was a member of the Black Hand, a forerunner of the Mafia in New York at the turn of the century. He and his cohorts were often hired to strong-arm garment district business owners into paying "insurance." They also intimidated immigrants into paying protection money, or made the occasional heist of a truckload of merchandise that showed up a few days later on the black market.

But, being good businessmen, they also sold their services to others on the outside for such nefarious activities as breaking up attempts to unionize, disposing of business competitors who couldn't be "persuaded" to leave the area, and sometimes burning down a building or two to make their point.

When a repeat client approached Alphonse with another job, it was just a continuation of a business relationship that was advantageous to both sides. Alphonse and his partners were well paid, and his customer got services delivered, on time and effectively.

Gus went back to the bar.

"Well, Gus, what did you say to those wops? They've quieted down quite a bit."

"Actually, boys, I feel a bit sorry for that poor guinea over there, the one with his hand wrapped up. Poor lad got badly burned in a fire a few nights ago."

Viko immediately perked up. Fire? A few nights ago? He turned and looked over at the man in question. Turning back, he asked Gus if he knew this Alphonse.

"I've seen him in here a few times, but he isn't a regular, prefers those dago places across town. Too bad about how he got burned. He was doing some kind of special job for someone, got five hundred dollars for it, but it may have cost him his hand. Between you and me, I prefer to stay away from those types. Those damned wops can be dangerous."

Viko's mind was on high alert. Coincidence? Perhaps, but one thing Viko had learned from working with Tesla is that there are no coincidences. Badly burned? A few nights ago? Paid five hundred dollars? Was this the man who torched the building? Had he stolen the transceivers?

He wanted to rush over and grab the man, beat him and question him. Why did you do this? Who paid you? Where is our property? He took several deep breaths and willed himself to relax, to calm down and think rationally.

Gus had said these Italians could be dangerous.

He'd heard this before. Small talk around the shop sometimes centered on *guineas* and *wops*. Viko had two Italian employees who usually kept to themselves and when together preferred to speak in their native dialects. But they feared their countrymen from Sicily, where violence and revenge was the norm. Viko, having his uncle's facility for languages, found it quicker and easier to learn Italian than to teach them English.

He ordered a fresh pint and took it over to the table where the three men were quietly talking. *"Alphonse, mi scuse, vorrei acquistare una birra."* (Excuse me; let me buy you a drink.)

Alphonse looked up with mild surprise on his face. Continuing in Italian, Viko said, "Gus tells me that you are badly burned. I am sorry to hear that. As a child I was severely burned on my back, and I know how painful it can be. I just wanted to tell you how sorry I am, and I know a good doctor who may be able to help you. Mind if I sit down?"

There was an empty chair at the table. Viko sat down and called over to Gus, "How about a round for everyone?"

At first they were suspicious of this stranger. However, since Viko seemed to be fluent in Italian, they were at least cordial, introduced themselves, and began to talk about their origins, describing the small village in Sicily where they grew up, and asked how Viko was able to speak their language so well. Viko explained how he used to run a tavern in Serbia and travelers from all over Europe would stop by, and he learned to speak several languages. This impressed them, especially that he would take the time to learn Italian when so many in New York disliked Italians.

It was obvious to Viko that Alphonse was in great pain. His eyes told of sleepless nights, and Viko could see that he winced whenever he moved his heavily wrapped hand. Viko could smell the stench of rotting flesh. This man needed a doctor immediately.

Continuing in Italian, Viko said, "Alphonse, my friend, please let me give you the name of a good doctor who can help you."

Alphonse did not trust doctors. He preferred Old World treatments for his burns. He was from a country where doctors were worse than quacks. They were usually the sons of the local don, and the only reason they had a doctor's license was because their fathers had demanded it, probably under pain of death to anyone who refused.

Viko was able to get Alphonse to open up about the injury. It had happened three days before in the early hours of the morning. He shattered his kneecap when he fell down a flight of stairs at the back of a burning building. He burned his hand when the kerosene he was using flashed and burned through his gloves.

Viko could feel his heart pounding in his chest. He wanted to lash out, crush the burned hand, and kick Alphonse in his shattered knee, but he forced himself to remain calm. He went one step further, carefully choosing his words. "That's terrible. You know, now that you mention it, there was a building fire over on Fifth Avenue just the other night about that time. I remember all the noise during the night."

Hearing that, Alphonse's eyes shifted ever so slightly; the other men at the table reacted by shifting in their seats, and then Viko knew—this man had set fire to his building.

"Alphonse, let me write down the name of my doctor for you. You need to see someone as soon as possible before the infection in your hand gets any worse." With that, Viko went back to the bar and asked Gus for a pen and paper.

He wrote:

Do not react to this note. Follow my instructions. That man is the one who burned down my building, I'm sure of it. Please go out to the street, find a policeman, and get him in here.

He gave the paper back to Gus, motioned for him to read what he had written.

He made eye contact long enough to assure that Gus understood, then took a second piece of paper and wrote *Dr. James Cartwright, 212 43 St., Second floor.*

He handed Alphonse the address of the doctor and said, "I know that you don't trust doctors, but this is America. He is the best and will help you with the pain and infection."

Alphonse was clearly grateful and replied, *"Grazi ifinite, grazie molte."* (Thank you very much.)

Gus lit a cigarette and stepped out onto the street. Viko and his new "friends" continued to make small talk, where to get the best Italian food in New York and such.

Moments later Gus returned with two policemen. Alphonse was facing away from the door and did not see the police enter, but the man to Viko's right, with a full view of the door, reacted immediately. He looked at Viko with hatred in his eyes.

"Bastardo!"

Viko got up and stepped back from the table and called to the policemen, "This man right here, the one with the hand wrapped, he's the one."

The policemen, both Irish, were good friends of Gus, and most evenings he made sure they received a pint of Guinness on the house. With no love lost for Italians, they drew their sidearms and approached the table. Everyone in the pub froze. Drawn guns in New York City were rare at the turn of the century, as the mere presence of police was usually all that was necessary to ensure order. The three men at the table, Alphonse included, sat perfectly still, knowing that for an Italian immigrant to challenge an Irish police officer could mean a quick death from the muzzle of a gun, or a severe beating later in a back cell at precinct headquarters.

Gus spoke first. He suggested to the officers that the men sitting at the bar should leave the pub. The officers agreed after asking Viko if any of them were suspect as well.

Viko said, "The only one that is suspect here is Alphonse."

While one of the officers stood back with his gun in hand, the two men who were with Alphonse were handcuffed and led outside to sit on the curb and wait to be taken to headquarters. The remaining officer nodded to Viko. "Ask him anything you want."

Viko sat across from Alphonse, being sure to stay back to avoid a painful kick under the table. The police officer, after frisking Alphonse and finding a nasty-looking stiletto, stood a few feet away.

"Alphonse, you set fire to my building. It was my property that you removed. The law will deal with you, but I want to know who paid you."

Alphonse stared murderously at Viko but remained silent.

Viko went on, "You have destroyed the life's work of my uncle, Nikola Tesla. You have ruined the crowning achievement of his career."

Nothing, he might as well have been talking to a statue.

The policeman said, "Do you really think he is going to tell you a damned thing? There's only one thing these guinea hoods understand—a good beating."

"I want to avoid that if possible."

"I've dealt with these wops for years, and the only thing they understand is pain. I've seen some of them beaten to death and they never uttered a word."

Viko didn't know what to do. He had to know who perpetrated this crime against him and his uncle. They had to be prosecuted. This was America after all, where those that committed crimes like this were brought forth and made to pay dearly for their transgressions.

Viko turned to the officer. "What would you do to get an answer from him?"

The policeman was eager to demonstrate. "Now that's a good lad, why didn't you ask me before?"

He pulled his nightstick from his belt and, walking slowly toward Alphonse, took a powerful swing at the table, hitting it with such force that the strong oak surface split open. Viko recoiled, his eyes wide with surprise.

Alphonse began to sweat; beads of perspiration ran down his face and he attempted to swallow. The hatred in his eyes was still there, but the unmistakable look of fear was mixed with it. The policeman stood back and tapped the nightstick against his hand.

He turned to Alphonse. "Are you ready to talk, wop?"

Alphonse hissed a string of profanity at him in Italian.

The policeman brought his club down on Alphonse's head, not with tremendous force but with enough speed to send a loud crack through the room and knock Alphonse to the floor where he lay trying to get his bearings.

Blood trickled down from the gash that opened on his head. The policeman's huge hand grabbed him by the collar of his coat and shoved him back roughly into the chair, causing him excruciating pain in his shattered kneecap and burned hand.

"That wasn't the right answer, you guinea louse." He threw the remainder of Alphonse's beer into his face. "Now that I have your attention, who paid you to burn down this man's building?"

Alphonse uttered the same curses.

The policeman shook his head as if in resignation and took a few steps back as a smirk of victory came across Alphonse's face.

"Viko, I told you that the only thing these animals understand is pain." And with that, he swung around and landed a bone-shattering blow on Alphonse's already splintered kneecap.

White-hot pain shot up his leg as Alphonse let out a scream that reverberated off the walls. His eyes rolled back into his head. His entire body went rock hard as every neuron from his knee to his brain burned with the intensity of a torch. He grabbed for his knee with his good hand and tried to double over but was pressed back into his chair. The policeman had his hand around his neck as Alphonse gasped for breath.

Viko was shocked at this display of brutality. He started to object but the look in the policeman's eyes told him to keep quiet. Gus, behind the bar, simply looked the other way and continued cleaning up. As Alphonse screamed, the two Italians outside looked at one another and then at the policeman guarding them; he was tapping his own nightstick on his hand while looking at them with contempt. They feared for their lives and said they didn't know this Alphonse, they just happened to find him on the street in pain and were simply trying to help him.

The cop smirked and shook his head. *Bullshit.*

Alphonse, delirious with pain, opened his eyes to see the policeman standing over him. This time his eyes showed nothing but fear. The defiance had been knocked out of him.

"Well, my guinea friend, we are waiting for the name of your employer, your *padrone.*"

He tapped the nightstick against his hand a few times, waiting for an answer. Alphonse began to shake his head no. The officer gently laid the nightstick against his bandaged hand. Even the slight touch caused Alphonse to recoil.

"Why, look here, Viko, it appears that we have found another good spot."

He raised the nightstick. As he reached the apex of his swing with his arm fully extended, he hesitated for a moment, looking at Alphonse as if to say "Well? Do we get the name?"

Alphonse's eyes were wide with fear. He could take no more pain. Where were his friends? If he talked, it would be certain death. The law of *omertà* had a single punishment, carried out in the most painful of ways.

The policeman began to count, "3, 2, 1."

Alphonse screamed out, "*No, non vi daro il suo nome, per favore non piu!*" (No, I will give you his name, please, please, no more!)

Although disgusted with the beating he just witnessed, Viko leaned forward as the officer looked on triumphantly. Alphonse had defecated and his bladder emptied. He smelled like a pig. Tears streamed down his face. The pain in his leg was unbearable. He knew he was signing his own death sentence. He cursed the day he joined the Black Hand, cursed the day he left Sicily, cursed God for not saving him from this pain, and cursed New York City.

Viko asked, in Italian, "One last time, the name, give me the name."

Slowly, and almost in a whisper, Alphonse said, "*Il suo nome e`, Senor Curtis, Mark Curtis.*"

Viko sat back, stunned. The information had to be correct. There was no way that this Italian immigrant could know Curtis, and it fit perfectly, too perfectly. He looked up at the policeman and nodded his head.

The last words Alphonse heard were vile curses spoken with a thick Irish brogue as the officer lashed out with his huge right hand, knocked out several teeth, and sent him sprawling across the floor where he was left unconscious.

Gus set the officer up with a pint of Guinness. He sat at the bar with Viko and asked, "So, do you recognize the name? Do you know who it is?"

Viko nodded. "Yes, as a matter of fact I do."

— ❖ —

"Morgan? *The* J.P. Morgan?" Robert sat astonished behind his desk, finding it hard to believe the story Viko had just related.

After learning the shocking news that Morgan's head of security, Mark Curtis, hired the arsonists, Viko wandered the streets through the night. He came to the steps of the American Citizens Bank and waited for the bank to open. He was a little unsteady on his feet from the previous night's drinking, but thanks to a large mug of hot black coffee he was regaining some steadiness in his shaking limbs. Despite his condition, the conviction in his voice was clear. Viko knew the identity of the arsonist and of the man who hired him.

Robert had listened attentively as Viko told of the previous evening. He shook his head in disgust at hearing of the policeman's behavior, but this was New York, and Robert had heard rumors that such things happened.

"I have come to you once again for help. Your advice has always been full of wisdom and thoughtfulness. How do I get Morgan? I know he put them up to this. The bastard must have found out about the wireless sets for *Titanic*. How do I get justice?"

"Unfortunately, Viko, you have been exposed to the modern world of greed and power. As you know from the lamp fiasco, Morgan is ruthless. His trusts block out competition, and when that doesn't work he resorts to violence.

"It is rumored he hires gangs of thugs to break up union activities, often leaving factory workers maimed for life or worse. He covers his tracks well, never being the one directly involved. But with this evidence you may be able to change things. I must add though, and I'm no attorney, you don't have any real evidence linking Morgan to this. All you have is the word of an Italian thug, an arsonist, and that Curtis's name was given up during a severe beating. I, like you, have to believe the path leads back to Morgan, but that is yet to be proven."

Viko shouted back, "Robert, what more evidence is needed? There is no other explanation—it has to be Morgan!"

"Viko, calm down. You're exhausted and have obviously been drinking. Get cleaned up and get some sleep, start thinking rationally. Do you have the name of the police officer who witnessed this Alphonse character giving you the name of Mark Curtis?"

"Yes, his name is Sean Murphy, and he agreed to corroborate my story. His partner's name is Padrick O'Leary."

Robert made an appointment for three o'clock with his attorney, sent Viko home to bathe and put on clean clothes, and asked him to write out the string of events. Robert knew that finding any evidence linking the fire back to Morgan would be practically impossible. Morally, Robert knew he could not just walk away from this to protect his own skin. He needed to help, even if it was at arm's length. Morgan could squash him like an annoying bug in any number of ways. But if his help might lead to justice for Viko and Tesla, then he was willing to take the risk.

Clarence Delmont, Robert's attorney, was in the conference room with Robert when Viko arrived looking and smelling much better. Viko handed Delmont a tablet with several pages of his neat script, detailing everything he could remember about the previous evening. Delmont asked Viko to retell the story of what happened. He and Robert listened quietly as the previous evening's events unfolded. He reacted with a pained "ouch" when he heard about the nightstick hitting the kneecap.

Viko added, "It's all written down for you."

"Have you included the policeman's name, rank, and precinct?"

"Yes, he is Sean Murphy, a beat patrolman out of the first precinct."

"This is good; I will meet with him." Delmont asked a few questions to clarify his understanding of everything and then asked Viko, "What do you want from me?"

"I want Morgan punished for this crime. I want our wireless transceivers returned, and I want full compensation for the damage that has been caused. I want Morgan exposed for the crook that he is."

"I understand your anger, Viko, but let me explain something. J.P. Morgan is arguably the most powerful man in America. Being able to prove that he was involved in this in any way will be very difficult, perhaps impossible."

Viko objected, "But Alphonse gave us Curtis's name. How could he have made that up? And Morgan had every reason to stop us."

"Viko, it isn't what we think happened, what is most plausible, even potentially apparent that will make a difference here. Justice hangs on what we can prove in a court of law. Even if we can positively pin it on Curtis in court and get a judgment, Morgan can simply deny any involvement. Where is the proof? I am sure that Curtis will not give him up, and remember Curtis has personal reasons enough to have planned this himself. After all, aren't you responsible for the burns he suffered in that Bronx fire?"

Delmont continued, "I am going to speak with the police officer and try to talk to this Alphonse character and his friends. I can assure you though that they will never talk in a court of law. Morgan has the best attorneys in New York, and most likely he has the ability to influence the outcome of court trials, if this ever gets that far. Viko, you may be correct that he is behind this, but getting to Morgan may prove to be futile. If nothing else, he will simply cause delays, effect gag orders so this cannot be discussed with anyone outside the case and simply drive you into bankruptcy with legal fees."

Viko looked at Robert, whose sympathetic gaze did little to settle the boiling fury inside his stomach. The son-of-a-bitch was going to get away with it. Morgan, that fat, arrogant bastard, was going to get away with the crimes of arson, theft, and endangerment of human life—scot-free!

Delmont said, "Give me a few days to look into this. Don't do anything until I get back to Robert. We will meet again and I will give you my advice."

Three days later, Robert, Viko, and Clarence Delmont were back in the conference room at American Citizens Bank. Viko was desperate to hear some good news.

Delmont began, "Two days ago, I went to the first precinct headquarters to speak with Officer Murphy. He did corroborate your story that Alphonse gave up the name Mark Curtis. Of course, he denied using any force to get the man to talk. However, he did agree that if it came to a court hearing, he would be available to testify on your behalf, which under other circumstances might be considered good news. I asked if I could speak with Alphonse and he became very nervous and cagey, not willing to give me a direct answer. I asked where he was being held, and Murphy told me to speak with the precinct captain.

"I went to the man in charge, Captain Steven Smith, who, after listening to my request, informed me that Alphonse Anacelli was dead. He was found in his holding cell, not breathing, the morning after he was brought in. They claim that he hanged himself with his belt. His death is being called a suicide."

"I don't believe that story for a minute," Viko interrupted. "Either they killed him or he's been hidden somewhere. His leg and hand were practically useless, especially after the beating he received. There is no way he could have hanged himself. To do that with one hand and only one leg, impossible!"

Delmont continued, "I then inquired as to the other two who were with Alphonse that night, might I be able to speak with them? At that the captain expressed complete surprise. He asked me, '*What other two? Only one perpetrator was arrested and booked, Alphonse Anacelli. And you might want to know he has quite a record of petty theft and suspicion of arson and murder.*'

"Viko, I don't believe it was suicide either, and of course we will never know. The code of silence among the police is very strong, and further, Anacelli could have hanged himself as part of the law of silence that those Sicilians live and die by. By killing himself he has proven he is an honorable man and his family can be proud of him."

Viko nodded. "What did you mean when you said that Murphy's corroboration with my story 'might' be considered good news in other circumstances? Why isn't it positive proof of my contention that Morgan's man set this up?"

"Because officer Murphy has disappeared. I went back yesterday to have him sign a statement and was told that he and his partner, Padrick O'Leary, have been transferred to a special detail in the police department, and I would have to speak to the police commissioner to locate them. I have attempted to reach the commissioner by telephone and was informed that he is away on police business indefinitely and cannot be reached.

"In other words, Viko, we have been stonewalled. I suspect that Morgan or Curtis have learned that we questioned Anacelli. At this moment, we only have your word as to what happened. None of us question that, but against the forces that Morgan has at his disposal, your chance of proving anything is virtually nil. I'm sorry, but there is nothing that you, I, or anyone else can do. Morgan is so isolated that we cannot get to him through the law, even if he is guilty."

Viko showed no reaction to these final words. He sat there quietly, slowly breathing and staring straight ahead. The words *there is nothing that you, I, or anyone else can do* echoed through the conference room, like the distant screeching of vultures descending on a helpless victim.

Something within the synapses of Viko's brain snapped. This was the final, fatal straw that shoved him over the brink into a freefall to the depths of darkness as reality dissolved into his own world of madness.

The room became gray and then blackened. Viko's mind was filled with roiling clouds as the demons of his dreams emerged from the darkness and floated about him. The demons were not taunting him as in his past nightmares. This time they were looking to him, pleading with their eyes. They moved apart and a pathway of glowing, bubbling lava formed, leading off into the distance where the likeness of Morgan sat on a throne of fire. The smoke filling the room seemed to emanate from Morgan as his throne slowly lifted into the air until he was looking down on an assembled mass of tormented souls who moved behind Viko, seeking protection and safety.

Viko heard voices. He looked into the faces of the demons about him and they began to mutate, to change—everyone he had ever known was before him, pleading for protection. Tears ran down his face as he saw his father and mother with their arms around little Djouka, blood pouring from the terrible gash running across the side of his father's neck. There was Juliet and Lilet, and behind them stood Aleksandar; even Josef, Karl, and Professor Lippmann were there. Off to the side he could see Katherine and Robert. Everyone he had ever known needed him, begging to be saved from the fate that Morgan planned for them.

And then, to Viko's astonishment, all the faces began to twist and bend grotesquely until only one face could be seen, the face of his uncle, Nikola Tesla, and with one voice they cried out: "Viko, avenge us!"

The demon on the throne spoke to him. *"You little pissant. Did you think for one moment that you could get to me? How pathetic you are, almost as pathetic as that fool you call your uncle. The name Tesla will be buried in the rotting dung of history."*

Viko shouted back, "I'll see you in hell, you bastard!"

The demons evaporated, the black clouds receded. The sound of his voice reverberated off the walls of the conference room, dissolving into silence as the image of a laughing, taunting Morgan, standing on the gleaming white deck of a huge black ship, faded away, disappearing into the mist that clung to the room.

"Viko, are you all right?"

A hand appeared through the wall of fog and touched his shoulder. "Viko, look at me, Viko, can you hear me?"

The white fog around him cleared, and standing there were Robert and Clarence Delmont. Robert's secretary held a glass of water.

Viko was drenched in sweat. His clothes clung to him as if he had just climbed out of a pool of water. He was cold and his skin had the pallor of white alabaster. His throat was sore and he spoke in a rasping whisper.

Robert said, "Viko, you frightened the hell out of us. What happened, did you have a seizure?"

Robert and Delmont had just witnessed the catatonic behavior that ran through the Tesla family. Viko had been as still as death. His eyes were open but unseeing. He had been like that for nearly twenty minutes when he screamed out "*I'll see you in hell, you bastard!*"

"What happened, why are you staring at me?" Viko rasped. He had no recollection of the scare he had just given everyone. "Why is it so cold in here? Have I been in the rain?"

Robert helped Viko out of his suit jacket and wrapped a blanket around his shoulders. They gave him a cup of hot coffee with a touch of brandy to soothe his raw throat. He sipped it and offered a whispered "Thank you" to Robert's secretary for her kindness.

As color returned to Viko's face, he sat there with a look of serious determination. Robert and Delmont sat across from him; it was obvious to them that the news Delmont had given him had pushed him over an edge. To Robert, the frightening similarity to behavior he witnessed from Nikola Tesla was alarming.

One word kept running through Viko's mind, repeating itself in several languages: *revenge, la vengeance, venganza, la vendetta, rache,* over and over.

In those few minutes of psychotic hallucination, he saw the solution. He knew how to get Morgan. He knew the Achilles heel that could bring Morgan down. How simple, how beautiful, how unexpected this would be! Morgan would be forced up against a wall, unable to find a way out, unable to do anything but admit his miserable little attempts to hurt Tesla. He would be forced to give Tesla the public accolades he so much deserved, forced to admit Tesla's superior intellect, and forced to confess that it was he, J. Pierpont Morgan, who directly ordered the destruction of Tesla's facilities, and who deliberately set out to ruin this phenomenal genius.

A smile spread across Viko's face.

"Well, Viko, that's better," Robert said. "Take another sip of coffee; it is good for your throat." Viko sipped the hot coffee and its warmth, aided by the brandy, soothed his sore vocal chords.

There was a knock on the conference room door. Robert's secretary opened it slightly and announced that the doctor had arrived.

"Dr. Braun, thanks for coming on such a short notice," Robert said.

Robert introduced them. "Viko, this is Dr. Braun, our family physician. I called for him when we feared that you were having some type of epileptic attack."

Speaking in a raspy whisper, Viko replied, "Well, doctor, I hope this isn't a waste of your time. Robert may have called you a little prematurely. I'm fine."

"Based on the sound of your voice, I disagree with you. You don't sound well at all. I want to examine you."

Viko's throat hurt like hell, he had a blanket wrapped around him, and his clothes were beginning to smell from the perspiration that had soaked into them. He didn't want to be poked and prodded by a doctor.

Robert said, "Viko, you may be the second smartest person I know, but I just witnessed every symptom of a seizure. Shut up, stop arguing with this man, and let him do his job. You are almost as pigheaded as your uncle."

This last statement made Viko laugh, which triggered a coughing fit that brought up phlegm tinted with blood.

A half hour later, he jokingly said, "Well, am I going to live?"

"Young man, you have ruptured a blood vessel on your vocal chords. Your blood pressure is 190 over 120. Your body temperature is two degrees below normal, and your heart rate is over 100 beats per minute. If you were thirty years older, you very well might have died from heart failure just now. You have suffered some kind of serious event. You need medical attention, and most likely you need to take a regular medication to prevent something like this from happening again."

Putting it all together, the doctor concluded that Viko suffered an epileptic event triggered by the emotional shock of hearing the news about Morgan, confirming Robert's suspicions. He left them with the instructions that Viko was to come to his office the next day for a complete physical.

Viko knew better. He didn't question the doctor's advice or his analysis; he knew exactly why his heart rate was so high and his blood pressure was off the charts. It was the excitement of knowing that Morgan was finally going to be exposed! It would be he, Viktor Tesla, who would bring it about.

Any consideration that Morgan may have been innocent, that the arguments put forth by Robert and his attorney may have had merit, dissolved into the fog of insanity that surrounded Viko.

Viko had given up control to his inner demons. Mr. Hyde shoved Dr. Jekyll brutally aside, and a path that would lead to the deaths of over fifteen hundred people began to be paved with hatred and cunning that knew no bounds.

BOOK 7

CHAPTER 38
Targeting *Titanic*

F rom that life-altering moment onward, Viko focused his energies on one thing only: revenge against his perceived enemy, Morgan. To Viko's distorted mind, Morgan's Achilles' heel was the ship *RMS Titanic*. With his photographic memory, he knew every detail of *Titanic*, especially the weaknesses in the ship's design.

He and Thomas Andrews were on a first-name basis and had worked side by side for weeks. Andrews had great respect for Viko and on more than one occasion had told Viko that if he ever wanted to join his staff of ship designers, he was more than welcome; it was an open-ended job offer.

Viko had crossed the Atlantic many times on the *Californian*. He spent hours on the bridge with Captain Lord and received a good education in sailing and in ship operations. On several occasions, when he was not busy in the wireless room, the ship's engineer used him as an assistant, performing everyday maintenance and repair.

Viko had his own supply of money, nineteen thousand dollars, funds deposited in banks after learning of Morgan's plans to take away the lamp production. He could operate independently for a very long time and put the money to work as he saw fit to carry out his plan for revenge.

— ◇ —

Viko had sent a telegram to Colorado the morning after the fire, and as soon as it reached his hands, Nikola Tesla made arrangements to return to New York, reluctantly shuttering his operations in Colorado Springs—for a third and final time.

After being met at Grand Central Station by Viko late on a Tuesday evening, Tesla stayed up all night listening to Viko relate the terrible events from the time of the fire up to the discovery of the perpetrator's identity.

Tesla was deeply shaken by the news. He had faced Morgan's wrath in the past, he knew of the man's power and his total grip on the financial institutions in New York, but he never suspected that the man would stoop to such a dastardly act. He could accept hard-nosed business decisions, but violence? Tesla in fact had misgivings that Viko's suspicions were anything more than that, just suspicions in the mind of a very angry and revenge-driven young man.

Viko's pain was obvious, and Tesla found himself more in the role of surrogate father rather than a colleague. He did his best to try to convince Viko that not all was lost, that they would move on, and that new and exciting days lay ahead. "Remember Viko, we still have the two original prototypes of the new wireless. I took them with me to Colorado so that I could use them in my wireless power experiments."

Viko had forgotten about the two early transceivers; they were not of the most recent design like the ones stolen during the fire, but they worked quite well. He also knew there was no way these could lead to a delivery to White Star Line, but perhaps they could serve another purpose.

Viko's plan was quite simple in concept, but complicated to carry out. It was to somehow stop *Titanic* mid-ocean and let her drift for days in the middle of the sea, filled with the world's most influential families, especially that bastard, J.P. Morgan. His contemplation of all those powerful people, their wealth and influence suddenly meaningless, unable to do anything but drift aimlessly, cold and hungry, brought a wicked smile to his face. He imagined Morgan screaming at the captain. He pictured Morgan cornering and brutalizing Ismay.

How fitting, the justice of it all. Would any of them realize that their own injustice to Tesla brought it down upon them? The person they should be screaming at and threatening to lynch would be right there among them, none other than the squat little man with the big red nose.

The basics of his plan were delightfully straightforward. Disable *Titanic*, cut off her communication, and let her drift in the open ocean long enough to cause a major panic. Let her *disappearance* become major news, let it evolve to a fever pitch of emotion, and then step in as hero and save the day, all in the name of Nikola Tesla. The North Atlantic was a huge empty space. Even a ship the size of *Titanic* would be lost, impossible to find, like looking for a needle in a hundred stacks of hay.

Viko moved ahead with a singular purpose as clear as the cool mountain air he had breathed in Colorado. No longer beholden to anyone, he began the deliberate and carefully planned steps to exact the revenge he so deliciously anticipated. As soon as the two transceivers arrived from Colorado, he took them to another building where no one but him would see them or work on them. He ceased shaving and grew a thick dark beard. He let his hair grow longer and obtained a pair of reading glasses. The natural disguise added ten years to his appearance and changed him just enough so that a casual acquaintance would not recognize him.

Viko sent a cablegram to Thomas Andrews at Harland and Wolff, inquiring as to the availability of the job offer tendered during his last visit. He researched the sailing schedule of the *Californian*, noted all its planned crossings to Great Britain for the next eighteen months, and verified that Stanley Lord was still the ship's captain.

Working alone, Viko altered the function of the transceivers. He had copies of work done by Tesla years earlier for the 1900 World's Fair at which Tesla demonstrated a small, remotely controlled underwater ship or "automaton" as Tesla called it. The transceivers were going to serve a new purpose, and Viko was altering them to become remote control devices, small complex "black boxes" that would bring a great ship to an unexpected destination in the North Atlantic and into a unique place in the history of ocean travel.

— ◌ —

Two months later he booked passage on the *Californian* under the name *Viktor Gracac*. He waited until they were a day out of New York and stood outside the door of the bridge late one evening. He approached the captain as Lord left for his room. Removing his glasses, Viko asked, "Tell me, sir, is this ship safe enough to cross the sea?"

Lord began to reply, but something in the voice caught his ear. "Viko, is it you?"

A huge grin spread across Viko's face as the two exchanged warm greetings.

Lord asked, "Why didn't you tell me you would be on board? We have empty first-class cabins; I would have gotten you into one."

"I don't want to be any bother; you have enough to do running the ship without looking out for me."

"Viko, you are never a bother. This ship is so solid, my crew so well trained, they could sail her without me. Now, what say we have a drink?"

As they enjoyed glasses of warm brandy, they exchanged stories of the past year and lamented the death of their mutual friend Harold Wittington. Viko offered to be of any assistance he could while on board, including operation of the wireless if the operator needed a break.

This was more than the renewing of an old acquaintance for Viko. He needed to be sure that he still had the friendship and camaraderie of Captain Lord. The use of the *Californian* was a critical part of his plan to disable *Titanic*, and he would need full access to the wireless room on some future night to carry out his plan.

He bid farewell to Lord and the crew of the *Californian* at the docks in Belfast and walked across the wooden boards of the pier to a carriage and a smiling Thomas Andrews.

After a hesitant moment looking at the heavy beard, Andrews said, "Viko, you have sailed so much, you look like an old sailor. Come on, let's get you to a room and then how about a pint?"

In a corner table of the local pub, Andrews began, "God knows that I need your help, but what brings you here? There must be better things for you to do in New York than come here and hang around a dirty old shipyard."

"You know about the fire," Viko said. "We have lost everything. I cannot tell you how disillusioned I am with America. It's not the golden land that everyone yearns for, but rather a den of cutthroat barons who hide behind the law and their riches. Oh, there is the illusion of freedom, but try to tread on their turf, their land, so to speak, and you learn quite quickly just how much control they have.

"I need a job. My association with Tesla in New York closes every door to me. I recalled your offer and, on a chance, sent the cablegram. Ships intrigue me, I am an expert in wireless and electricity, and I offer my services. And please note my last name is *Gracac*, not *Tesla*."

Although there were well over a thousand men working in and around the *Titanic* and her sister ships, the name *Tesla* would jump off the page if Morgan or his bean counters were monitoring employment records. *Gracac* would simply blend in, another nondescript name in a business where dozens of employees might be added or dismissed weekly.

Over the course of the next several weeks, Viko completed tasks assigned by Andrews related to the installation of the new Marconi wireless built for *Titanic*.

Viko saw the Marconi wireless assignments as providential. Another part of his plan was falling into place. *Titanic's* Marconi wireless was the most powerful radio set yet manufactured for seagoing use. The large cumbersome size worked in favor of Viko's plans. He needed a space where he could install a simple yet effective explosive device that when activated would sever the connection to the antenna and at the same time do significant damage to the transmit coils, damage that could not be repaired at sea. *Titanic* would be unable to send messages.

He made a few subtle changes in the placement of the large cumbersome chassis and coils, creating the space he needed to fit in a small explosive charge. It would be connected to the ship's antenna, the perfect receiving device for the detonating signal he would send on a future fateful night.

The other part of his plan was not as easy to carry out. Viko needed to bring the ship to a stop, and do it so completely that the damage would be permanent, not repairable at sea. He recalled a conversation he had months earlier with

Captain Lord. Lord had explained that a ship without a rudder would wander aimlessly at the mercy of the current. Protocol dictated that a steamship's engines must be shut down and the ship call for help in the event of the loss of a rudder or rudder control mechanism.

Viko focused his plans on the steering mechanism. The huge propulsion steam engines, with a combined output of fifty-nine thousand horsepower, were much too massive to disable. It would be impossible to take out all three. But the steering remotely controlled from the bridge—that was the weak link, made especially so because of Ismay's meddling with the ship's design. There was no redundancy. True, Andrews did everything possible to make it invulnerable to damage or failure, but a properly planned and executed destruction of a critical part could render the great ship uncontrollable.

The responsibility for the steering mechanism went to Andrews's most senior manager, Osgood Meineke, a German émigré renowned for his mechanical wizardry, with years of experience in the installation and design of ship rudder mechanisms.

Viko needed to locate the weaknesses in the complex mechanisms of the steering system. He recalled seeing its basic outlines. A small steam engine, located in the stern, turned the rudder. If he could damage the engine, or somehow damage its controls, then he could render *Titanic* uncontrollable.

Once again, the hand of fate took Viko and led him to the answer he was seeking.

Thomas Andrews had many ways of motivating the work crews as they went about their dangerous daily work. There was a standing offer that any group which completed a major installation ahead of the already accelerated schedule would be treated to a Saturday night at one of the many pubs that thrived near the shipyards in Belfast. The effect of this offer was to create a competition among the many groups of men who scurried about the ship each day.

As the twelve-hour workday drew to a close on Friday, August 22, 1911, shouts went up from two groups aboard the *Titanic* superstructure. Viko led one of those groups. His nine workers just completed the initial installation of the main wireless assembly, three days ahead of schedule. Meineke headed up the other group. They had installed the large steering wheel and connected it to the complex rheostat that would send the electrical control signals to the rudder-control steam engine, and like Viko's group, were ahead of schedule.

The two groups commandeered several tables in Dargan's Pub Saturday evening. Andrews circulated among them shaking hands, greeting them by name as they cracked jokes, cheered each other, cheered Harland and Wolff, cheered *Titanic*, and especially cheered Andrews, who in his usual self-effacing style told them, "No, it is you who should be honored here. You have done all the work." Which of course just brought more cheers and shouts from the group.

Viko knew of Osgood Meineke, but the two had never met. After spending time with his crew of men, Viko went up to Meineke and in perfect German said, "Congratulations on a job well done. Let me introduce myself, I'm Viko Gracac."

Meineke shook Viko's outstretched hand, replied with a simple, "Danka, I didn't know you were Deutsch."

Viko laughed. Continuing in English, he explained that he was actually from Serbia, currently an American, and learned German at the University of Prague. Meineke nodded in approval and replied, "Well, you could have fooled me. Your German is flawless."

Meineke took another swallow of Guinness and frowned into the glass. "Too bad these Micks don't know how to make beer. I miss a good German brew."

As the two stood there chatting, Thomas Andrews joined them. The three found a quiet table, sat down, ordered more ale. "You two are doing a great job; I wish I had a few more like you to head up work crews," Andrews said.

Meineke asked Viko, "What are you doing aboard the ship?"

Andrews jumped in and answered the question. "Viko here is a damned good electrician and is installing the Marconi wireless."

"An electrician you say? Tell me, Viko, have you ever worked on motor controls?"

Being careful not to appear overly anxious at this unexpected opening, Viko replied, "Oh, I have a little experience, perhaps I can take a look—that's of course if Thomas doesn't mind."

Viko was among the top electrical experts in the United States. He had the knowledge and the ability to resolve the most complex of electrical problems or designs.

Andrews explained, "Osgood is installing the rudder control. In fact just yesterday they finished the installation of the ship's wheel and part of the rheostat mechanism." He turned to Meineke, "I didn't know you were having any difficulty. What's the problem?"

Meineke replied, "No problems, Thomas, just that this new idea of an electrical rudder control has me worried. I have never seen one like this before."

"Viko, I want you to spend a few days with Osgood. You have done about all you can do for now with the wireless. Go ahead and take a look at the steering electrical controls. I will stop by on Wednesday and the two of you can brief me on your findings and recommendations."

As Viko walked the few blocks to his room, his step was light and his fertile mind was alive with possibilities. Once again, fate had opened a door for him, giving him the access he needed to carry out the second part of his plan.

CHAPTER 39
Viko the Terrorist

Viko was given a detailed overview of *Titanic's* steering controls, from the ornately carved wheel on the bridge to the thirty-ton rudder at the rear of the ship. Meineke pointed out every weak spot in the system, describing in detail how damage in those places could render the rudder immobile.

Viko listened to all of Meineke's concerns with fawning concurrence. He shook his head in mock agreement, but he had found the weakest link in the steering chain, one that would be impossible to repair at sea, and one that would be child's play to damage. He was delighted! The designers of *Titanic* never considered acts of sabotage; such possibilities simply did not enter their minds. Who would deliberately do anything to endanger the ship or the lives of its passengers and crew?

He had all the information he needed to carry out his plans to stop *Titanic*, but there was much to be done to carry it out.

The *Californian* was in port in London and would be returning to New York in two days. It was critical that he be on board. Viko couldn't simply walk away from *Titanic* and his crew as such behavior would appear irresponsible.

The next day he burst into Thomas Andrews's office looking appropriately distraught. He explained that Nikola had been severely burned in an electrical accident and there was fear for his life. He needed to leave immediately. Thomas understood, offered his concern, thanked Viko for all the help with the wireless and the steering control, and with a warm handshake bid him a safe journey.

As Viko left to catch the ferry to London, he was surprised that he could be so convincing with his lies. It seemed strangely effortless for him to speak in half-truths and outright fabrications, because at one time he had been scrupulously honest. He had changed. He kept reminding himself that the only thing that mattered was to succeed in his mission to bring Morgan to his knees, and *Titanic* was the key to it all.

Viko arrived in New York late in the afternoon of a fall day in 1911 and went directly to his apartment at 28 E. 12th Street. He took a hot bath and went to sleep. He once again descended into dreams of revenge. He welcomed his nightmares. The demons in his dreams had become his friends and mentors, constantly reminding him of his purpose.

Obtaining explosives in New York City in 1911 was an easy task because of the ongoing construction of high-rise buildings. Beginning with simple squib detonators, working in the sub-basement of his secret building, where the small explosions could be muffled, he perfected his remote charges. He made the necessary changes in his remote transmitter and receivers to include the fail-safe circuitry that would ensure no premature detonations.

Three weeks later, he completed the assembly of the explosive charges, one for the steering mechanism, one for the Marconi wireless, and a third to be used as a trial run.

Ideally, he would have made two of each detonator, using one of each as a test device and the other as the tactical explosive. But he felt that if he tested just one, he would have the assurance that his plan to stop *Titanic* would be successful. Unfortunately, his reasoning was flawed.

— ❖ —

He packed his test explosive and detonator into a cushioned suitcase, boarded a New York Central train, and traveled north to the quiet Hudson Valley town of Peekskill. Located in the rugged hills just east of the Hudson River Gorge, Peekskill was a short distance from remote uninhabited valleys. It also happened to be just across the Hudson River from the US Army officer training college, West Point.

Residents of this area were accustomed to the sounds of rifle and cannon fire as the cadets went about their training exercises. One more explosion would not rouse suspicion or concern.

He checked into a small hotel and nearly had a heart attack when the bellman clumsily let the suitcase slip from his hand. Viko watched helplessly as it tumbled down a flight of stairs. Fortunately, it didn't detonate, nor did its cover fly open revealing its deadly contents.

At two-thirty the following morning he quietly left the hotel through its back door, mounted the horse he had rented from a local equestrian center the previous evening, and using a flashlight to show the way, rode out of town following a remote logging road deep into the woods famous for the tales of Rip Van Winkle and the Headless Horseman.

The moon was full. It was deathly quiet except for the soft crunch of the horse's hooves on the gravel. It brought back memories of his short time in Colorado and his love of the outdoors and horses. He decided that when this was all over he was going to move west, find a small ranch, and relax for his remaining days. This early morning, however, he had serious work to do.

After traveling for what he reasoned was three or four miles, he reined in the horse, dismounted, and found an old tree downed by decay. He placed his shaped charge, the same design that would shatter the steering mechanism of *Titanic*, in a location near a huge limb not yet touched by the decay. He fastened it down just as he planned to do on the ship and nervously connected the trigger mechanism. He rode a mile back in the direction he had come.

He stopped the horse and patted its neck. "Take it easy, boy." Viko watched as the horse's ears turned back to hear his voice, and repeated, "Good horse."

He reached down into the saddlebag and located the trigger switch that would energize one half of the activation signal. He pressed the button and held his breath in anticipation. Nothing happened. He breathed a huge sigh of relief. This confirmed to Viko that the explosion could not be set off by an unintended radio pulse. Without both halves of the unique activation signal, the trigger mechanism would not operate, a precaution that ensured an unwanted premature or accidental detonation of the explosive charge.

After once again reassuring and calming the horse, he activated both switches and a muffled roar and brief flash of light came from the direction of the charge. The horse reared on its hind legs, startled by the unexpected blast. It was followed by the sounds of hundreds of squawking birds taking flight and many small animals scurrying away. Viko was able to control the horse. He calmed it with his soothing voice, patting it on the neck and repeating over and over "It's alright, calm down, boy."

Viko let the surrounding woods quiet down and listened for any sounds other than those of the gentle breeze in the trees and an occasional mockingbird practicing its repertoire. Hearing nothing that would cause alarm, he worked his way back to the downed tree. Much to his satisfaction, the tree limb, easily ten inches in diameter, had been neatly severed from the trunk.

"Not bad work, don't you think?" Viko said in satisfaction as he looked at the results of his handiwork. The horse didn't express an opinion but seemed anxious to leave, pawing at the ground and snorting, probably frightened by the smell of burned cordite residue.

Viko only planned to test one of his explosive designs, and he chose the more powerful of the two. The shaped charge that was to disable the Marconi wireless was of a different design, smaller and with less destructive power. He should have taken the time. This was the single error made in his otherwise elaborate and detailed planning.

Arriving back in Peekskill just before dawn, Viko left the horse tied in front of the equestrian center, took the saddlebags with him, and walked to the hotel. He gathered his belongings from his room, found his way to the train station, and boarded the next train into the city. As he sat there among the early morning commuters on their way to the city, he overheard someone complaining about

West Point and their nighttime training exercises. He had been awakened at a quarter to four in the morning by an explosion. "And that must have been some huge cannon; sounded like it was over here in our woods."

Viko smiled to himself.

CHAPTER 40
Viko's Final Farewell

Viko made his final plans for the trip back to the shipyards of Harland and Wolff and his target, the *RMS Titanic*.

It had been several months since he had set foot into the rebuilt location of Tesla's New York operation, and his disappearance was cause for concern. Tesla and Viko occasionally met at their apartment, but there was little communication between them.

Tesla was concerned by the sight of Viko. The change in his appearance, the heavy beard, the glasses, and the cap that covered much of his face all raised the specter that Viko was trying to hide himself. He certainly had the right to change his appearance, but when added to the total secrecy regarding his activities, his long unexplained absences, and his general surly mood it was obvious that something sinister was happening to Viko. He was no longer the talkative, helpful young man befriended by everyone. His eyes, normally bright, smiling, and steady, were like dark glowing embers set back behind thick-rimmed glasses, and they darted about as if constantly on the lookout for danger.

Nikola, Robert, and Katherine discussed the changes in Viko over dinner one evening. Tesla was very concerned as he watched Viko's personality change.

Katherine suggested that they invite him for dinner, and together they might be able to draw Viko out, to find out what was troubling him.

Two days before Viko was to sail back to Ireland for his final deadly work on *Titanic*, Katherine invited Tesla and Viko to dinner. The timing could not have been worse for Viko, but Tesla forced him into accepting by cornering him early one morning as he was sneaking out to his secret facility. Viko was left with no alternative but to say yes. He feared being found out if he protested, and he could not allow that to happen.

They arrived at the Johnsons' at seven and were greeted by Robert. He knew of Tesla's concerns for Viko and had heard of his change in appearance, but even with this knowledge, seeing the full beard and glasses, he looked at Tesla and mouthed "Viko?"

Tesla shrugged. "Meet the new Viko. I told you he's changed."

Robert let out a slow exhale. "That you did, but I was not quite prepared for the difference in him." He then shook Viko's hand, and as he led them into the library added, "I can't wait for Katherine to see you. This should be interesting."

Viko said little. Parts of him feared that he would say something that would give a clue as to his plans, and the other parts were controlled by the *new* Viko—parts that preferred to remain quiet and at arm's length from others. Robert poured them glasses of wine.

As they sat there chatting, the sounds of children's voices could be heard. They entered the room in a rush and squealed with delight as they saw Tesla, who bent his tall frame down to smother them in hugs and kisses. They turned to the bearded man next to him and clung to their mother, looking at him suspiciously.

Robert knelt down with them and explained, "This is Uncle Viko." He motioned for Viko to bend down, and Robert took their small hands and rubbed them against Viko's beard. Their fear evaporated instantly as he gently rubbed his bearded cheek against their tiny faces. They burst out laughing, shouting "That tickles!" and immediately begged him to do it again.

For her part, Katherine looked wide-eyed at Viko, and a smile came across her face. "Why, Viko, you look just like a sailor. The beard does you well. You are more handsome than ever. Do you have a girl in every port?"

Viko turned a bright red as he flushed with embarrassment; he always had trouble with compliments, and those that came from the women in his life were the hardest to take.

Katherine excused herself to put the children to bed. The three men sat down in the library. Robert refilled their wineglasses and turned to Viko. "Nik tells me that you have been off by yourself for some time now. What new wonderful thing have you got up your sleeve?"

Viko caught a quick glance between Tesla and Robert and suspected that this dinner was meant to be more than a pleasant evening. They were going to spend the evening prying information out of him. Voices within him told him to be on guard. He could do nothing to let anyone know that he was leaving for Belfast in the morning, nor could he give them the slightest clue to his intentions.

"I've needed a little time to myself, time to think and to consider my future."

Tesla spoke up. "Viko, I could use you at the laboratory. The men miss you, and when you are around we get so much more done."

Annoyed at being cornered like this, Viko replied, "Well, Uncle, perhaps you might learn something from that. If you could learn to follow through on things, if you could stop from messing everything up by flying off in all directions with your crazy ideas, maybe things would run better."

Robert jumped in. "Viko, that isn't necessary. Nik is just looking out for your welfare. We are all just looking out for your welfare. What is going on with you? Why the change in appearance? I have never known you to be so sullen."

Viko glared at Robert. They were trying to learn his secret, one that must be protected at all costs. "I am about something that will benefit my uncle more than anything he has yet accomplished. I cannot discuss it for reasons that will become obvious in the near future."

He carefully placed his wineglass on the table beside him, paused for a moment, and took a deep breath. "Please respect my privacy, that's all I ask."

Robert wouldn't let it go; he had pushed Tesla past the edge in the past and foolishly felt that he needed to do the same to force Viko back to some sense of normalcy. "Viko, you need to listen to us." Both Tesla and Robert leaned in toward him as Robert asked, "What are you up to? We are your friends and your family; we have a right to know."

That was all Viko could take. Jumping up from his chair, he shouted at Tesla, "I have spent the last twelve years of my life trying to save you from yourself. You have ruined every chance, walked away from opportunity after opportunity. My life is my own now—leave me alone!"

He opened the door to leave, paused, and said to Robert, "Goodbye. Thank you for your hospitality and your friendship. I regret it has to end this way."

CHAPTER 41
The Final Solution

A s the *Californian* left the shelter of New York Harbor and headed east along the southern shore of Long Island, Viko stood at the stern looking back at the receding skyline of the city. He did not regret the previous evening's events. He was on a quest to restore the name of Tesla and to avenge the destruction caused by Morgan. One thing was certain in his mind: no one would wonder or care where he had disappeared to, and more importantly, no one would ever find out until he accomplished his mission. He had taken care to leave a detailed letter complete with all his plans and documents behind for Tesla to find at a later date.

Off to the port side of the ship Viko could just make out the slow rotation of the lighthouse at Montauk Point at the eastern tip of Long Island. He stood there for hours, lost in thought.

The crossing proceeded without incident, and Viko settled into the normal routine of the ship, sharing the duties of the wireless room with Peter Evans to keep himself busy.

He spent much of his spare time on the bridge continuing his education in the art of sea navigation. He found that he enjoyed working with the ship's crew, made up mostly of sailors from England and Ireland who seemed to have been bred for a life at sea. These sailors were uncomplicated men, the salt of the earth, or perhaps the sea. They were the type who could take quick measure of a man and, if inclined, become lifelong friends. On his earlier crossings on the *Californian*, Viko had met all of them and had come to know them on a first-name basis. He joined them in their card games and could cuss, joke, and drink with the hardiest of them. He knew the locations of the best pubs in Liverpool, London, and Belfast, and when in port would often frequent those places, preferring to be among the loud boisterous crowds.

Viko didn't think himself in any way superior to the common sailors who bore the brunt of the work on board the *Californian*, and this led to some important friendships that would aid him in his final preparations for *Titanic*. While sharing pints with his shipmates in places like Dargan's Pub near the Harland and Wolff Shipyard, it was common to hear dockworkers and sailors complain about lousy working conditions, low pay, overbearing supervisors, and all the usual bitching that went on among common laborers. But it was also here that Viko learned the names and positions of various men who held berths on the ships, especially the ones who were vying for positions on the new ships *Titanic, Olympic,* and *Britannic.* With his infallible photographic memory, Viko filed away the information for future use.

In Ireland, ready to return to his duties on *Titanic*, he reported for work on his first Monday back at the docks. As he walked along the railing of the first-class promenade deck, Viko was surprised to see the amount of progress made in his absence of just five weeks. Everywhere he looked men were installing fixtures, painting, and riveting huge structures in place; *Titanic's* majesty seemed to be taking shape before his eyes.

"Impressed, Viko? It's amazing to me, even after all the times I have seen this happen, just how quickly the outfitting takes place. She is going to be a glorious ship, I tell you, the finest to ever sail the seas." Thomas Andrews was justifiably proud of his creation, and especially when he could show it off to a knowledgeable colleague like Viko. They met earlier that morning at Andrews's field office on the dock next to the ship. After the usual pleasantries, Andrews remembered why Viko needed to leave in such a rush. "How is your uncle?"

The question caught Viko off guard, and it took a few seconds for him to recall that his excuse for rushing back to America had been a ruse, an electrical "accident" that caused Tesla to be severely injured. He stammered for a moment, quickly recovered, and explained, "He's pretty sore and has some nasty scars, but appears to be recovering nicely. Hopefully he will be a bit more careful the next time he gives one of his high-voltage demonstrations."

Andrews brought Viko up to date.

"We completed the testing of the rudder controls last week, and several of the suggestions you made have been installed. Meineke expressed his appreciation for the insight you offered. We are ready to seal the bridge floor over the controls, and we need to do it as soon as possible as Meineke is quite concerned that the salt air is going to cause corrosion. However, I asked him to wait until you returned before fastening the floor in place."

Viko was fortunate to have returned when he did. Another few days and Meineke would have sealed the floor of the bridge, riveting the heavy steel plates in place and making any access to the vulnerable controls impossible.

Viko said, "I'll take a look at it right away. When can we have electrical power operating? I want to observe the operation of the rudder and also operate the wheel myself. If I can have eight hours, I'll have more than enough time."

Keeping track of the work crews and the status of their work assignments on *Titanic* took a staff of thirty-two people. Andrews devised a huge billboard type display, with scaffolds and walkways that gave clerks access to its gigantic surface. The display was set up in a warehouse near the ship. Andrews as well as other executives could stand on the far side of the building and watch as the status was updated hourly, twenty-four hours a day. It looked like a miniature image of the ship. Various colors were used to indicate progress or completion. Runners spent the day going back and forth between the ship and the warehouse bringing progress updates to the billboard managers, who kept detailed notes and directed the scaffold climbers to change colors at coordinates on the huge display. Green indicated that a given task was completed; yellow meant a maintenance procedure, and red was for problem areas. Andrews enjoyed watching the display as the ship slowly turned to a solid green as the sailing date approached.

Andrews took Viko across the room where he could see that the electrical generator section was yellow in color. They went to a desk clerk, Timothy DeForest.

Andrews's reputation as a friendly but demanding chief designer preceded him, and he greeted DeForest with a warm handshake and a friendly "Good morning, Tim. Is everything as hectic as usual down here?"

"No more hectic than usual, sir, and I assure you that we have everything under control—well, as under control as we can manage."

"Let me introduce you to Viktor Gracac, Viko for short. He has been immensely helpful with electrical work. He needs to run a few tests before we seal things up, but the electricity seems to be unavailable. When will it be restored?"

DeForest looked through a pile of papers that were located under a yellow paperweight, and pulled out a work order. "This was issued late last night. It seems that the brushes in a generator are being replaced. The replacement brushes could not be located until a half hour ago. Completion of the repair is predicted to be eleven o'clock this evening. They've put a second shift on to be sure that it is done before midnight."

Andrews and Viko went to the observation tables, poured two cups of tea, and considered the options.

"Meineke is adamant that we get that compartment under the bridge floor sealed up no later than tomorrow morning, and I agree with him," Andrews said. "The men have been waiting to rivet the covering plate in place, and Captain Smith is upset that the bridge cannot be completed with the floor plate open like it is. As I see it, there is only one option to get your testing done. Are you willing to come in at midnight and work through till morning?"

At midnight the ship would be deserted. No one would be anywhere near the bridge. Viko could send his helper home early and do his deadly work in private. Fate had stepped in again in his favor, and another piece of his plan was falling into place.

Viko said, "No problem. Just arrange for one of Meineke's men to meet me on the bridge at midnight. Tell the night watchmen that we will be on board and that the rudder will be moving. I will stay as long as needed."

They parted with a handshake. Viko went to his room, located the wooden crate that contained his explosives, and hired a carriage to take him back to the warehouse. He put the crate on a hand truck and wheeled it over to DeForest. "Tim, this box contains the tools that I'm going to use tonight to test the steering mechanism. Can you arrange to have it delivered to the bridge for me?"

"I would be glad to arrange that for you." And he proceeded to have the box labeled: **DELIVER TO BRIDGE – PRIORITY**

DeForest called over one of his runners. "Take this to the bridge right away. Don't let it out of your sight until it's up there."

As the crate was wheeled away, DeForest said to Viko, "Things can get misplaced on this ship, and if this crate goes to the wrong place, it could take weeks to locate it. With my man delivering it you can rest assured that it will be there when you need it."

A light drizzle was falling when Viko returned to *Titanic* late that night. It was eleven-thirty; he was early for his appointment on the bridge, and he paused for a moment to take in the magnificent sight before him. As he stood on the dock looking up at *Titanic,* Viko was struck by its festive appearance. The ship was aglow from stem to stern, illuminated by hundreds of brightly burning electric lights that looked like little halos suspended in space in the mist that surrounded them. The freshly painted white walls of the upper decks reflected the light, making them appear in brilliant contrast to the black hull glistening with moisture as the mist and rain settled on its surface and ran down the sides in its unending cycle back to the sea. The distant hum of the steam-driven generator was the only sound save the gentle lapping of the waves against the hull of the ship.

Even on a cold foggy night it was obvious that this was a special ship.

There were few men on board as Viko found his way to the bridge and located his helper for the night, Sidney Black. The bridge was eight stories above the dock surface, and at this height, the chilling effects of the rain and a gathering breeze caused both men to wrap their coats a little tighter. Viko looked around the bridge, and over on the port side, against a wall, he spotted his wooden box and silently thanked Timothy DeForest for his efficiency.

Black had a thermos of hot coffee with him, and as he poured each of them a cup, he commented, "Too bad we don't have something to add to this on such a miserable night. It would take the chill out of our bones."

Viko sipped the hot black liquid. "Well, if we're quick about it, we can be done here in a few hours and get home to our warm beds."

Viko explained his testing plan for the rudder controls. Black added a few suggestions of his own and the two set about the night's work. Viko headed aft to the lower deck where he could observe the rudder mechanism in action. About fifteen minutes later, Black turned the wheel four turns to the port side and then a full eight turns back to starboard before returning the wheel to its original position. Viko watched as the steam engine came to life and performed flawlessly, effortlessly moving the thirty-ton rudder.

Viko was impressed with the large mechanism that moved with such ease and precision, but he was secretly delighted that there was no redundancy. Any failure in the single rudder control at any place along the way would render *Titanic* uncontrollable—precisely what he needed.

His reason for being on board this fog-shrouded night had nothing to do with his concerns about the operation of the steering mechanism. He was here for the dual purpose of installing his explosive devices and the activation of a unique homing beacon.

Viko went back to the bridge and asked Black to do a final inspection of the cable installation and wiring that connected the bridge controls to the rudder motor, a job that would easily take two hours. Viko remained on the bridge to verify that every part of the mechanism was well protected with the corrosion-inhibiting lubricants that Meineke had specified.

Black left to start his inspection. Viko, after waiting a few minutes to ensure he was alone, opened his crate and carefully removed the shaped charge that would disintegrate the control mechanism and sever its connections to the rudder control engine. He lowered himself and his materiel into the tight quarters of the cavity below the deck and began the task of mounting the explosive charge. He used a hand-operated drill to put three holes through thick iron brackets. A full forty-five minutes passed by the time the last hole was completely finished.

As he was bolting his deadly package in place, he heard voices and footsteps as people approached the bridge. They were arguing about something. He could make out a few words as they stood just outside the entrance to the bridge for what seemed like an eternity. In his cramped position, Viko dared not even breathe lest he be discovered. The arguing stopped and then there was silence. The eerie quietness of the ship caused him to become very nervous. Where were they? Had they entered the bridge?

Several minutes passed before he heard footsteps receding into the distance.

Viko relaxed. Whoever it was had left the area, and he was quite sure they hadn't seen him, but he had lost precious time. He checked his pocket watch and saw that Black would be returning in a half hour. Time was running out. If anyone discovered his plot it would mean disgrace, prison, or hanging, but worst of all, failure. He could not let that happen.

Working as quickly as he could, he finished mounting his explosive package in place, tightened the bolts as hard as his fatigued muscles would allow, strung the wire antenna out and tied it to the support beams, and scrambled up out of the hole. He went to the wheel and turned it both ways to be sure its operation was not affected by his *additions*. When it turned normally and he could see the large mechanism was following the wheel's rotation without interference, he threw his head back and exhaled.

But he was not done.

There were a few more tasks in his plan and tonight was the ideal time, in fact perhaps the only time for him to act. He went back to his crate and removed a small powerful magnet, went to the ship's compass, located a bolt relief on the lower front side of its pedestal, and inserted the magnet up into the hole where it fit snugly and clung solidly to the iron assembly. He checked the compass reading and saw that it had shifted ever so slightly to the south—perfect.

Any navigator following the directions supplied by the compass would be unknowingly heading northwest from his intended heading.

Viko wanted *Titanic* to be to the north of normal shipping lanes, with less of a chance for accidental discovery as it drifted aimlessly in the North Atlantic.

He stepped outside the bridge, enjoyed the feeling of the cool mist on his face, and, for the first time since Black left, allowed himself to relax. He looked around at the huge expanse of the ship in its final stages of outfitting. He felt a strange sense of pride. Even though he was moving inexorably closer to the day he would bring this behemoth to an unscheduled stop in the middle of the ocean, he had taken part in the decisions that went into its design. *Titanic* was one of modern man's historic accomplishments, a glimpse of wonders yet to be created in the twentieth century.

Viko looked back into the bridge and was suddenly alarmed. The bridge lights were burning brightly. A bulb located near the wheel illuminated the explosive charge he had just installed. Two hours had passed. Black would be back at any moment. He frantically looked for the light switch but couldn't locate it. To complicate matters, as a safety precaution the bulb was inside a wire frame enclosure. He couldn't remove it. He thought of simply breaking the glass, but that was impossible because of the heavy-gauge wire frame that surrounded it. He looked in vain for something long and thin that would fit through the closed knit wire mesh—nothing.

His brain raced for a solution as he heard Black's footsteps echoing off the steel deck of the ship.

He frantically looked around for a tool of any kind.

There it was on the floor before his eyes. He picked up his mug of cold coffee and threw it at the bulb. Just as Sidney Black stepped into the bridge, the hot surface of the glass shattered into thousands of tiny particles and the hot filament, finding a rich supply of oxygen-laden air, burst into a bright flame and in a fraction of a second burned away as the superheated carbon threw out an impressive array of sparks. "My God, Viko! Are you all right? What the hell was that?"

Neither Black nor Viko could focus for several seconds. All they could see were bright spots superimposed on their vision.

"I tell you, Sidney, those Edison bulbs are dangerous," Viko said. "Did you see that thing explode? I almost crapped my pants. The bulb must have cracked from the filament heat."

They stepped out into the night air to catch their breaths, relaxed for a couple of minutes, and proceeded to review their notes regarding the inspection. Black was surprised to see the perspiration on Viko's face. It was quite cool and it seemed odd that someone working in such temperatures would show signs of exertion.

"Viko, are you all right? You look like you have a fever."

"Thanks for your concern, but I was standing right under that damned light when it exploded. It must have frightened me more than I realized!"

Viko's secret was still safe. But he was not sure what workers might see in the light of day when they arrived in a few hours to rivet the final floor plate into place.

"Sidney, this opening in the floor is dangerous and a night watchman might accidentally fall and get injured. Help me move the plate into place, and I will leave a note for Meineke's morning crew that it is ready to be riveted."

Working together they were able to muscle the quarter-inch-thick cover plate into place where it belonged. There was a loud clang as all two hundred fifty pounds of it fell into place.

They walked back to the gangway that would take them to the dock and were about to start down when Viko stopped. "Damn it, I forgot to leave the note. I told Andrews I would leave a message behind. Without it they won't rivet down the floor. I'd better go back and take care of it."

Viko did nothing by accident or omission. He was not finished with his plans for *Titanic*. He told Black to go ahead without him, said goodnight, and walked back toward the bridge.

The ship was deserted except for the occasional sleepy night watchman who might happen along. Viko timed his activities to avoid inspection rounds. He went back to the bridge, scribbled out a note to the attention of Thomas Andrews and Osgood Meineke. He went to the wooden box that continued to sit discreetly in the far corner and removed the last two items, a small explosive intended for the Marconi wireless, and his special *black box*. The wooden box was discarded over the far side of the ship, falling silently seventy feet to the water below, making a splash that no one heard, becoming just another piece of flotsam drifting about the Belfast harbor.

The wireless room was two levels above and about a hundred feet behind the bridge on deck A. All the exterior lights on the deck were off. Viko went up two flights of stairs. Certain that he could not be seen, he turned on his flashlight and found his way to the wireless room. He was pleased to see that several of the screws that held one of the large panels were missing. He patted his pocket, smug in the knowledge that he alone knew their whereabouts.

He placed the explosive into the spot he prepared for it, directly above the main transmit coil. When detonated, it would sever the antenna connection and shatter the structure of the coil, cutting off *Titanic*'s ability to communicate with the outside world. Even if they managed to restore the antenna connections, they would only be able to listen as the world searched for them. Repairing the transmit coil would be impossible at sea. He made the necessary connections to the ship's antenna and put the panel back in place.

He was not quite finished.

Moving in the shadows, Viko worked his way to a staircase that led down the entire depth of the ship and quietly descended to the central boiler room where a crew of four sleepy men was maintaining a single boiler. Under his right arm was the final piece of his intricate plan, the first *black box* ever conceived. Using his photographic memory as a guide, he recalled the location of a spacious storage closet against the port wall of the ship. Inside, with the door closed, he moved several shovels aside, sat down, and began his last installation. He opened a vial of powerful glue, smeared it on one side of the black box, carefully wiped the ship's wall to remove dirt and moisture, and pressed the box firmly into place. He held the box for several minutes, allowing the glue to set. He uncoiled an antenna and glued it to the wall, once again pressing it into place as the glue dried.

He operated a switch on the box, placed his hand against the ship's wall, and felt it vibrate as the box emitted high-energy sound pulses directly into the iron wall. A faint "chirp" could be heard each time.

He was done.

On a future date, radio signals from an FM wireless transceiver, once intended to promote *Titanic*, would emit unique radio signals directed against the great ship. Explosive charges would stop and silence her.

A unique acoustic sounding device would secretly provide her location, but only to someone who knew how to listen.

Early in his career, Nikola Tesla had experimented with resonant devices that could produce powerful sound waves, the types of waves that could travel vast distances through the dense medium of seawater. Viko had located Tesla's experimental data and, unknown to Tesla, had made his black box using this technology.

Viko left the ship. He walked several hundred feet and turned to look back at the great ship. The mist grew heavier and a blanket of fog was settling over the ship, rolling in from the bow. As the fog advanced toward the stern, *Titanic* appeared to be drifting away and floating into oblivion. He watched the ship disappear from view, an omen of the disaster to come.

Viko raised his collar against the chill and the drizzle, turned away, and walked into town and the welcome warmth of his room.

He lay there in the darkness overwhelmed with all that he had accomplished. He had arranged for a world-shaking seagoing "accident." He savored the sweet taste of revenge. The *Titanic* missing! And only he, Viktor Gracac, would know what happened or how to find it. All those giants of finance missing, J.P. Morgan included, unable to be located. That was the sweetest taste. All their money, all their power, all their influence, all would be meaningless—they would be unable to help themselves.

Nikola Tesla would be the most surprised of all. He would not be able to ignore the anonymous cablegram from London. It would contain a few key words, and in those words he would find the secret to locating *Titanic*.

When the man Morgan and Edison dismissed, the man they tried to stop, who they treated like the rabble of the street, Nikola Tesla, directed the rescue ships to her freezing passengers, all that Viko had accomplished would be worth the sacrifice. That would be the crowning moment. Morgan would be forced to admit his crimes—Viko would have his revenge.

Viko crawled out of bed after a sleepless night. Rest could wait for a more convenient time. He arrived at the shipyard along with the thousands of men who would soon be swarming over *Titanic* like so many ants. He went directly to the planning warehouse. Andrews was standing at his desk in a heated conversation with his supervisors.

Andrews was saying, "I know what you are saying, and I agree with you, but I have no choice in this. We must remove thirty-two of the lifeboats. That son-of-a-bitch has done it again. I will work on this and do my best to restore the boats, but for now they have to go. Have them taken to warehouse 3A, and cover them to keep them in good condition. The davits stay as they are, no changes."

The men who were gathered around began to walk away muttering to themselves. Andrews sat down and shook his head in disgust.

Viko had never seen Andrews so upset. Considering that this might not be a good time, he turned to leave when he heard Andrews call him. "Viko, finally, a friendly face. Please tell me that you have good news for me. How did it go last night?"

"I didn't want to interrupt; it looks like you have your hands full this morning. I can come back later."

"Just a part of the job, one that I really hate, but sometimes I have to do asinine things to satisfy our customers."

"The inspection went well. Everything looks as good as it can, and the rudder control worked flawlessly."

"Thanks. That bastard Ismay is going to drive me to drink with his damned changes. I convinced him eighteen months ago that *Titanic* should carry forty-eight lifeboats. He was wandering around the promenade deck yesterday. When he saw the lifeboats in place, he went berserk. He has demanded that we remove thirty-two of them so that his first-class passengers can have more room to walk around. If he had his way, there would be no lifeboats at all on the damned ship.

I pray that this ship never goes down or hundreds of people are going to lose their lives."

All talk of steering and wireless was forgotten. The progress on board *Titanic* continued, each step moving her ever closer to her one and only sailing date.

CHAPTER 42
Revenge or Disaster

V iko's plans for the *Titanic* rescue hinged on his ability to locate the stricken ship in the vast North Atlantic. If all went well with the detonation of the two explosive charges, *Titanic* would simply disappear at night somewhere between Southampton and New York. Unable to control the direction of the ship due to the loss of rudder control, the captain would be forced to shut down the steam engines and let the ship drift, hoping that someone would find them. The wireless operators would sit at their stations listening as the world searched for the ship, unable to send for help or inform rescue ships as to their location.

The sudden loss of communication from *Titanic* would cause a worldwide panic as the news spread that she could not be located. Financial markets would go on red alert as the number one financial leader, J.P. Morgan, was reported missing. The relatives and friends of her wealthy passengers would converge onto the offices of White Star Line demanding answers.

Whenever he let these scenarios play through his mind, Viko would salivate with pleasure. What fitting justice for those who thought nothing of stealing a man's property, especially the property of his famous uncle, Nikola Tesla.

Viko's ultimate vision, his dream come true, would be the day that none other than J.P. Morgan himself, taken shivering and hungry from the decks of the stricken *Titanic*, stood before Tesla and apologized and admitted publicly that he tried to destroy the very genius who saved his life.

Viko was so driven with his need to destroy Morgan that the potential for disaster never crossed his mind, or if it did, was dismissed by the hype that *Titanic* was unsinkable. His mind was as sharp and creative as ever. But his ability to weigh right and wrong, to measure the potential harm he might be instigating, was gone, shoved aside by his psychotic need for retribution. The same mental forces that caused the depression in Ana Tesla and Christina Gracac, stealing from them life-giving energy and from their children maternal love, surfaced in Viko. But in Viko, the depression turned into seething anger, held in check by his intelligence and cunning until the day his revenge could be taken properly.

CHAPTER 43

April 11, 1912
New York Harbor—
Viko's Final Goodbye

V iko stood on pier thirty-nine awaiting his final crossing to Great Britain, looking up at the gleaming iron hull of the *Californian,* wondering if he would ever set foot on American soil again. Most of the crew was aboard, the cargo had been loaded, and in a few hours her passengers would arrive for the crossing to Southampton and then on to London. It had been raining for the past several days, but this morning dawned to beautiful pink clearing skies with a light westerly breeze sending a few nimbus clouds skipping across the blue canopy that spread above him. Rain had washed away the grime of New York.

The major news around the shipping world was taking place three thousand miles away on the other side of the Atlantic. Newspapers could write of nothing else as they tried to outdo each other with stories of the world's first "unsinkable" ship. The subject of course was the maiden voyage of *RMS Titanic,* scheduled to sail on her first crossing on April 11. The articles published in the *Times* and the *Post* ranged far and wide in their coverage, some describing the detailed mechanical marvels of the huge ship, her propulsion system, and the unique watertight compartments. Others concentrated on the impressive list of passengers lucky enough to be sharing this unique moment in history. The list was more like the invitees to a swank society gathering than the manifest of a ship about to set sail. The newspapers were full of details of their dress, jewels, and most recent visits to European royalty and health spas, and a myriad of social trivia that was devoured by the endlessly curious public.

Viko had been in New York for three weeks and was very careful to remain out of the sight of anyone who might know him. The culmination of his plans was just a few days away. He had to avoid his uncle at all costs, knowing full well that Tesla's keen senses would cut through any alibi he could muster to explain his disappearance for the past six weeks.

Sleep, an escape he rarely enjoyed, was more difficult than ever. So much had been done: intricate plans were in place, explosives had been installed on *Titanic*, the black box awaited—the fulfillment of his dream was nearly upon him. He was working around the clock to ensure every contingency was thought out, every potential stumbling block was removed, and everything humanly possible was done to achieve the ultimate success he hungered for.

Viko tested his acoustic receiver and microphones several times until he had satisfied himself that they would work flawlessly, especially in the harsh environment of the open sea. When finally pleased with their performance, he moved everything to a storage locker at Grand Central Station.

He wrote a long letter to Nikola Tesla, adding to the instructions he had written out weeks before, explaining all he had done to disable *Titanic*. He wrote over fifty pages of what turned into a manifesto, justifying the deed he had accomplished, all for reinstating Tesla to the place of prominence he deserved.

Prior to returning to America just a few weeks earlier, Viko had been offered a position on *Titanic* as chief electrician for her first voyage. After that, a future at Harland and Wolff was his for the taking. His ideas for ship electrical design and application of new technology coupled with his extreme concerns for safety brought him directly to the attention of Edward Harland.

Viko wasn't expecting such an honor, and when it was first offered he had second thoughts about his plans, knowing full well that after *Titanic* was located adrift in the North Atlantic and the destruction of her mechanisms was discovered, he would be suspect number one. He asked for some time to consider the offer, and rather than turn it down he simply disappeared one day, going back to America and setting his *final solution* on its irreversible course.

He had withdrawn his remaining money from the Manhattan banks. The money would be his only means of support. He would have to remain in Europe for years. He made plans to contact his uncle on May 1, 1912, giving him detailed instructions to locate the key to a locker at Grand Central Station. The rest would be up to Tesla himself.

Viko boarded the *Californian*, secured his trunk containing the radio transmitter that would stop *Titanic*, and went to the bridge where he found the officers and Captain Lord standing around the map table discussing a serious matter.

They were considering altering their planned course from the shorter northern route to a more southerly passage, opting for safety rather than a fast crossing. News reached them from the crews of three ships that just arrived in port, one from Queenstown, the other two from Norway. They were reporting heavy pack ice. It had been an unseasonably warm winter and large amounts of ice had broken off from Greenland.

Viko was quite certain *Titanic* would be taking the shorter northern route. Prior to his final departure from Ireland, he had been party to conversations between Captain Smith and Thomas Andrews. Bruce Ismay was interjecting himself into the navigational plans for her first voyage. His latest demand was that *Titanic* set new speed records on her first voyage. He wanted to do the crossing in three and a half days, perhaps even three. To perform such a feat *Titanic* would have to run twenty-four hours a day at maximum speed, putting undue stress on her huge steam engines. In addition, Captain Smith would need to take the shortest route possible, the northernmost crossing from east to west.

In order to placate this latest idiotic demand, Smith had compromised and ordered that the northern route be taken. But he stipulated that *Titanic* would run no faster than 75 percent of maximum speed. He reasoned that they could avoid icebergs. He was following the well-offered advice from Thomas Andrews that sustained travel at any faster speed would damage the engine bearings, and it could take up to six months to replace them.

It was critical to Viko's plans that the *Californian* and *Titanic* pass near each other as they traveled in opposite directions. Viko knew that eastbound and westbound ships on the same route usually passed close enough to be in visual contact, a distance of perhaps five to six miles, certainly close enough for his radio signals to penetrate the steel hull of the ship. Viko also had a more personal reason. If they were close enough, he would be able to witness *Titanic* slow down and stop—a sight he desperately wanted to witness.

Just then Peter Evans, the *Californian* wireless operator, came in with a Marconigram. "Sir, just received this from the *Cedric*. You might want to look at it." The *Cedric* was about an hour out on its journey to New York. It had taken the southern route across from Queenstown and had encountered a surprising amount of ice along the way.

Lord read the message and handed it to his second officer, who read it through. "Well, what do you think, what route would you take?" Lord asked.

"Sir, it seems that no matter how we make the crossing we are going to encounter ice. I suggest we get the trip over with as quickly as possible and take the northern route. Seems it won't make much of a difference; ice is everywhere."

Captain Lord asked everyone around the table for their opinion, and the general consensus was a northern route with extra lookouts and extra caution. Viko breathed a sigh of relief as Lord made the final decision and the ship's navigator began to draw out the planned route.

Lord then spoke to Peter Evans and Viko.

"Viko, since both you and Peter are here, I would appreciate your assistance with the wireless on this trip. I want at least one of you on the wireless every minute, twenty-four hours a day. We need to send and receive a constant flow of communication with other ships. All information about ice is to be brought to the bridge immediately. I want two shifts. Peter, you will be on duty from eight in the morning to eight at night. Viko, since you are usually up all night, can you man the night eight-to-eight shift? Consider yourself a crewmember and your ticket money will be refunded."

Viko agreed. Part of his plan was to be in the wireless room alone at night; he just didn't know how to make it happen.

Unknowingly, Captain Lord had just aided him in his plans for *Titanic*.

— ◊ —

The *Californian* was steaming eastward at a steady fourteen knots, making her way across a choppy North Atlantic. It was just past three o'clock in the morning on April 13. Viko stood by the railing outside the door of the wireless room looking up at a spectacular display of stars. His mind wandered through the history of the past seventeen years of his life. Had it really been that long since he was lifted from the misery and pain of life in Salonia? How had he arrived at this moment in his life?

He had studied at the feet of the master, Nikola Tesla. He learned the brushstrokes of this new science of electricity. He had traveled the world in pursuit of dreams that would never come true, and decided it was time to stop dreaming. He found it hard to accept that this genius he worshiped was a very little man struggling hopelessly against forces, and he would never prevail. Those forces were as vast as the heavens that spread above him that cold April night. But in just a few days those forces would be wandering these same chartless waters helpless against one not-so-small man, Viko Tesla.

Viko went back to the warmth of the wireless room, slipped the headphones back over his head, and continued listening to the wireless traffic between unseen ships and the shore towers that dotted the New England and Carolina coasts. There was little traffic at this early hour, but as he sat there a string of dots and dashes came through and he was sure that the name "Ismay" was one of the words. He reached for his pad and pencil and began to take down the message. It was indeed from Ismay; they were at sea and he was contacting his office in New York with details of his arrival. As a courtesy, Marconi operators relayed messages on to the receivers in New England, who in turn would forward it to New York. *Titanic* was at sea and, if on its original scheduled course, was traveling in his direction. Based on the time included in the message, Viko deduced that *Titanic* set sail as originally scheduled and was about five hundred miles out of Queenstown.

The rest of his watch was quite busy. No sooner had he sent the message from Ismay than he received an entire string of Marconigrams that sounded like greeting cards. *Titanic* wireless operator Jack Phillips was sending personal messages from passengers. Simple messages were being sent like: "HI HAVING A GREAT TIME" or "THE TITANIC IS A WONDERFUL SHIP WISH YOU WERE HERE," with an occasional business message mixed in.

Viko was filling up his Marconi forms so fast that he hardly had time to forward one before the next came in. He was annoyed at this frivolous use of wireless communication and found it questionable in light of the need to keep the wireless channels open to important messages about ice in the area.

Later that morning, Peter Evans arrived at the wireless room to begin his eight o'clock morning shift. Viko was busily relaying a pile of trivial messages.

"What's all this?"

"Peter, you are going to be busy. Would you believe these are all from the *Titanic*? Personal messages that have tied up the wireless most of the night."

Viko got up, stretched, and handed Evans a pile of unsent messages. "Here, have fun!" He turned and left to get breakfast and some sleep.

Viko was surprised that he was able to sleep at all. Each hour brought him closer to the moment when he could turn a switch and several miles away *Titanic* would be forced to stop. He had planned everything perfectly. He was particularly proud of his tampering with the ship's compass, just a few minutes of a degree off true north, but multiplied by thousands of miles it would put the ship ten to fifteen miles north of its assumed position. Even if they did manage to send their coordinates off by the wireless, they would be directing ships to the wrong location.

After a short nap and a good meal he wandered around the ship, paused occasionally to watch a group of dolphins swim alongside, and marveled at their ability to keep pace with the ship for hours on end. Perhaps they thought the *Californian* was just a big dolphin, but more practically he figured they were probably just looking for any table morsels that might be dumped into the sea with the ship's garbage.

He busied himself with whatever small chores might catch his fancy and finally found his way to the bridge. Captain Lord and his second officer were placing small wooden squares on a map of the Atlantic spread before them.

Viko looked at the map. "Can I assume that these wood blocks are representative of ice?"

Lord nodded. "Right as usual. Evans has brought three Marconigrams with ice reports, and as you can see, ice is directly in our path. We may reduce our speed; it's too soon to tell though. I want you to be especially mindful of ice reports tonight and bring them to the bridge immediately."

Viko reported to the wireless room a half hour before his shift was to begin.

Evans said, "I received a message from the Cape [Newfoundland's most easterly wireless station] that they were receiving *Titanic* quite well. I stopped the message relays. But the messages have kept right on coming, never heard anything like it. The wireless rarely stops, and at least two ships are complaining to the *Titanic* operators for tying up the channels. But it hasn't helped a bit. They act like they own the airwaves."

"Have you told them about the ice warnings?"

"Me and every operator for a thousand miles, and not one reply from *Titanic*."

Similar conversations were happening in the wireless rooms and bridges of at least a dozen ships plying the North Atlantic. The ships' crews were acutely aware of the dangers of the sea, especially the stormy North Atlantic during late winter and early spring when ice added another measure of danger.

Titanic wireless operators Jack Phillips and Harold Bride, experienced men in their own right, had been specifically directed by J. Bruce Ismay that passenger messages would take precedence over all other traffic. This directive was unknown to Captain Smith, the only man on the ship who had the authority to issue such a directive, and it blatantly flew in the face of safety and common sense. Ismay was interfering with everything and anything *Titanic* related, just as he had done since the first pencil was put to drafting linen in the design department of Harland and Wolff in 1907.

Ismay had threatened Bride and Phillips that their jobs hinged upon following his orders. They continued transmitting the trivia that poured into their wireless room from excited passengers anxious to try this new method of sending letters for twenty dollars per Marconigram. Sitting off in the corner was a stack of messages from other ships containing the locations and details of ice. Neither of them took the time to reply to wireless operators scattered across the ocean acknowledging the ice warnings.

This situation continued until the morning of April 14.

Captain Smith happened by the wireless room to inquire how things were going and was handed a dozen notices of ice on the route ahead. Demanding an explanation as to why he wasn't informed immediately of such danger, Phillips reluctantly informed him of Ismay's directive about passenger messages. Ten minutes later there was quite a buzz going through the first-class lounge about Captain Smith and Second Officer Lightoller bodily grabbing Ismay from a game of cards and dragging him to the captain's cabin, followed by an intense but muffled screaming match that could be heard through the walls.

CHAPTER 44
April 14—Early Morning

Dawn broke on a smooth sea, one of the smoothest seen by any of the crew. The choppy windy weather that followed them the first days of the trip subsided, leaving the ocean surface like a mirror, the only disturbance being the wake created by the *Californian* as it steamed eastward at a steady fourteen knots. The wireless traffic about ice intensified during the night. One ship, the *Liverpool*, was surrounded by pack ice and had stopped until daylight.

Viko stood outside the door looking out to sea through a pair of binoculars, hoping to spot the ice that everyone was talking about. He had seen the water temperature readings and was surprised at how cold the water had become. Two days earlier it had been thirty-six degrees. The most recent readings showed that they were now in water at twenty-nine degrees.

During the night Viko had relayed four ice messages to *Titanic*. He asked for their coordinates. Captain Lord was keeping track of all the ships in the area to better understand the extent of danger posed by the ice. *Titanic* was less than seven hundred miles away and steaming directly toward the *Californian*. Viko calculated the closing distance and determined that they would pass within visual distance around nine p.m. Perfect! This day, April 14, 1912, would be remembered in history as the date the *Titanic, man's greatest mechanical marvel,* would disappear off the charts only to be rediscovered a few weeks later by Nikola Tesla, just in the nick of time to "save" her passengers from the cold of the North Atlantic.

No one on the *Californian* or *Titanic* knew that an ice field the size of Rhode Island floated in the path of both ships.

Peter Evans arrived for his day shift at eight o'clock. He looked awful. His eyes were red, he had wrapped himself in every warm article of clothing he owned, and yet he shivered uncontrollably. When he coughed he sounded like a barking seal. Viko took one look at him and put his hand on his forehead. Evans was burning up with fever.

"Peter, for God's sake, man, get yourself back to bed. I'll send the ship's doctor down to see you."

"But Viko, you've been up all night. It's not fair; who will be on duty?"

"Don't worry about me. I can stay up for days if I get enough coffee. We need you alive. Now get back to bed."

Viko hurried to the bridge and told Captain Lord of Evans's condition and his intention to remain on duty throughout the day. He poured himself a large cup of hot black coffee, and as he went back to the wireless room he shouted over his shoulder, "Have someone bring me something to eat and a pot of coffee."

Lord turned to his second officer. "Give me more men like Viko and I would have the finest crew on the sea. Go arrange for the doctor to see Evans, and have the galley send a plate to Viko—and don't forget the coffee."

Viko couldn't believe his continued good fortune. He and only he would have complete control of the wireless room all day and into the night. He would be able to set up his special transmitter without interference or fear of discovery, and he was in a perfect position to keep track of *Titanic*'s location.

As the day wore on, the wireless traffic became heavier with ice reports coming from ships and from the station at the Cape. The trivial messages from *Titanic*'s powerful transmitter continued, but at least now her operators were replying to the ice reports. Curiously, *Titanic* had yet to report any ice.

Viko left his watch just after noon to take ice warnings to the bridge. He found everyone looking off the port side of the ship, pointing north and commenting on the size of the iceberg just seen by one of the spotters in the crow's nest. Never having seen an iceberg, Viko went over and joined them. On the horizon he saw the sun's reflection off the brilliant white side of the ice. It was about ten miles away, and even at this distance it looked impressively large. Viko borrowed a pair of binoculars to get a better look and was surprised at the berg's craggy, jagged appearance.

Captain Lord gave a low whistle. "That's a big one, Viko, the kind that can take down a ship. They say that less than 10 percent of an iceberg is above the water. Can you imagine how big that thing is?"

Just then the spotter called down, "Dead ahead, on the horizon, large berg."

They all went to the front window of the bridge; the second officer shouted out, "There it is, just coming into view."

From the crow's nest, the spotter called down again, "Off to starboard, several small bergs."

The sea was dotted with small floating pieces of ice, ranging in size from a few hundred pounds to perhaps a ton, too small to do any damage in themselves but serving as messengers that their large relatives were not far away.

"Hold a steady course and speed," Captain Lord said to the officers on the bridge. "You have my authority to slow the ship if the ice gets any heavier. Viko, get back to the wireless and report the large bergs."

On the way back to the wireless room Viko made a stop in his cabin to retrieve the small trunk that contained his transmitter and tools. Back in the wireless room, he covered the trunk with a piece of canvas and began to transmit the locations of the ice. He received messages from six ships thanking him for the information and one asking for a clarification. Surprisingly, he did not get a reply from *Titanic*. He was quite sure she was on the same heading they were and would pass quite close to the ice they had just seen.

It was late in the afternoon when Viko noticed the change in rhythm of the *Californian*'s steam engine. Lord had ordered the speed reduced slightly to ten knots. In the past two hours, they had spotted six more large bergs. Passengers on deck were commenting on the beautiful icebergs, one of them less than two miles away. There was a flurry of excitement as the spotter in the crow's nest pointed out three seals hitching a ride on the berg, and people were straining to catch a glimpse of them.

Viko remained on duty as the traffic became busier. *Titanic* was once again sending a long series of personal messages, and her powerful transmitter was causing interference with ships' attempts to communicate regarding the ice. When the *Liverpool* wireless operator asked that they stop the trivia until the ice was passed they got a terse "MIND YOUR OWN BUSINESS" from the *Titanic* operator.

In the early days of wireless ship-to-ship and ship-to-shore communication, there were very few, if any, protocols for communication. Marconi was busily building his transceivers, in actuality copies of Nikola Tesla's design, and was equipping both ships and shore stations with them as fast as they could be produced. These were simple devices. One operating channel spilled over into adjacent channels, and if you happened to have a receiver in the vicinity of one of the more powerful transmitters, all channels would be affected and garbled messages would result. Just about everything that created sparks—lightning, motors, switches—was a source of annoying interference.

There were no international agreements on language, distress calls, prioritizing of messages, or emergency channels. The response of the *Titanic* operators, when asked to cut down on the personal messages, may have been rude, but there was no precedent dictating procedures under such conditions. Inasmuch as they were annoying other ship operators by interfering with important safety messages, they posed a greater danger to themselves, their passengers, and their ship. And as time would show, the consequences would be disastrous.

Viko started to take messages to the bridge and ran into a steward bringing him a hot meal and a message from the captain. Viko didn't realize how hungry he was until the aroma of hot roast beef reached his nostrils and he found himself salivating. But as soon as he read the message that Captain Lord was sending, any thoughts of eating quickly left his mind.

"CALIFORNIAN HAS SLOWED TO FIVE KNOTS. ICE CONDITIONS EXTREME. CAUTION IS ADVISED."

The slower speed, the second reduction in the space of just a few hours, was going to affect his timing for the close passage near *Titanic*. He quickly sent off the message as a general CQD (All Stations - Distress). He sent a direct message to *Titanic* asking if they were going to reduce speed. He received a terse reply indicating that *Titanic* was maintaining a steady twenty-four knots and to leave them alone. The strength of the signal that blasted through his headphones told him that they were closer than before.

Viko did some math. He figured they would be at their closest at around ten-thirty p.m., about an hour and a half later than he previously calculated. It would give him additional time to prepare his transmitter. He relaxed a little and poured another cup of coffee.

Waiting until darkness had descended, just after six Viko removed his small transmitter from the trunk. He opened a service panel on the Marconi wireless and located the antenna connection, verifying that it would reach his transmitter's connection.

He was ready—it was just a matter of time.

His food was cold, but the growling from his stomach told him he'd better eat something. Viko had not eaten for at least a day, except for a half-gallon or so of coffee. He wolfed down the large plate of food.

As his body began the task of digesting the roast beef and potatoes his eyelids grew heavy with fatigue. He had been running on adrenaline, and as his body returned to normal it craved rest. The steady ticking of the dots and dashes in his earphones was hypnotic. He leaned back in his chair, felt the gentle vibration of the engines massaging his sore back, and nodded off to sleep.

Viko awakened with a start. The *Californian* was deathly still. There was no engine vibration. He ripped off the headphones and hurried to the door. It was bitter cold. The sky above was black velvet, dotted with millions of points of starlight, split down the middle by the Milky Way—a breathtakingly beautiful sight.

He looked aft. There was no wake wave behind the ship. They were floating freely with the gentle current. He had never experienced a ship being this still except when tied up at a dock. He pulled out his pocket watch: ten-twenty p.m.

He had been asleep for nearly two hours. When did the ship stop? Why did it stop? Did he miss the passage of *Titanic*?

He ran to the bridge and rushed in to find Captain Lord and two officers standing around the table shaking their heads.

"Captain Lord, I am sorry, I fell asleep. Why have we stopped?"

"No need to panic, Viko. We stopped about an hour ago. We shut down the engines at nine-fifteen and are just maintaining one boiler for heat and electricity. We're surrounded by ice. We'll wait until daylight before we proceed. We've turned on all the ship's lights so no one will run into us out here, although I think that's unlikely. Any captain in the area will stop for the night also. I'm letting everyone get a good night's sleep since there is little else we can do. I suggest that you turn in also."

Viko hurried back to the wireless room, his mind a maelstrom of emotion. Was it possible that he came this far and an ice field would thwart his plans? Had *Titanic* stopped also? How far away were they? Had he missed his chance? Was all the planning and work for nothing?

He put on his earphones and heard yet another frivolous message from *Titanic*. Now he was angry. How could these idiots tie up their wireless for hours on end like this? He keyed his transmitter, using the CQD prefix, informing *Titanic* that the *Californian* had stopped for the night due to ice and requested their status.

He received an abrupt message in return: "LEAVE US ALONE WE ARE WORKING THE CAPE. YOU ARE BLASTING US. WE ARE AT 41° 18' N, 49° 40' W STEAMING AT 24 KNOTS."

They were about thirty miles away, steaming toward the ice field at full speed. Viko had to warn them: "MAJOR ICE FIELD AT 42° 22' N, 51° 22' W."

Only to get in return: "I SAID LEAVE US ALONE."

They can't say they weren't warned, Viko thought to himself.

He did some mental figuring and determined that *Titanic* would be closest to them later than originally thought, most likely at about eleven-thirty-five. There was no longer a need for the Marconi wireless that night. Viko disconnected the antenna wire and connected it to his transmitter. He turned on the power and saw the glow from within its vacuum tubes confirming that everything was ready.

Only one more hour to wait for the event he had planned for months.

He stepped outside, closed and locked the door, and went to the galley for coffee. A few crewmembers were there, mostly men from the boiler room. Two other crewmembers were assigned the job of night watch, but when a ship is stationary there is nothing to watch so they sat in a corner playing cards.

"Viko, what are you doing up at this hour?"

"You know me, can't sleep. I'm going to wander around the ship for a while, check for incoming messages, look at the stars until I get tired enough to go to bed. What are you guys up to?"

"We're supposed to be on watch, but fully hemmed in by ice. Who in their right mind would continue traveling tonight, especially with no moon or waves? We might wander around the deck occasionally but probably spend the night right here. It's colder than hell out there."

Viko, assured of complete privacy, walked back to the wireless room. He sat in his chair, placed his pocket watch on the table in front of him, and watched the seconds tick by. The hot coffee tasted good but not as sweet as the revenge he was about to inflict on a man who thought he was above the law. A fat little man was about to learn the true meaning of fear.

Just ten minutes to go.

Viko stepped out into the cold night air—it invigorated him. He looked around. The lights of a ship were coming into view off to the east. He lifted his binoculars to his eyes.

Four stacks, the ship had four smokestacks! The rate that coal smoke was coming up from three of them and blowing straight back indicated that she was steaming fast. It had to be *Titanic*.

One minute to go.

He went inside and held his hand near the transmit switch and watched the secondhand step precisely around the face of his timepiece. The seconds ticked by—forty, thirty-nine, thirty-eight, thirty-seven. Time seemed to stand still. After what seemed like an eternity, the moment arrived, eleven-thirty-five p.m. Viko's finger hovered over the switch.

There was a moment's hesitation—"Morgan, this is for you."

His finger pressed down with firm determination. The circuits within his transmitter came alive and sent a series of powerful electrical signals traveling up to the *Californian's* antenna. Silent deadly pulses of electromagnetic energy raced into the atmosphere, reaching out for three unique receivers hidden in *Titanic's* structure. Wireless operators in the area heard a strange warbling sound as the electrical pulses sped through the "ether."

On the bridge of *Titanic* the wheel suddenly fell limp in the hands of helmsman Robert Hitchens as a loud WHUMP was heard from beneath his feet. Everyone in the bridge turned in the direction of the sound as the faint odor of burning insulation wafted through the bridge.

In the *Titanic* wireless room, Jack Phillips was in the middle of a frivolous transmission when the panel in front of him seemed to reverberate like a snare drum. He was exhausted and frustrated and was not sure what he just heard, if anything. He continued keying in the Morse code but was aware that something had definitely changed. The usual authoritative sounds that came from the powerful transmitter were now more like soft whispers.

A message from the Cape came through: "TITANIC. WHAT HAPPENED? I HAVE LOST YOU. PLEASE ACKNOWLEDGE."

Phillips repeated his message but once again received the reply: "TITANIC — SIGNAL IS VERY WEAK."

Viko went out onto the walkway and watched *Titanic* through his binoculars. Nothing seemed to happen for several minutes, and then he noticed a definite slowing of the ship's progress. The smoke from her stacks no longer trailed straight out behind her, it was rising at an ever-increasing angle and after nearly five minutes was going straight up.

He had done it, he had brought the beast to a stop, and in the middle of an ice field where no one would dare to venture.

He went back to the wireless and put on the headphones. The only sound was a gentle hissing: no transmissions from *Titanic*.

Mission accomplished!

Viko went back outside to watch as the *Titanic's* crew and passengers began to realize they were stranded.

CHAPTER 45

April 15, 4:00 AM—*Californian*

Viko felt no remorse for the passengers on board *Titanic*. The spectacle he had witnessed during the night as *Titanic* tried to get someone's attention was amusing. Why would they fire rockets into the air? Were they that frightened just because they had to stop? He was delighted that the two crewmembers assigned to the watch on the *Californian* had stayed in the galley all night. He didn't want the *Californian* finding *Titanic* so quickly. No, that was not part of his plan. *Titanic* and all on board needed to drift for a few weeks.

He had watched as the great ship's lights were turned off around two-thirty in the morning, most likely at the urging of Thomas Andrews. He would be the one with the most common sense. He most likely had convinced them that they needed to conserve fuel until they figured out what to do about their predicament. All had been quiet for the past hour and a half. Viko sat in front of the Marconi wireless and listened, but there was nothing at all, no ships, no land stations, no sounds of wireless traffic of any kind.

Something was wrong. There was always some minimal communication activity, even in the middle of the night.

He glanced down at his transmitter under the table. He had forgotten to reconnect the antenna to the Marconi wireless! He stared in disbelief at the mistake he had made.

No wonder he heard none of the familiar dots and dashes always coming in from a distant ship; he had spent the night listening to nothing but the hiss, that ever present noise, a sound like the rustling of leaves from within the receiver. His Marconi wireless was not able to receive signals because the antenna was not connected. He had been in the dark, literally and figuratively.

"What have I missed? What has been going on?" Viko muttered to himself.

He reconnected the antenna. A wireless signal was in the process of coming in. It was from a ship named *Carpathia*.

Carpathia's operator was in contact with the Cape, asking for the last known location of *Titanic*. *Carpathia* was closest to the *disaster*. What disaster?

Carpathia was steaming north at full speed to come to the rescue of *Titanic's* passengers. They also wanted to know how many lifeboats they could expect to find in the water.

Survivors? Lifeboats? This line of questioning made no sense. Why would the passengers leave *Titanic*? Even when disabled, she was still a warm and safe place. As he continued to listen to messages from *Carpathia* to the Cape and to other ships attempting to reach her location, Viko began to piece it together. *Titanic* had foundered. Captain Rostron of *Carpathia* was asking for help from anyone who knew of the whereabouts of *Titanic* when she sent her last message, "WE ARE GOING DOWN AT THE HEAD." and then cut off before it could finish.

Viko understood. *Titanic* must have been close to ice when he disabled the steering. The ship did not stop right away as he predicted it would but rather ran head-on into the ice field. Twenty-four knots! At that speed the damage must have been immense, too much for even the mighty *Titanic* to endure. He couldn't believe his ears, but the great ship was gone, on the ocean floor twelve thousand feet below.

Viko knew of the limited number of lifeboats and the concerns of Thomas Andrews.

How many people had he killed? How many innocent lives—fathers, mothers, and children—went down? How many froze to death in the water? All because of him, Viko Tesla! How many were out there right now on the freezing ocean in lifeboats or clinging helplessly to floating pieces of wood?

He could listen no longer. He ripped the antenna wire from the Marconi wireless.

He screamed in anguish. What hatred drove him to this point? He could not contain the boiling emotion that was exploding within him. He grabbed a hammer and smashed the transmitter that had caused this tragedy. He crammed it into the trunk, ran outside, and with all his strength threw it as far from the ship as he could, watching as it fell to the ocean and sank out of sight.

"I must help them. I have to find them and tell them that help is on its way. Off to the east, that's where they are. It's not too far, only a few miles. I have to get to them."

Viko took off his heavy sea coat and shoes and threw them into the water. The cold of the night spurred him on.

"I must hurry!"

He climbed to the top of the railing, took one last look back at the wireless room where he committed this terrible crime, and dove into the water. He was a powerful swimmer and began to swim through the subfreezing water, ignoring the hundreds of tiny needlelike stabs penetrating his skin. He swam away from the *Californian* and off toward the east where the first pink rays of sunlight illuminated the floating mountains of ice, shedding light onto a surreal ocean graveyard.

And the greatest irony of all, the one purpose of his plan of revenge, now turned to one of murder, was that his enemy, J.P. Morgan, was somewhere back in Europe, not among the multitudes of bodies frozen to death and floating silently on the ocean currents.

CHAPTER 46
April 15, 10:00 AM—
Aboard *Carpathia*

C *arpathia*'s Captain Arthur Rostron and *Titanic* Second Officer Charles Lightoller stood together in the bridge of the *Carpathia* looking out at the ice field that surrounded them.

"Are you sure there are no more lifeboats?" Rostron asked.

"Quite sure, there were sixteen on board when we sailed, plus the four collapsibles we were able to launch, and all are accounted for."

"By my count we have brought about seven hundred people aboard."

Hearing this, Lightoller put his head in his hands. "My God, there were twenty-two hundred people on board; all those souls, drowned or frozen to death—I can still hear their screams for help."

Rostron put his hand on Lightoller's shoulder. "You have done all that can be done. Get below and get warm. We will continue the search for survivors, but in this cold water I doubt we will find any alive."

Lightoller left the bridge. As *Carpathia* moved cautiously ahead, the crew continued to scan the water for signs of life. An hour later, the two crews out in the rescue skiffs rowed back, reporting that no living people could be found.

Rostron turned to his crew: "Well, what more can we do? Those few that we have found floating are dead. It has been nearly eight hours since *Titanic* went down; there can be no one left alive out there. Get underway and let's get these people to New York."

As the second officer was about to send the command "ALL AHEAD ONE-QUARTER," a shout came from a crewmember standing near the starboard rail. He was looking off to the west and spotted a body in the water. At first he thought it was a dolphin, but no, someone was in the water—he saw movement.

They put one of the rescue skiffs back in the water and within minutes pulled the nearly lifeless body of a man from the freezing water. His skin was deep blue, his hair and full beard encrusted with ice. He was not wearing a life vest. At first they thought he was dead, but when he opened his eyes and tried to speak they bundled him in as many blankets as they had on the skiff and got him back to the ship.

Carpathia's doctors were certain he would not survive, but by the next morning he was still breathing and they were able to get him to take warm liquid. Miraculously, he recovered. He suffered no long-term physical effects of several hours in subfreezing water, but he never spoke to anyone as they tried to find out who he was. He would mumble, appearing to be in a trance, trying to speak. At times he would say something that sounded like "organ," at others "curt" The only complete word he could form was "uncle." But mostly he simply stared at others, or his eyes seemed to focus on some unknown image that only he could see. He occasionally shook his head; otherwise he was quiet and motionless. But when he was left alone he would become very agitated, his behavior bordering on violence. They had no choice but to restrain him.

They never determined his identity and, most surprisingly, no one remembered ever seeing him onboard *Titanic*. *Carpathia*'s overworked doctors surmised that he was suffering from severe emotional shock from the trauma of the sinking.

When *Carpathia* docked in New York, he was the last survivor taken from the ship. There was no one waiting for this strange man. With no other options, and over seven hundred other *Titanic* passengers to deal with, Captain Rostron arranged for him to be admitted to a local asylum for the insane, hoping that rest and treatment would restore his mind.

EPILOGUE
1943

T he wars in Europe and the Pacific were raging. Each day brought news of the advancing armies of the Third Reich and Imperial Japan. The lives of young American men were being wasted at an alarming rate. And from Europe came unbelievable reports of German exterminations of "undesirables": Jews, gypsies, the elderly, and anyone else that the madman Hitler had a whim to eliminate.

Nikola Tesla, now in his eighties, lived as a virtual recluse in his rooms at the top of the Waldorf-Astoria. He was a beaten man. All of his wonderful inventions and creations had been stolen, altered, and their credit given to others. People like Marconi, Edison, and Steinmetz, all dead, but credited with radio, AC power, the "newly" invented and highly secret RADAR, and on and on, all of which had been his original ideas, and it was so easily proven, but no one cared. Untold millions of dollars had gone into the pockets of Morgan, Westinghouse, and Astor, all money that was rightly Tesla's.

Over forty million AM radios graced the homes of Americans who sat by them each evening listening to Edward R. Murrow's reassuring voice report on the progress of the war, as they anxiously hoped to learn the fate of their son or father or husband in some far-off hellhole of death and destruction.

Instantaneous news from thousands of miles away was delivered over this miraculous medium of wireless communication, given to the world by the genius of a forgotten, beaten old man and stolen by Marconi and the greedy barons of the financial world, bent only on enhancing their already huge fortunes.

Tesla was gaunt, frail, and despondent. His closest friends were dead. Except for his beloved white pigeons, he had no one. Those few people who did see him in his last days remember him fondly with birds perched on his arm eating seeds from the palm of his hand, talking quietly and lovingly to them in his native tongue.

It was January 7, 1943. Tesla once again allowed himself his one connection to the past, his reminder of how great he had been. He went into the sub-basement of the hotel where his trunks full of notes, writings, drawings, and manuscripts were kept. He found solace in these interludes. He would read and reread the hundreds of *New York Post* clippings reporting his latest accomplishments, or his original treatise on AC power, its edges still showing the scorch marks from the suspicious fire that had destroyed his laboratory so many years ago.

Of great pain to him was his correspondence with the US government when he tried to tell them of his experiments with death rays, remote-controlled torpedoes, and methods of creating massive destruction through his principles of mechanical resonance and acoustic location. Those blind fools! If only they had listened. If only he had not been stopped by their unfounded fear and prejudice toward him. These horrible wars would be over by now. No foreign power could beat his inventions. But alas, all to no avail.

On this cold winter day, sitting in the solitude of the Waldorf-Astoria's basement, Tesla searched for and found his designs and treatise on the remote-controlled torpedo, or as he had called it, the "automaton." He had not seen this in many years, and why he would look at it now he was not sure, but for some reason he was attracted to it. As he began to leaf through his sketches and notes from so many years before, he was surprised to find a large envelope among his notes—one he did not remember.

Puzzled, he opened it, finding that it contained several of his notes on the new wireless system, now called FM, that he and his lost nephew Viko had stumbled upon thirty years ago. He was puzzled. His perfect photographic mind had lost none of its sharpness. He knew something was wrong. *What are the notes about FM doing in here? They don't belong here! Was someone into my things? Have those bastard government agents been here again? Have I no privacy at all?*

As he bristled with rage and pain at this further violation of his life's work, he turned a page and immediately recognized Viko's handwriting on a sketch that was not his.

Memories of his nephew flooded back. He realized it must have been Viko who mixed things up. Viko, his brilliant protégé. His heart was filled with an overwhelming wave of sadness for the lost Viko.

He remembered the citywide search for him. How he had simply disappeared one day, never to be heard from again. Tesla had engaged every means, every agency, had inquired everywhere as to his whereabouts. In fact, Tesla had raised the specter that Viko, knowing and understanding the intimate details of all of Tesla's work, had been kidnapped or killed by a foreign government, or even by the US military. And of course all of this fell on deaf ears.

The pain of Viko's disappearance lifted slowly as his reverie drifted through their past enjoyable days and evenings together, as Tesla continued to leaf through the papers in front of him. How curious, he thought, as he realized that the drawings depicting his underwater acoustic experiments were marked up with notes regarding an acoustic homing device. *What had Viko been thinking about, and why hadn't he discussed this with me?* After all, they were each other's best sounding boards.

Stuck between two of the drawings Tesla found an envelope, sealed with wax and addressed "To the Greatest Mind the world has yet to know, My Uncle, Nikola Tesla." Tesla smiled at this, thinking *so typical of Viko.*

Tesla opened the envelope, which crumbled slightly at the edges; it was obviously very old. Inside he found a letter, written on Tesla's original stationery from so many years before.

As Tesla began to read, his smile turned to a frown and then to disbelief. This wasn't real. This could not be. Detailed in front of Tesla's unbelieving eyes were Viko's plans to disable *Titanic*. It went on to explain and ask forgiveness for his behavior that had so confused and upset everyone.

My Dearest Uncle Nikola:

I am sure that by now you know that a few days ago the ship Titanic disappeared from the seas. Let me assure you that she is afloat but wandering helplessly about the North Atlantic awaiting a savior to rescue her. You are to be that savior. For you see, it was me, operating alone, that disabled the ship and destroyed her wireless. She cannot communicate; no one knows where she is. I simply placed two simple explosives on board and detonated them from the Californian a few miles away. Her steering is destroyed. I did this all for you.

I am so sorry that I did not say goodbye to you, but you would have stopped me. You are a great man, my dear uncle, but you are a coward. You are so naïve. You live not in this world of corrupt men but in your world of science and dreams and childish trust. It has pained me deeply to watch you beg them for money, to give away inventions worth millions for mere pennies, when it is they who should be begging from you.

How many times did I plead with you to be stronger? How many times did I beg you to let me negotiate for you? But no, you did it all for the "good of the world." But what has the world done for Nikola Tesla? What has that bastard Morgan or that pig Edison done except conspire against you? And what about that thief Marconi, what about him?

Your moment in the sun is upon us. If you go to my private laboratory, you will find a key to a locker at Grand Central Station. There you will find an acoustic receiver and special underwater microphones. I have placed an acoustic sounder on board the Titanic that can be heard for thousands of miles. The sound it makes, like the sound of a chirping bird, will guide you to her. Once you locate her and her wealthy passengers, the world will look at you as a deity and the likes of Morgan, who has done the most to destroy you, will offer you a fortune, but more than that, he will acknowledge your greatness and his sins against you.

And on it went. It was written in their Serbian language to prevent accidental discovery.

Of course Tesla remembered the *Titanic* sinking. Anyone who had been in New York in 1912 had followed the newspaper reports from that first *New York Times* headline telling of the collision with the iceberg and the loss of life all the way through the daily reports of the trials that Senator William Alden Smith conducted. In fact Tesla had been interviewed by several reporters and asked his opinions of the claims that *Titanic* had been "unsinkable." His reply, published in the *Post*, was brief and sobering: *The events of April 15th answer that question with unquestionable accuracy.*

Tesla stared at the letter in utter disbelief as it went on to tell of Viko's plans, to explain exactly how it would be done, and that he, Viko, would exclaim to the world that the great inventions of Nikola Tesla were greater than the money and the power and the influence of all others. Of how he was certain that finally Nikola Tesla would be given the credit, the position, and the power to realize his ultimate dream of wireless power to the world.

Tesla put the letter in his pocket, locked up his notes for the last time, and in a stupor got up and went back to his rooms at the top of the hotel. His normally erect posture was gone. Those who saw him pass through the lobby hardly recognized him. Charles Vinder, the desk clerk on duty that day and a longtime admirer of Tesla, commented later that "Tesla looked like a walking cadaver."

In his room, he took one last look at the letter, placed it in his fireplace, and burned it along with the plans for the acoustic sounder that Viko had drawn up. He went to his two pigeons, lovingly took them to the open window, and let them go, telling them to go forth, have babies, and forget him.

Closing the window, he slumped into a chair, buried his head in his hands, and began to sob. His dream had always been to help mankind. He wanted nothing more than to take the burden of labor off the backs of men and women and let them experience the art, the poetry, and the beauty of this world. And yet his creations had been used unknowingly to cause the deaths of 1,517 innocent men, women, and children.

Two days later he was found dead in the chair, and even though he was eighty-one at the time, those who found him commented that he looked twenty years older.

The ultimate twist of fate in this story of hatred and revenge can be found in a rumor that continues to persist. Morgan, on his deathbed in 1913, in an apparent moment of contrition, ordered that a trust fund be established ensuring that Nikola Tesla would be provided with housing and food for the remainder of his life at nothing less than New York's finest hotel.

ACKNOWLEDGMENTS

For years I would occasionally mention to people that I had an idea for a conspiracy novel based on the *Titanic* disaster. Thanks to all those who expressed an interest in this frighteningly possible scenario and whose encouragement convinced me to sit down and write.

I would like to thank the following people who took the time to read my first drafts and give me valuable feedback and critiques: Roger Basham, Jon Claitman, Don Coe, Rod Girard, and Gary Neidhardt. Particular thanks to Tom Allen for his insightful comments regarding terms and verbiage used at the time of *Titanic*, as well as granting me permission to use his name as one of my characters. Thanks to all members of the Golden Pen Writers Guild of Santa Clarita, California, for their constructive critiques, which have helped me become a better writer and grammarian, and with special thanks to Pat Kraetsch for the hours of proofreading and many suggestions that helped clarify word usage. I must also remember Judith Buntin, Stan Clough, Christine Hermann, Nancy Perkins, Nancy Senger, Marty Stephens, and Dianne Wheaton of the *Wednesday Night Gang* for their encouragement and constructive criticism.

Two editors at Morgan James Publishing, Angie Kiesling, and Katherine Rawson are amazing. Both offered excellent suggestions and clarifications, and pointed out a few of my boneheaded errors. Every fiction author should have the privilege of working with you two.

Words alone are not enough to thank book coach Judith Cassis for her encouragement, insight, editorial corrections, and guidance through the entire process. Judith, you are a gem. Thank you for the endless hours spent poring over the manuscript and the many suggestions that clarified and improved the story. This book would not exist without you.

It seems obligatory for an author to thank his wife. However, in this case it goes far beyond an obligation; it is a small attempt at compensation for wading her way through five rewrites. Her endless patience was a gift through the entire process. Her critiques have been insightful and helped immensely in telling this tale of *what might have happened*. Thank you, Sherron, for the hours you spent alone with the TV while I sat in my den, hunting and pecking my way through this thing. You are the love of my life.

AFTERWORD

Dangerous Betrayal is a work of historical fiction.

I have been interested in the *Titanic* disaster ever since I first saw *A Night to Remember* as a child. However, the tragic reality of the event was most brought alive for me by the movie *Titanic,* starring Leonardo DiCaprio and Kate Winslet (1997). Somewhere along the line I began to wonder—was it truly an accident?

My purpose in writing this story was threefold. The first was to entertain. I know of few things so intriguing or entertaining as conspiracy theories. The second was to point out amazing coincidences between *Titanic,* her backers and passengers, and the life of Nikola Tesla. When I first had the idea for this scenario about fifteen years ago, it was just a whim. But as I read and studied both subjects, the coincidences were amazing. The third purpose was to make a statement about how brilliant ideas can be turned into terrible methods of death and destruction. For example, Einstein's theory of relativity revolutionized physics, but also led to the atomic bomb. He didn't intend that.

There is a large community of people, myself included, who believe that Nikola Tesla was one the world's most significant inventors. He was one hundred years ahead of his time, and his contributions to our lives today are immeasurable. Just think of the world without AC power, radio, television, or the basic element of all electronic digital communications, the *AND gate.* All of these were originated by a man of incredible intellect who died a pauper's death on January 7, 1943. History has unfortunately given credit for most of his work to others. It is not my intention to detract from his greatness, however, *Dangerous Betrayal* does reflect his contributions to his own obscurity.

Any connection between the sinking of *Titanic* and Nikola Tesla is entirely fictitious and the product of the author's imagination. His nephew Viko did not exist, nor did his sister Christina (Viko's mother), as well as several other characters used in telling this story. J.P. Morgan was a famous banker and industrialist whose methods (and those of other financial barons of the age) are accurately depicted as the story unfolds. Although scheduled to be on *Titanic's* maiden voyage, a last-minute change in his schedule caused Morgan to remain behind, most likely saving his life. He died in 1913.

Among those reading this book may be relatives who lost family members in the *Titanic* disaster. If this book has in any way caused pain or discomfort, it was most certainly not my intention.

ABOUT THE AUTHOR

William (Bill) Blowers is a retired engineer who turned his love of reading and writing into a second career. The recipient of Technical Academy Awards and co-author of *Waiting at the Train Station*, he directed his inventive abilities to the successful creation of novels, business books, short stories, poetry, and numerous newspaper stories. He and his wife Sherron, along with their shih tzu Abby, live in the historic town of Newhall in California's Santa Clarita Valley. *Dangerous Betrayal: The Vendetta That Sank Titanic*, is the result of his lifelong fascination with the *Titanic* disaster.

CPSIA information can be obtained
at www.ICGtesting.com
Printed in the USA
FSOW01n1458060116
15485FS